A Citizen

This edition first published 2017 by Fahrenheit Press

10 9 8 7 6 5 4 3 2 1

www.Fahrenheit-Press.com

F 4 E

A Citizen Of Nowhere

By

Seth Lynch

The 3rd Republic Novels

Fahrenheit Press

For Isla, with love

CHAPTER ONE

Paris, 1930

I am a citizen of nowhere, escaped from the tribe, an Englishman living in Paris. My head beats like the drum roll before an execution. Why does my hand hurt?

A coffee follows a cigarette. My head beats like the drum roll before an execution. Why does my hand hurt?

A coffee follows a cigarette, then some orange juice and a breakfast of bread and jam. My kitchen is small with a table, a tiny stove, a basin and a cupboard. French cuisine is famous but they don't actually cook - that's what restaurants and bistros are for. In Paris the kitchen is a place to drink coffee, smoke, and be thankful you don't live in a stinking hotel anymore. It's silent here, aside from the constant dripping of a tap. For over a year I lived next door to a room used by prostitutes. The novelty of hearing them wears off fast. Well, it's early and my blessing has now been counted.

The wintry sun casts long shadows across the kitchen. My coffee pot sits on the stove and shines like a jewel in a magpie's nest. I should have shaved by now. I'm thirty-four years old; there are many things I should've done by now. Not so many as the things I've done and shouldn't have. Unshaven or not, I shall go out for my bread and jam.

'What makes you think you are welcome here?' André, the waiter and proprietor, stands arms akimbo as if acting in some Molière play.

André is an unpleasant creature. He has a pot belly and the lingering smell of horse-flesh soup. I'm not certain if he eats it or bathes in it; either way if he gets too close I feel like vomiting. His hair is Italian-black and shorn away at the sides. It also sprouts from his ears and nose. His skin glistens through a film of sweat and grease which grows deeper through the day. If this café weren't so damn close to my bed I'd never come here. André is punishment for my laziness.

'I know I'm not welcome, André, but my money is, so cut the crap and fetch me some bread and jam. Bring coffee too.' I take out a Gitane, light it, and make a dismissive gesture with my free hand.

André huffs as he leaves. At least he didn't spit on the floor first. He has all the pride of his profession but little of the skill and none of the tact. What does it matter if I turned over a table and punched some half-wit? It wasn't André's fat ugly lip I'd left dripping with blood. He saunters back with a small stick of bread and a pot of strawberry jam on a metal tray. As if parodying the more talented waiters in the established restaurants, he holds the tray with one hand above his head. The coffee cup he holds in his other hand; he'd spill it otherwise.

'Who's that girl over there?' I ask.

'I don't know, I don't care. She has a coffee and she's been nursing it for an hour. So, whatever else you may say about her she fits in well here.' He walks off before giving me the chance to question him further.

The woman has a pallid complexion with exceedingly dark eyes. She looks like the kind of girl Keats would think about before sighing and jumping out the window. I'm not too good with ages but I'd say she's in her early or mid-twenties. Damn! She's caught me looking and has turned away. A subtle enough defence, and if we lived in gentler times it may have been enough to deter me. I've faced German machine gunners, withstood artillery bombardments that went on for days, and I've seen human flesh hanging from trees, being picked at by carrion crows. A cold shoulder doesn't cut it any longer.

'Mind if I sit here?' I ask pulling out the seat opposite her and sitting on it.

Up close she is much paler than she appeared from across the café. The only bright colour on her face comes from a trace of lipstick. Her body is thin framed, with small breasts and only the slightest intention of a waist. The prostitutes in Arras had looked like this after a couple of years on starvation rations. She could be a drug addict; they tend to wither away, the colour going first and then the flesh. Her eyes are too alert for an addict.

'I mind, but does it matter? You look like a pest. Are you a pest?'

She lights a cigarette, refusing my offer of a light with the shake of her head. She turns to face away from me and looks out of the café door. It comes to something when, rather than look at you, a woman would rather watch a rag and bone man's horse taking a crap.

'Pest is a matter of perspective. I'll leave if you really want me too.'

'I really want you to.'

'How can any of us know what we really want? We should analyse your dreams and try to understand your subconscious longings and desires.'

She rolls her eyes and mutters something I don't quite catch.

'Look, mister, I'm not interested in you. If you want to be of help you can tell me how to get to rue Challot.' She starts pulling her coat on and lays a few coins on the table. I glance at them briefly. They make for a pretty slight tip.

'I can do better; I can show you the way,' I say moving alongside her.

'How would that be better? Are you going to go or am I going to call the flics?'

'I live at 24 rue Challot - it's just around the corner. I'll leave now and you can follow me, we don't have to walk together.' There comes a time when you have to admit defeat.

'Oh Christ! I might have known it. A detective would be the sort of low life who tries to pick girls up at breakfast.'

3

'Not exclusively at breakfast.'

'Not exclusively girls either I'll bet.'

'Then you'll lose your bet. Wait a minute... how did you know I was a detective?'

She fumbles in her bag and produces my business card: Salazar Detective Agency, 24 rue Challot. I'd handed them out around the cafés and a few bistros a while ago. Well, business is business, and I could use the distraction.

'You're in luck; I do discounted rates for pretty women.'

'I really couldn't give a damn,' she says. 'I guess you're all going to be as bad as each other so there's little point me trying to find someone else. Let's go, monsieur Salazar, and please don't try to touch me: and if you can help it, don't talk to me either.'

I leave some cash for my breakfast then follow her out of the café. She's waiting for me to take the lead. A Citroën automobile pulls up and parks on the side of the road opposite us. Why would anybody with an automobile choose to drive it here? A knife sharpener moves from building to building, he's doing a good trade too by the look of him. The wind picks up and sweeps along the road, ignores my overcoat, and enters my bones. I hate the cold.

'It's not far,' I say, 'a couple of streets from here.'

My potential client tags along in silence. I'm going too fast for her but she doesn't complain and I don't slow down. 'What's your name?' I ask the question over my shoulder as she's now beginning to lag behind.

'Marie Thérèse Poncelet.' She holds out her hand for me to shake. I stop to take hold of it and then continue walking at a slower pace.

'Pleased to meet you, mademoiselle Poncelet. Would you mind if I call you Marie? I'm going to anyway - I can't stand all the Monsieur this and Madame that carry-on. The formality reminds me of school and the army.'

'I don't care, monsieur Salazar.'

'My name isn't monsieur Salazar - it's Salazar.'

I can see my building so I point it out to her.

'So, Salazar is your first name. It's odd that you called the agency Salazar Detective Agency. If your name were Jean, would you have called it Jean Detective Agency?'

'If my name were Jean I would rename myself Salazar and the agency would be as it is.'

'Is your real name Jean then?'

'No, it's Salazar.'

We reach the steps to the front door and I pull the key from my waistcoat pocket.

'Before we enter I want to make something clear to you,' she says.

'What?'

'This,' she says and pulls out a silver dagger. The sun causes it to twinkle in her hand. 'If you try anything, I'll stab you in the eye.'

'I'm not going to try anything, Marie, and I'd appreciate you putting that away.' Seeing the blade has left me feeling uneasy. It isn't the idea of her attempting to stab me which I find disturbing, it's the thought of breaking her arm if she tries it.

At the top of the first flight of stairs we pick our way through the dismantled pieces of my bicycle which are scattered all over the floor. I'd taken it apart in a fit of enthusiasm intending to clean and grease every moving part. I'll put it together again when the level of frustration at not being able to cycle is greater than my laziness.

My office is on the first floor. On the second floor, together with some rooms in the attic, is my apartment. The ground floor is occupied by Filatre, a notary, who doubles as my landlord.

I open the door to my office. 'In here,' I say.

I hadn't been expecting anyone so the place is a mess – I'm not a man who cleans from habit or custom. Books and magazines are scattered about the floor. On the desk there are four part-finished coffee cups on as many saucers. One saucer has been doubling as an extra ashtray. The ashtray itself is overflowing on the window sill.

I pick a jacket and a book off a chair and tell Marie to sit in it. She pulls an unfiltered Gauloise from a packet, not a case, and lights it. She doesn't offer me one nor does she attempt to find an ashtray. Smoking her cigarette, she sits and looks at the corner of the room near the window. I stand to one side of her and feel like a waiter; does she want me to take her order? I notice that, within the darkness which surrounds them, her eyes are a pale blue. Her dress, of good quality, is a little frayed and has splashes of mud on it. She has slung her coat over the back of the chair.

I offer her a scotch which she declines. I take a glass for myself. I watch as she lights a second cigarette, leaving the first, still burning, balanced on the edge of my desk. I ask if she would care for an ashtray. She flashes an ever-so-quick smile but says nothing. I bring over the one from the window sill and place her cigarette amongst the dead butts already there. It continues smouldering.

'If you only wanted to sit and smoke you could have stayed in the café.' I walk over to the door and open it. She'd called my bluff with the ashtray; I'm intent on regaining the upper hand. 'You don't have to stay.'

'I want to hire you. That is if you can spare the time from your rigorous cleaning routines.'

The ash from her cigarette falls on my parquet flooring. Why does that disturb me more than my fallen ash by the window sill? I close the door.

'Try to tell me, without embellishments, in as few words as possible, what it is you need me for.'

'I would like you to find somebody.' She speaks to the space I'd occupied before going to the door.

'Who?'

'A man - Gustave Marty.'

'Go on.'

I take my seat at the desk, get out my notebook and begin jotting down the salient points. When she has finished I read them to her: 'Gustave Marty, believed to be in Paris. Aged 29. Ex of Namur, Belgium. Height: One metre seventy. Dark haired and tanned. Was or is a stockbroker.'

'That's about it.'

I ask why she wants to find him. She tells me to mind my own business. I detail my fees and she pays for two weeks up front along with a retainer. There's nothing about her which suggests she can afford this. The dress she is wearing needs repair; she only bought a single coffee at the café and then left a minimal tip. When I'd named my price I'd been expecting her to haggle – then, as a favour, I would accept her reduced offer. Now I feel like a penny-pincher. This money means a lot less to me than it must do to her.

'You are not French are you Salazar?'

'No, I am English. Does that bother you?'

'Finding Marty matters to me, you do not.'

With that, and a curt goodbye, she departs, leaving behind a slight scent of lavender.

CHAPTER TWO

I stand at the window and watch as Marie walks up the street towards the boulevard St. Germain and the Métro station. A nanny pushes her charge along the street in large black perambulator. A window cleaner has set his ladders up against a building half-way down the road. The cleaner is on the pavement smoking a cigarette and talking with a man who looks like he's on his way home from work at the market. Two autobuses try to pass each other in the road as a man sitting in a horse drawn cart throws insults at them. At least I assume he's insulting them - I can't hear what he's saying but those gesticulations would look odd accompanied by pleasantries.

Marie walks with a hesitant gait making her easy to pick out as she begins to merge with the crowds near the boulevard. From here she looks as if she's challenging people. It's as if she isn't certain she has the right to be walking down the street but is doing it anyway. Earlier, when she'd told me to mind my own business, she'd cocked her head slightly as if daring me to ask more. I didn't - there are only two reasons why a woman wants to track down a man: he either did her wrong or owes her money. I wonder if her hand is still clutching that silver dagger.

I fall back into my chair and begin spinning myself around. I'd carry on all day, but my head objects after thirty seconds. I feel dizzy, an unpleasant sensation which does provide a slight distraction from life – other slight distractions from life: lighting a cigarette, drinking, narcotics, cycling, hashish, chasing women, and now chair spinning. A further distraction: sticking my nose into other people's business.

The euphoria of getting a new client evaporates when they leave the office. Once they are out of sight I feel reluctant to begin. I've come to realise my reluctance stems from a strong aversion to this work. Generally speaking I have an aversion to all work. If I could sit content all day for months on end I would. Unfortunately I'm cursed and the curse forces me to seek distraction. For a time I lived a playboy lifestyle. It lasted until the day I came to in a grotty flat in Limehouse, London. I was cold with a foggy head and lying on a dirty bed with a corpse on either side of me. The corpses had been living breathing human beings a few hours earlier when we'd smoked our opium pipes. Soldiering provided four years of diversion. It also beat and twisted my brain until I could think of nothing but dying. I'm not like the younger generation where everything is a drag and life a series of yawns. I find contentment in boredom. It comes down to this: I'd rather spend two hours waiting for a train with nothing to read than sitting in a trench waiting to go over the top. But boredom stretched to infinity is death.

I read from my notebook: Gustave Marty is or was a stockbroker. That means just about nothing. Since the crash of twenty-nine, brokers are either richer than ever or destitute. If he's among the ones who lost it all he could be in the cemetery. If he is, then the death will have been recorded somewhere. Unless he died in a back-alley and lay undisturbed for a few days. If the city authorities found his corpse, half-eaten by rats and rabid dogs, they'll have slung it into an unmarked grave without as much as a by-your-leave. The real problems will come if he's a down and out: then he could be anywhere. One thing I know for certain is that everyone notices a tramp walk by, but nobody notices who the tramp was.

I doubt that Marty would have reached that level of destitution yet, unless he ploughed all his money into American equities. I'm sure the crash will hit us soon enough but as yet it's only the American colonists of Left Bank who are suffering. With their dollars drying up back home it's only those with jobs in Paris who remain. The cocktail sluggers are leaving and you can hear people speaking French in-stead of American down on the boulevard Montparnasse. That doesn't mean the all-night parties and crowds on the terrace have given up the ghost. There are still some English and American die-hard hedonists there, partying away, unconcerned by events around them. Then there are the ones who were already broke when they arrived and are happier being broke in Paris.

I go downstairs and fill Filatre in. Apart from being good company, Filatre also has a list of researchers I can use. These researchers will check the death registers. They will also check employment records, marriage records and newspapers; they will visit the prefecture to find out if Marty is registered as an alien worker; they will even go to the Belgian embassy and enquire within. They do the general plodding and time-consuming reading - I get a summary and a bill.

Having made a few telephone calls, and engaged a researcher named Hervé, I settle down to an evening of chess and wine with Filatre. Due to our shared lack of clients we spend a lot of time playing chess. Neither of us is in need of money so we studiously ignore the fact that we have scant work to do. We could claim to be living a life of leisured refinement if it weren't for the different ghosts and demons which haunt us. I say we are men who could never be happy. Filatre replies: I could, if only things had been different.

'What's she like, your client?' Filatre puffs on his tiny black pipe and keeps his eyes on the chess board as he asks his question. Is he doing this to distract me? The sneaky so-and-so would ask a question like that to stop me noticing I have a piece in jeopardy. I scan the board for a good five minutes before replying.

'I had to resist bundling her into a taxicab and taking her to an opium den. She looked like she might enjoy it.'

'She is pretty then?'

'She is, but not in the classical way. She could easily have gotten work in those German Expressionist movies; lingering in the background as Dr Caligari attempts to hypnotise her sister. There's something desperate about her which I can't quite place. This is not the desperation of an addict or of a woman who has lost a loved one.' The silence is immediate and filled with ghosts from Filatre's past. I bite my lip and mumble something about the game. He hides it well but I can tell it's too late from the way the shadow of his head is moving gently up and down over the board. I'll win this game now and the victory will rot in my mouth.

The next two games are played in a silence disturbed only by the frequent clinking of the wine bottle against the glasses. I decide to stretch my legs and stroll around Filatre's so-called office. At one time there would have been a throng of clients visiting these rooms. Clients who would have been impressed by the floor-to-ceiling book-shelves stocked with the latest leather-bound law books. The painting of the Jardin Du Luxembourg in the Winter Time would have been new and the portrait of Marshal Ney a piece worthy of comment. Gentlemen sporting huge moustaches would have sat at Filatre's desk and smoked cigars as they discussed their business. Filatre had two partners in those pre-war days; they occupied the rooms I've taken. There were secretaries and assistants too. This building was once a hive of legal activity.

The chaise longue under the portrait of Ney is no longer a decorative item. As well as being worn and tatty it doubles up as a place to sleep. A crumpled orange blanket lies across this makeshift bed. Filatre spends as many nights sleeping in this building as I do. Unlike me, however, he owns a small house somewhere out in the countryside beyond the grasp of the city. His morning cleaner does a good job; picking up discarded clothes and taking them to be laundered, bringing croissants, and making him coffee for breakfast. Without her assistance I'd hate to imagine what this room would look like, or smell like - probably like mine.

Candles are burning on the mantle shelf above the open fire place. The ornate clock in the middle of the shelf keeps good time, when Filatre remembers to wind it up. The fireplace has retained some of its former elegance. A quick clean to remove the soot and it would be as good as new. Amongst the clutter deposited on this shelf sits the only photograph of his wife on display. I'm sure there are others at home or even in his wallet. Judging by her dress and that hat I would say this picture was taken around 1912 – only eighteen years ago and already she looks like someone from another age. She is wearing a formal dress which reaches to the floor. If her corset had been pulled a fraction tighter it would've cut her in two. She's staring straight at the camera and has the bored, serious, look people have in old photographs. I used to hate having mine taken; being told not to move, not to scratch my nose, not to blink, not to sneeze. I would rather have sat for an oil portrait, it would have been quicker.

Filatre is sitting back in his chair and watching me – must be my move. He's recovered his composure. This is most pleasing; Filatre has the uncanny ability to set me off. I can think of no worse a scene than two men sat over a chess board weeping. I take my seat and scan for any crafty traps he may have set.

'One of the things I do like about you, Salazar, is that you're such a faker.' He begins put-putting gently on his pipe which is always a sign that he's confident of victory.

'I'm no such thing,' I say without looking up or giving too much thought to the conversation. I can see he has my knight in a tight spot, although I could exchange that for a bishop, so who cares.

'Your name isn't really Salazar; at least it isn't the name you used to sign the lease.'

'Quite correct, Salazar is a name I have taken, it is not the name I was given.'

'When you speak you sound like a Parisian. There is some ambiguity about the district, but Parisian all the same. You are not a Parisian though, you are English.'

'Also true - I don't try to hide my heritage. I am thirty-four years old and have lived in Paris for the last ten years. I also spent four unpleasant years in north-eastern France. In all that makes for fourteen of my years in this country. Should I reach the age of forty I will have spent twenty years in France and so equalled the time I lived in England.'

'Your passport is British is it not?'

'My passport was issued by the British government but my heart does not recognise these unnatural boundaries.'

'You claim to be a detective too.'

'I am a detective; we've been talking about my latest client.'

'How many clients have you had so far? You may include this one in the total if you wish.'

'This case brings the total to three. I've never claimed to be an experienced detective.'

'But you do, you do. I have seen you with your clients, and when you go out. You drop your pleasant, civilised, persona and adopt a rough-edged, bawdy one.'

'It's not a persona: more another aspect to my personality. Part of me is happy to play chess and while away my days in quiet contemplation. I have another part which rages and burns. I'm sure Freud would put it down to my relationship with my father and I wouldn't contradict him.'

'So you are not a fraud. Misunderstood perhaps?'

'I don't know about that, we none of us are what we seem at any given moment. The man sitting placidly at his desk - copying from an insurance ledger - may become a raving drunk at six pm. The banker shouting at his staff and foreclosing on a mortgage may spend his spare-time pressing wild flowers. It's this understanding which has allowed me to see that your innocent looking bishop is preparing to kill my rook.' I move my rook to safety and allow the knight-bishop exchange to take place.

'There isn't much glamour in it,' I say. 'I knew I'd have to spend hours in the rain spying on people. I knew that I'd have to go around buying information from corrupted bureaucrats. I thought I might also get to spend some time drinking cocktails with sparkling ladies in chic hotel bars. There's none of that though. Detection is really quite a tedious occupation.'

'I don't believe there's much glamour in any job. Perhaps a jazz guitarist or a tango instructor: there may be some glamour in their work.' Filatre starts puffing rapidly at his pipe; that usually means he's made a blunder.

*

I find sleeping difficult. At least I find it difficult when I want to go to sleep. Come the morning, sleeping is easy. In a café at three pm, with people bustling all around, a coffee cup held in my hand, and I can nod off without a problem. At night, in a darkened room, wrapped up in my blankets, sleep evades me. I read and smoke until my eyelids begin closing of their own accord. The book slips from my fingers and I begin to drift off. I begin and go no further. Without the distraction of the book my mind begins to race. I think of my new client. A feisty woman with those eyes like sapphires hidden in a peat bog. Her sepulchre face with the hint of red about the lips stares down at me from the ceiling.

Filatre is right: I am too bawdy. André is right too: I am a bastard. I ought to learn how to talk with people again. I manage it with Filatre and him alone. During the war I always got on with my fellow officers. In those days our environment always provided a good opening for conversation. Aside from Filatre I know hardly anyone anymore. If I visit a café I drink and read then leave. I don't try to make contact. I shuffle about in a blinkered isolation, lost in the lonely world of my own paranoia.

I'll try to talk to a least three different people every day; preferably women. Having made this resolution, my mind relaxes and I fall asleep.

CHAPTER THREE

Breakfast at André's, what a delight. I take my usual seat near the window. He arrives at my table with bread, jam, coffee, and orange juice. I've placed this order nearly every day for six months - this is the first time I haven't had to ask for it.

'OK, what's the game?' I break open the bread and inspect it for broken glass.

'Isn't this what you wanted?' he asks.

It's hard to define exactly what happened to André's face as he spoke – it could be he smiled.

'What I want has never troubled you before. Why are you still hanging around my table? Normally, once the food's been deposited, you make good your escape.'

'Perhaps I am turning over a new leaf. I wish only for my customers to be happy.'

'If you keep this up any longer I'm leaving. What is it? Tell me and be done with it.' The orange juice smells like orange, and the coffee like coffee, so I feel safe taking a drink.

'All right, I want to know what happened with that girl yesterday. She looked as if she was as repulsed by you as the rest of the world is. Then you left and she followed you up the street like a loyal puppy. How did you do it?'

'André, my dear fellow, you shall never know.'

Realising I'm not about to start gossiping, André leaves me in peace. I could have exploited his curiosity to get breakfast on the house. To do that I would've had to endure his company – that's a price I'm not willing to pay. I drink my coffee, eat my bread, down the juice and light up a cigarette.

This morning I'll visit the prefecture at the Hôtel de Ville. If Gustave Marty is operating at the Paris Bourse he must be registered with them. This is something Hervé could do but I fancy a walk. Before leaving I take the café copy of the local paper and have a read. During my second cigarette I remember my resolution from last night. If I can speak to someone in here I'll have the whole day to find another two.

I replace the paper in the hanging rack near the door, return to my table, and scan the room. You couldn't pick a worse place to start a conversation. The people here know me and they would no more desire my company than I desire André's. I sit back down and subject the faces I don't recognise to further scrutiny. The clientele get uglier with each passing day; what beautiful person, when confronted with André's visage, would wish to eat in here?

There are two women I haven't seen before. They look like dishevelled harpies. Each of them has a man, almost certainly their husbands, sitting in glum silence at their side. One fellow is looking absent-mindedly at a bottle of gin behind the counter. The other is being scolded - no doubt for getting the wrong jam or forgetting to put sugar into his wife's coffee before his own. He glances in my direction and catches my eye. I nod at him. He returns with a smile and for a brief second he is away from her; we are talking about sport and buying each other beer. Ah! But no, Monsieur, I do not believe she loves you really.

With no suitable candidates in the café I cast my gaze out to the street. There may be an elegant woman who, despite the early hour, needs escorting to a cocktail bar - if only she could find a suitable fellow like me to do the escorting. No such person exists in my line of vision. If she did I'd probably get her as far as the front door of the Ritz before the orderlies from the insane asylum swooped down to take her back into custody.

I'm about to return to work, satisfied that I've made a slight effort at changing my ways, when I notice a skinny lad watching me from up a side road. He is trying to make himself appear inconspicuous by smoking and looking the other way. To make sure he's watching me, I switch to the seat opposite. Then I take out a cigarette and position my cigarette case on the table to act as a mirror. The metal is dull so the reflection isn't clear. Yet I can see he's still watching me, and I don't like it one bit. He's either a mugger or he's acting as lookout while my apartment is burgled. Judging by his lack of subtlety I'd say he's not used to spying on people. I'll use that inexperience to trap him.

Without formulating a plan I leave the café and make my way home. I ought to get into the habit of carrying my revolver. As I get closer to my apartment I light a cigarette and take a look into the large front window. I don't have a clear view from here but I do see Filatre walk into sight smoking his pipe. He pulls a book from a shelf and stands there skimming through a few pages before replacing it. I take a look behind me and see the guy waiting at a street corner. He obviously isn't the lookout for a burglar, so what then?

I cast my cigarette into the road and walk off casually. My stomach begins twisting and dancing with excitement and nervousness. Soon I'll engineer a showdown. From this distance the lad doesn't look physically strong but he could be carrying a knife or even a pistol. If he is, one of us will come to regret it.

I do have moments of paranoia - particularly at night - when I think people are following me. On those occasions it's a feeling, I never actually see anybody. This time there is a man of medium height wearing a dark jacket on my tail. Leading him along the road and taking indiscriminate turns here and there, I spot him trying to hide behind pissoirs and plane trees. There is no doubt that he's following me.

I turn up a side street, then jump down a few stairs towards someone's basement apartment. This is a residential street and most of the occupants are out at work. Down here I'm partially obscured from the road. Although I know I am hidden, I feel certain he's watching me, preparing to slit my throat should I drop my guard. I hear his approaching footsteps, confident as they come around the corner. He walks past the stairway then pauses. If he turns around he'll see me and I'm vulnerable down here. I must act fast. Without thinking I creep quickly up the stairs and leap at him. I lock my arms around his legs and rugby tackle him to the ground. He lets out a yelp of surprise and topples forward on to his face.

I stick my knee into the middle of his spine and put some weight into it. His arms begin flailing. I grab one and wrench it up behind his back. With my left hand I take hold of a clump of hair from the top of his head and force him to his feet. I march him down the stairs where I'd been hiding. It's dark down here and stinks of piss and rotting vegetable matter. I push him against the wall and give his arm a vicious twist. He screams out in pain. Nobody hears, or if they did they choose to ignore it. I let go of his hair while keeping my grip on his arm. He struggles so I give his head a shove. The side of his face hits the wall.

'I'm going to ask you some questions and you're going to answer. If you don't, or I don't like your answers, I'll break your arm. Then I'll break your other arm. Then your legs.' I press his face hard against the wall and put my mouth up to his ear. 'Who are you?' I whisper.

'Stefan Silvestre.' His voice is quavering and I can feel his body shuddering.

I reach around to feel inside his black jacket. No gun, no knife. I get his wallet. I release his arm and punch him in the kidneys. As he wallows about on the floor moaning and getting his suit dirty, I go through his papers. If he isn't Stefan Silvestre he's carrying a forged library card. He's too inept to be a real threat. I recognise the address on the card; it's a stinking Montmartre side-alley. From what he's carrying I get the following: occupation, student; age, 20; marital-status, single; nationality, French. The wallet is old, made of brown leather – there's no money in it. Stefan is lying on the floor crying. I can see a hole in the sole of one of his shoes.

He's plugged it with cardboard which has also worn through.

'Get up and tell me why you've been following me.'

He groans and holds on to the wall for support as he climbs to his feet. He looks resentful of the rough treatment whilst being resigned to it. I feel like punching him down again for being so pathetic. I look away for a moment as a pang of guilt erupts in my chest.

'I wanted to find out why she was with you,' he says.

His right cheek is grazed and his bottom lip is bleeding.

'Why who was with me?'

'Marie, she came to see you yesterday.'

'Who sent you?'

He pauses, so I slap him across the face. It's a reaction to the guilt I'd felt - a reminder that now is not the time for sentiment.

'Nobody sent me. I watch out for her, that's all.'

He starts blubbing and puts his arms over his head to shield himself from further blows. I want to hit him, to intimidate him into talking. Instead I crack. I give up the tough guy routine and pass him my handkerchief. Turning his face from me he takes it and uses it to dry his eyes. From his defensive actions I can see he's expecting me to strike him again.

'I haven't finished with you,' I say, 'but I'm not going to hit you unless you attempt to run away. Once you've finished sniffling, we're going to a café. I'll get us something to eat and you can answer my questions. I warn you though, and I don't care who might be watching, if you give me the run-around I'll break your scrawny neck.'

For some people wine is a greater aid to talking than violence.

We sit in a café in Montparnasse where the city sprawl rubs up against fields and pastures. This café is frequented by goat herders. They stop off here before going door-to-door selling their cheeses. Nobody pays us the least bit of attention: we are city folk, and despite living within the city limits, these are country folk.

Stefan is moody and sulking. I withstand his silence and keep his wine glass topped up. He gulps it down, smouldering with anger. I've made a serious mistake - rather than grow talkative he looks more likely to unleash a lot of pent up rage. He's definitely the sort who'd stick a penknife in your back over some inconsequential slight. I don't take my eyes off him. I wait and smoke, trying not to think too much about what happened down those stairs.

'So, what is she to you?' I ask.

'Nothing.'

'Nothing; yet you come spying on me because she visited me yesterday.'

He shrugs like some pétanque player after an indifferent shot. We sit in silence again for a little longer. He drinks more wine, I light another cigarette.

'More than nothing, everything.' He speaks to a remaining slurp of wine in his glass.

'I see – you're jealous.'

'No, not of you, a detective!' He turns his body away from me whilst folding his arms and crossing his legs. 'I followed her after she left your office. You didn't leave with her. Your connection to her is professional.'

He's turned so far he is almost talking to me over his shoulder. He must have realised this is odd because he turns around to face me again. His arms and legs remain folded and crossed. There's a large bruise forming around the cut on his cheek.

'You saw all that and still, the next day, you come and follow me.'

I call the waiter over to buy some cigarettes.

'I am jealous. I am jealous of everyone and everything. It comes and goes. If she rides on the Métro I think "so what". Then I start thinking about the other people there, the men, ogling her, perhaps making her laugh. Fear and frustration consume me like fire. I want to be the one who makes her laugh, not strangers. And you know what women are like.'

The wine is working. I refill his glass. 'Go on, what are

they like?'

'It would only take some cocky bastard and who knows... She may go off with him. He'll be the sort of guy women fall for, shallow and confident, full of sweet words. She'll fall for his spiel and allow him to defile her.'

'You've confused defiling with fucking.'

'No, defile! She should only sleep with men who love her and that sort of man loves none but himself.'

'Don't be an arse, Stefan. Women and men should sleep with anyone who can bring them pleasure.'

'She should be with me!'

'I made her laugh you know,' I say, lying. She hadn't even smiled. Stefan falls silent. 'Yeah, and she kissed me whilst we were talking. I think she goes for tough guys. I had to push her away. Even when she was leaving she asked me to make love to her in the hallway. I was tempted; after all she's totally edible.'

'You bastard!' He stands up knocking over his chair and swaying slightly.

'Calm down, Stefan. I doubt she's laughed at anything or anyone for more than a year. I've never met a more frigid woman than your Marie.'

'You're still a bastard.' He sits down again.

'No, my friend, I'm much worse than that.'

Other than his infatuation with my client I get nothing of interest from him. I ask about Gustave Marty - he knows nothing. The mention of a man's name gets him paranoid, imagining Marie in the arms of yet another unknown man. It may be worth tracking him down again in a week or so to see what he's been able to find out. I order some food which Stefan eats without pause. When he finishes, I let him go. It's almost sad - that lad following around a girl who has no interest in him. I guess these nihilistic obsessions fill the gap left by the death of God.

CHAPTER FOUR

The hand I'd used to hit Stefan with is throbbing. I stretch out the fingers before contracting them into a fist. I repeat the process a few times. Another glass of wine is required to ease the pain. The waiter brings over my drink and gives me a look. My school masters used to give me the same look. Back then it meant: I don't have enough on you yet but I'm getting the cane out in readiness. I'm sure the waiter believes I've been having a violent lover's tiff with Stefan. I imagine he could believe a series of things stranger than that.

From the café it's a five-minute walk to the Gare Montparnasse. It takes me ten. My legs are stiff; they are used to walking or cycling, not jumping up and down stairwells. I ride the Métro to the Hôtel de Ville station. This is the part of Paris where the tour guides lead the sightseers before finally letting them hit the strip clubs of Montmartre.

The Hôtel de Ville itself is a grand building which has stood on this spot, in one form or another, for over six hundred years. The flag of the Republic flutters from a pole on the roof. The building could easily be mistaken for a grand seventeenth century palace - an emblem of Parisian pomp and optimism. The large expanse in front of the building allows folk to walk about with their hands in their pockets asking strangers for money.

I cross the square to the entrance. If I close my eyes, and listen to the bustle of people on the busy road behind me, I can imagine the Communards marching through the streets holding burning torches. Government forces open fire on the crowd; they retaliate by sending the torches cascading through the night sky onto the building. Please, when I open my eyes, may the building be in flames. There is no fire, only a gentle drizzle and pigeon shit on the grey slatted roof top.

The splendour of the building does not influence the monotony of the work going on inside. Forms are completed, signed and countersigned. Copies are made and dispatched to department heads. To wit, all the mundane workings of the French bureaucracy. To think Robespierre was shot in the jaw in this very building.

I enter through the grand front door and a near-deaf man asks me what I want. Why give a man who is hard of hearing the job of enquiring after my purpose? He is not too old, probably fifty. His hands tremble and his head jerks to the left sporadically. These tics and his overly officious manner are a good line of defence; he has been strategically placed to deter visitors.

It doesn't take a detective to work out why he is like this. I decide to make him my first conversational victim of the day. If I do this right I may even get the information I'm after.

'Was it at Verdun?' That's as good a place to start as any.

'I was at Verdun,' he replies. 'The second offensive under General Pétain, a true hero of France. Unlike the other snivelling bastards who led our troops.'

'I'll drink to that, sir!' I say. There aren't many generals who came out of that war with any credit but Pétain is among them.

'Marne was where this happened.' He taps his ear. 'A shell exploded not four metres from me. Since that day I have had to put up with a constant high pitched squeal. I hardly sleep nowadays, how about you?'

'I sleep, until the dreams begin...'

I tell him about Passchendaele. I'm not sure why I picked that and not, for instance, the Somme. Each day of the war contributed to the mix of nightmares. Fear came from the bombardments and the charges across No Man's Land. The nightmares though, they came from everywhere; seeing body-parts amongst the scrub after a shelling, or a corpse - seeming to smile amongst a pile of the dead. My nights in a hospital tent were more terrifying than charging the German lines. On a charge there was always the chance of a quick death.

The man introduces himself as Lucien. We reminisce about the bad times as if they were good times. By giving me his full concentration, and turning so his right ear is pointing towards me, he is able to catch what I'm saying.

'Come with me, sir, the person you need is over here.'

Lucien leads me to a man sitting at a small counter tucked away in the corner. Unlike nearly every other spot in the room there is no queue here. Lucien explains that I am a Tommy and a good sort. The sitting man looks to be fine at first, aside from his rapid blinking. His hair is neat, nicely parted in the centre and slicked away from his forehead. He is wearing a clean jacket and a freshly pressed shirt. His Charlie Chaplin moustache is well groomed. There are no ink stains on his cuffs and his nails are unbitten.

The deaf man leaves us and the one behind the desk reaches out to shake my hand. I lean over, as he doesn't stand, and notice he has two stumps in place of legs. This pair must be part of the work for veterans programme; every company has to employ a small percentage of the living dead. He introduces himself as Jacques.

'Well sir, if Lucien says you are a good sort then a good sort you are. How may I help you?'

Finding an official who wants to help is miraculous. The rest of the room is packed with people being frustrated by contrary clerks. Ah! I get it. This man is going to do all he can to help but I'll soon discover he is an incompetent nincompoop. I'll smile politely as he spills papers all over the floor. Then I'll have to pick them up for him because he is incapacitated. Eventually I'll leave knowing less than I did when I arrived and he'll be calling out, 'remember to ask for me if you need anything else.' If I ever come here again he'll buttonhole me and I'll never be able to speak to a competent, if begrudgingly slow, official again.

'Gustave Marty, hey?' He drums his fingers on the desk and looks up at the corner of the ceiling. 'Give me ten minutes please. Wait here, or if you prefer go to a café and return in half an hour. That'll give me plenty of time to go through the records. Lucien will recognise you when you return and he'll bring you straight here.'

On saying this he lifts himself off his stool and into a wheelchair. I watch as he disappears through a doorway at the back of the office. I don't want to leave in case I can't get back in again. Sitting at the desk, alone, looking at an empty stool, I begin to feel foolish. I take his advice and head out to find a café.

Being in the centre of Paris, finding a café is easy. Having a choice makes things difficult. I can see a perfectly good café across the rue de Rivoli. There are large windows for those inside to gaze through and a few seats out front for those who want to pretend it isn't freezing. The trouble is it's on the other side of the road and there are far too many automobiles - I want a coffee, not a half-hour wait for a break in the traffic. I sometimes visit a café on the Île de la Cité – that's about five minutes from here. I cross the Seine to the island and take a side road which meanders off behind the Notre Dame cathedral. Sightseers are filling up the other cafés on the island. This one is left for the locals and people like me who spend their time roaming the city.

Thirty minutes later I reappear at the Hôtel de Ville. Lucien spots me and disengages himself from a woman who is talking at him. He guides me through the crowd to Jacques as if I am the British ambassador. As he turns to leave I tuck a few francs into his breast pocket. Jacques looks pleased with himself and is pointing at a sheet of paper on his desk.

'Did you find something, Jacques... or has The Girl from Havana asked you out?'

'I found something, monsieur Salazar. I found a total of four Gustave Martys. I didn't catch the age of yours.'

'I'm not certain, younger than me, say between twenty-six and thirty-two.'

My client had told me that Marty is twenty-nine, but I don't want to restrict the list of suspects yet.

'Oh, well in that case I have three Gustave Martys. The fourth Marty has started drawing his five hundred franc war pension. That puts him between fifty and fifty-five.'

Jacques produces a ruler from under his desk and neatly crosses something out. I lean over to take a look at what he's working on. I fear my prediction of Jacques's incompetence may be coming true. Is he really going to give me a piece of paper with the name Gustave Marty written on it four times?

'Well there you are then, monsieur Salazar.' He hands me the sheet and my heart sinks. 'You will see that I have numbered the Martys one to four. Number four has been struck from the record, leaving one to three. Here,' he hands me three more sheets of paper, 'are pages numbered one to three.' He takes the fourth sheet, scrunches it up, and casts it into a waste paper basket behind him.

'Good shot, Jacques.'

'I can't afford to miss,' he says. 'There is a name and an address and, where known, an employer. These are the Martys I could find in Paris as of last month. It is possible there have been more who have come and gone. If you need me to track those I will require further information, such as a date of birth.'

'This is fantastic, Jacques.' I reach over to give him a fifty franc note.

'Much appreciated, monsieur Salazar. I would have done it for free but I feel a lot happier this way.'

We shake hands and he wishes me good luck. I exchange nods with Lucien on my way out.

Once back outside I skim through Jacques's notes to make sure they aren't all gibberish. They aren't, so I trot along to the café near Notre Dame to study them in detail. The café is empty. I retake the seat I had used earlier. I pull the three pieces of paper out of my pocket and place them on the table. I'm mystified by the separate key page with Gustave Marty written multiple times on it.

The first page gives an address near the Champs-Élysées. It is an apartment on rue Balzac not too far from the Arc de Triomphe. The second is an obscure address over in the south-west of the city on the Île Saint-Germain - a man might go there if he were trying to hide. Why else would he go there? The third address brings me out in a cold sweat: rue de la Ferme 7. Saint-Denis.

Images from Saint-Denis flash through my head. It's like swallowing a fast acting poison. The desperation I'd felt in those times comes rushing back and kicks me in the guts. Those were suicide days. I thought I could pretend they'd never happened. I push the papers away. The air in the room is thinning out and I can't see the café anymore. Am I still here? I call out for the waiter and see a man standing somewhere, perhaps a mile away. A voice echoes from the void, 'Monsieur, monsieur.' Where am I? From instinct I mutter, 'bring me wine, red wine.' I'm going to be sick. A glass of wine appears before me. I down it and say, 'more'. I hope there is someone near enough to have heard me. Another glass appears and I take a few sips. Gradually the café comes back into focus. The waiter is standing nearby with a concerned look on his face. 'I'm okay thank you,' I say. The waiter nods and returns to the counter.

I don't know what has just happened. I feel as if I've been abused in some way. Saint-Denis was a hell I never wish to visit again. For two years I existed in that desolate wasteland. The streets disgusted me, the people repulsed me. I was down-and-out living hand-to-mouth in a revolting one-roomed apartment. Every day was a continuous battle against cold and hunger, my only distractions being cheap wine and the occasional screams emanating from the street. Days and nights would pass with nothing to mark them out. I'd lie in my bed for hours on end without sleeping or moving, just looking at the ceiling, the wall, or the dead flames that once lived in the fire.

If Marty is living in Saint-Denis then he is welcome to it. I'll go there last if I go there at all. Île Saint-Germain first, that address strikes me as unnaturally suspicious. No, rue Balzac off the Champs-Élysées should be first. That is a stockbroker's address. The island is where a man hiding would live. Is Marty actually hiding? If someone who knew me twelve years ago tried to find me today they would have a fine time going about it. Perhaps I ought to place one of those intriguing advertisements in the newspapers: Gustave Marty, ex of Namur, please contact Salazar for personal advantage.

I take out some coins to pay for the wine and toss one of them. It spins on the table before landing olive sprig up. That's decided then – I'll go to Île Saint-Germain first. There is no Métro station near the island so I'll take a tram for the final leg of the journey.

Life goes on hold when you are riding the Métro. Feelings and thoughts evaporate at the pay gates and don't return until you reach the surface. Is it a result of being underground? Do miners live their lives in this state of limbo and is this what makes their work bearable?

I try to plan what I'll say to Marty when I meet him. All I can think to do is ask if he is from Namur. If he says 'yes' then I'll bid him good day and take his address around to Marie's place. If he says 'no', how will I know if he is telling the truth? I can't attack or threaten him. If I had a camera I could wait outside his home and take a photograph of him when he comes out. He would have to look straight at me and hold the pose for a few moments as I exposed the frame. I could ask his concierge about him, she's bound to talk to me - so long as I keep the money flowing. If Marty has been living there all his life I'll be able to rule him out. Yes, I will start with the concierge, claiming to be a long lost friend trying to track down my old pal Gustave.

Fresh air, what a blessing. A slight drizzle is falling as I climb up into the carriage. I don't care – after my twenty minutes in the Métro I feel like a convict released after years of imprisonment. The tram slips along at a fair old rate, screeching on the bends and rattling the bell whenever a horse cart comes into view. From in here I can keep an eye on the city and experience the weather. There isn't a lot too experience. The journey is so quick my legs don't get cramp from the tiny space I've had to force them into.

Not too far from the tram stop is a bridge across to the pointless island. The city already has two perfectly good islands with the Île de Cité and Île Saint-Louis. Those can boast Notre Dame, Sainte Chapelle, and the benefits of a central location. This island has warehouses, anonymous buildings, and a rundown park. Should I ever need to hide out I'd come here and then leave; I'd rather get caught than live in a dump like this. If Paris is a beautiful woman then this is her elbow.

While crossing the bridge I develop a strange longing for the Métro. I stop and lean over the railings to look in to the river. At least it isn't Saint-Denis. That thought cheers me enough to continue across with a spring in my step. I walk around looking for the hidden beauty which once attracted painters like Courbet. Parts of the East-End of London are like this, without the park but with opium dens and good old fashioned boozers instead. I have fond memories of journeys around there - before the incident with the corpses. Ah! I am already walking along Marty's street. It's a few minutes past three pm on a Wednesday afternoon, Marty ought to be out at work. That will leave me plenty of time to talk to the concierge. I wouldn't normally rate my chances of success there; however, my visit to the Hôtel de Ville has left me in a positive mood.

CHAPTER FIVE

As I walk along the barren streets, wind blowing straight into my face, I think about how depressing it must be to have to live here. There are no automobiles and few people are about. They could use a café to brighten the place up. Something with lights, music, and laughter.

This place could easily have been a small Breton town. Two women are standing, hands on hips, at the end of the road talking. Despite the lack of any other visible activity there is a lot of noise. Running along the side of the island are a number of warehouses. They must be unloading a barge or two over there.

The front door to Marty's building has been left open. Inside, the flooring in the hallway consists of red ceramic tiles. My steps make loud clipping noises. A bicycle is leaning against a wall. Someone has been taking care of it – the chain and mud guards are clean, the tyres are nicely inflated, and the bell is glimmering. I wonder if it's ever ridden.

A wooden staircase to my left leads upstairs. There must be another one somewhere leading down – a building like this will have a dingy cellar. To my right is a typical concierge door - the bottom half is closed and the top half is open allowing her to listen out for anyone coming or going. I take a few steps towards this doorway when the concierge herself appears.

'You're too late young man - she's gone. Now sling your hook and don't come around here again.'

She folds her arms, defying me to speak.

'But, my dear lady, it is you I came to visit.'

'Rubbish! If you haven't come sniffing around for that tart on the second floor then you must be a salesman. I don't want whatever it is you're offering and I certainly don't need it.' She leans over the door to look me up and down. 'Where are your samples?'

'I don't have anything to sell, madam. I am looking for an old friend of mine called Gustave Marty. I was informed that he lived here.'

This gives her pause for thought and during the pause I make it the rest of the way to her door.

'Monsieur Marty indeed. And why wouldn't you look for him at work if you two are such good friends?'

'That's just it, Marty and I are old friends who have lost touch. I know he lives somewhere in Paris. But I don't know if the Marty who lives here is the same Marty I used to knock about with in Belgium.'

'I see. In that case you will have to wait until six o'clock, which is when he comes home from work. You can't wait here. You'll have to go outside. And I don't want you loitering around the entrance, either.'

'It's a bit too cold to wait outside for three hours, is there a café nearby?'

'Near enough, although probably not near enough for you. Cross the bridge and keep on going, you'll come to a café. Eventually.'

'Perhaps I might be allowed to wait in his rooms.' I reach into my jacket and pull out my wallet.

'I don't think so.' She shakes her head without taking her eyes off the wallet.

'I realise it would be an imposition, perhaps I could compensate you for the trouble?'

I remove a twenty franc note and hold it towards her door.

'Well, monsieur Marty is a good tenant and I shouldn't want to inconvenience one of his friends.'

She takes the money and gives it a once over. I almost expect her to bite the corners like it's a Spanish doubloon.

After satisfying herself that

The note is genuine she leads me up three flights of stairs. On each level I look down the corridor and each time I am faced with the open door of the WC. Thankfully none of them are occupied. We reach Marty's apartment where she pulls a key from her apron and unlocks the door. She then leaves and I am free to enter Marty's apartment alone. I'm glad there is no concierge in my building; Filatre would never let anyone into my private rooms for twenty francs.

The front door enters directly into Marty's living quarters. It's a sparse affair with a dining table in the middle and four chairs around it. The floorboards are in need of a varnish, some of them are in need of replacing. A small corner section of the room masquerades as a kitchen. Judging by the pans piled up on the side I would say that Marty does not eat out. There are no taps above the sink which means no running water; I wouldn't have expected there to be in a building like this. The only door leading off this room, other than the one I came in through, leads into Marty's bedroom. I enter and take a look around.

He has a cot bed, which has been neatly made up. Near the window there's a washbowl with a mirror hanging above it. The leather strop for his razor is attached to a nail in the window frame. On the bedside table is a photograph of a young woman in her late teens wearing a flowery dress. She stands in a dusty village square; it's somewhere French and warm-looking. At a guess I'd say a town near Toulouse or Bordeaux. If this Marty is the one I am looking for then she is too old to be his daughter and too young to be his lover.

The apartment isn't the sort of place a stockbroker would live in. If he is still a broker then this is too plain, too far from the city, and too impoverished. I should've asked the concierge where Marty works. I go back to the living room. There's nothing here that reveals any more of his identity. A volume of Baudelaire's poetry has been discarded on the dining table alongside yesterday's newspaper. I spy a cupboard in one of the corners of the room and decide to examine it. Pieces of paper tumble to the floor as I pull open the top drawer. The entire drawer is stuffed full of receipts and scraps of papers with household accounts scribbled on them. I forage around and find a brown folder containing some official documents. A birth certificate: Gustave Paul Marty, born March 13th 1910, Castelnaudary in the department of Aude. Down south, probably where that girl is in the photograph. I follow Jacques's example and cross his name off my list.

I give the concierge a wave - she rolls her eyes. The wind has picked up and is now escorted by a misty drizzle. I feel tired and want to sleep. If I pull my hat down and lift up the lapels of my coat I could lean against that wall and get ten minutes kip. There aren't too many people around on this island and I don't think there will be until six o'clock. Maybe I could sleep for an hour. The misty drizzle turns to rain. If I sleep outside now I'll get soaked. There was a time when I had spots around the city, in parks and under bridges, where I could go and sleep. It helped that I was dressed like, and looked like, a tramp. The only people who ever disturbed me were other tramps and they soon learnt to leave me alone.

Instead of riding to the Métro station I could stay on the tram – it would take me within half a mile of home. No, it's nearly four pm, if I go home now I'll fall asleep and I won't wake until eight or nine. Then it'll be too late to go calling on strangers.

I ride the Métro to the stop at Concorde where I change trains to ride under the Champs-Élysées. Three stops along and I arrive at one end of the rue Balzac. Whilst disliking the Métro I can't fault its usefulness.

In contrast to the island, people here are in abundance; gathered in doorways or crowding into cafés. They are also sitting in automobiles and driving up and down the road tooting their horns. There are quite a few of them in vehicles parked along the street. They pay a premium to live in the centre of Paris, have all its amenities within walking distance, and then they go and buy themselves expensive automobiles.

Rain is falling heavily so I scurry along keeping close to the buildings. Here the pavements are wider than elsewhere and lined with trees. The road between the pavements is wider too – creating the spaces you don't find in other areas of the city. This is where the politicians and lawyers live. The bankers, the stockbrokers, the business executives, and doctors live here too. There are also the well-to-do artists, the ones who have made it, like Picasso, alongside the owners of the fashion houses. If the whole district sank like Atlantis, we might miss the doctors but we'd get by.

A doorman stands to attention outside Marty's building. I hadn't bargained on that. He eyes me suspiciously as I approach.

'Lovely weather,' I say.

I knew it was a mistake as the words were leaving my mouth. Don't converse with the staff – it never goes down well. He doesn't reply or step from the doorway or open the door. 'I'm a friend of Gustave Marty's,' I add.

'Monsieur Marty is not at home, sir. If you would care to wait you may do so quietly in the lobby.'

He gestures towards a black leather chair in a sparse-looking lobby area. I'm not going to sit in there twiddling my thumbs like an expectant father.

'Do you know where I can find him?'

'He's right behind you, sir.'

I turn to see a man approaching on a noisy motorcycle. I say motorcycle but this looks more like a bicycle with an engine strapped to the top tube. He rides the machine right up to the door before jumping off. He is sporting a brown pilot's jacket and a brown leather cap with goggles. If I hadn't seen him arrive I'd have been searching for his aeroplane.

'Park it up for me, Hugo,' he says to the doorman.

'A gentleman is here to see you,' Hugo replies.

I touch the brim of my hat by way of introduction.

'Really, well come in out of the rain, why don't you.' He beckons me to follow him inside. 'What did you want to see me about?'

This could be the Marty I am looking for. He looks about the right age, late twenties. He has the poise of somebody with money, although I would have pegged him as being from a rich French family. I can't ask him straight out if he is Marty from Namur in case he asks why I want to know.

'I am not certain if it's you I am after,' I say. 'I am looking for a man named Gustave Marty.'

'Are you indeed? I am Gustave Marty, so it must be me you are looking for.'

'That fact will require some conformation, sir.'

'If my word is not good enough for you, then,' he opens the entrance door, 'I say, Hugo, what is my name?'

'Monsieur Marty, sir.'

'There you are, or would you like him to confirm the Gustave part too?'

He is grinning now and gives his jacket a good shake, flicking rain everywhere.

'Please understand, monsieur Marty, that I do not doubt your name. I have been asked to find a particular Gustave Marty.'

'Why is that?'

'He has been left a sizable inheritance by a great-aunt in Belgium.' Sometimes my best ideas are formed in my mouth.

'Sizeable, hey. I don't recall having a great-aunt in Belgium. How much was it exactly?'

'I am not at liberty to reveal that information, sir, but, I assure you, it is a sizable sum. The Gustave Marty I seek was raised in Namur, Belgium.'

'Drat, that puts me out of the running; I was born and brought up in Paris. Still, I may be related, after-all how many Gustave Martys can there be?'

I smile politely. I knew it wouldn't be him because I so wanted it to be him. I'm destined to go on seeking Gustave Marty like a modern-day King Pellinore after the Questing Beast.

'Are you all right, you look a bit peaky?' he says.

'Fine, thank you,' I reply.

'Would you care to come upstairs? I can offer you a cognac and a chance to dry off.'

Anything to delay my trip to the city's northern slums. Marty leads me to a clanky elevator. I have never really enjoyed riding in these contraptions. They are noisy and slow. I could get up these stairs in half the time it has taken us to ride and I wouldn't be dangling by a thread four storeys up. We ride to the top floor where I follow Marty along a corridor to his apartment.

Once inside we enter a huge room with windows stretching from the floor to the ceiling. The rain has stopped and I can see straight across to the Eiffel Tower, up north to the Sacré-Cœur, and across at the roofs of all the buildings of Paris. Marty hands me a cognac and takes my coat which he hangs over a hot radiator. He comes and stands next to me at the window.

'Beautiful, isn't it,' he says.

'It can be. I like the changing colour of the roof slates as the rain starts evaporating,' I say.

He puts his arm around my waist and moves closer. I push him away.

'Don't play hard-to-get. I know why you came here, Morineau sent you. All that stuff about great-aunts indeed. Come on, take off your clothes, let me see that sizable inheritance.'

'Look, mister, if you touch me again I'll break your arm.'

'Come on, don't play the fool now, I don't care for the hard-to-get act.' He steps forward and tries to kiss me so I sock him on the jaw. He staggers back, holding his chin.

'You miserable bastard. What did you do that for?'

'I wanted you to take the hint.'

'You could have pushed me away. A kiss wouldn't have hurt, but this did. I want you to leave.'

That's one of his wants I can satisfy. I leave him sitting on the settee rubbing his jaw. I feel pretty rotten and I would have liked to have finished my cognac. I shouldn't feel too bad; I did say no and he didn't listen. I could call the police and have him locked up. Although I would then have to testify in court and I wouldn't want that. I wouldn't want that at all.

CHAPTER SIX

By the time I hit the street I'm in a foul mood. The incident with Marty hasn't helped. That's not all of it though. With two possibilities struck off my list I am down to the final Marty. The Saint-Denis Marty.

During my time in Saint-Denis I lived in a fog of depression. Lack of food, lack of sleep, lack of warmth, all contributed to the downward spiral. I was reduced to crawling the street in rags, living off rancid food and poisonous wine. All this is to glamorise my time there. The hardship, the starvation, it was all a distraction from the interminable boredom. Every waking second was thumped into my head and played over and over until it lost all meaning. Then the next second would begin. I kept company with two war cripples, so disfigured nobody else could tolerate the sight of them. There we were, in the gutter, children too frightened to look at us. Three men tramping from street to street with piss-stained pants, waving our fists at the sky. Three men, who, with our very souls, helped to win the war.

I've got to snap out of this. Saint-Denis is a name on the map, I won't invest it with supernatural powers. I shan't revert to my past ways the moment my feet dirty themselves on its streets.

To survive in this game I need my wits about me. I can't afford this self-indulgent wallowing. I'll also need to dress down. For the Saint-Denis trip I'll take my knuckle-duster.

I'll strap a knife to my leg an inch above my ankle. Most importantly - I'll wear my holster and gun.

The rain has cleared up and there is nowhere I need to be, so I'll walk home. When you hold no purpose, and time is no constraint, the city can intrigue and lure you. I move from street to street on whims as all thought of the various Martys slips away. I obtain a state of relaxed semi-contentment tinted by curiosity. The closer I get to home the more I deviate through side-alleys and back streets. The evening is pleasant now and warm for a change, perhaps spring has finally arrived. I like to imagine that I'm encountering all the different aspects of life in the district; I can be foolish that way sometimes. I am encountering the life that comes out during the day: there is another city which exists at night.

I gaze through apartment windows and watch the plays being enacted there. Some stage sets are empty, the occupants of the apartments not yet returned from work. I would love to travel beyond this view from the street, to know more about those glimpsed lives. Even if I were to float into those rooms, and hover unnoticed up by the ceiling light, I would still not be fully satisfied. I need to know the thoughts passing through their heads - what dreams are these people enjoying or enduring?

I spy a tatty and intriguing red door. The door is in a redbrick building under a brightly painted sign reading 'Café Copenhagen'. The building is dilapidated and incongruous; there aren't many redbrick buildings in Paris. This one could have been transported here direct from Limehouse: certainly Sherlock Holmes must be disguised as a tramp and hiding inside. Perhaps it is a place where enchantresses gather. Small enclaves of women who spend their nights casting spells across the city, enticing young men to take a walk across the bridge of suicides.

The physical aspect of the building is uninviting to the point of repugnance. I am compelled to enter. If my feet should attempt to walk away I would turn myself upside down and walk there on my hands. Diversions are found in low dives.

Nervousness causes me to hesitate as I cross the street. I curse this cowardly sentiment without moving forward. Eventually curiosity overwhelms all other feelings and I proceed. I stand in the empty street before the tatty red door. There is no indication that the place is open. Nor indeed is there any contrary evidence, so I give the door a push. It creaks and opens into a dank corridor which slopes away towards a faint light. Stepping into the darkness I encounter a pungent smell which indicates that this hallway must have been used for pissing in on more than one occasion. Without delay I head for the faint light emanating from a doorway.

I push the door open and enter a cellar room which has been converted into a café bar. The place feels as if it were deep underground, a forgotten vault in the Parthenon, though I can only be four or five feet below street level. The smell here is pleasant; predominantly a coffee and tobacco medley infused with the unmistakable aroma of marijuana. I linger in the doorway, allowing my eyes to adjust to the dimmed lighting. A gramophone plays a scratchy rendition of Crazy Rhythm which blends with the conversations going on near the bar. Then there is just the music.

There are five customers in the café plus one waiter. I take a seat at a table by the wall towards the rear of the room. By doing this I am seated at the furthest point from the other customers, who are either looking at me or talking about me. My every action is scrutinised. The waiter arrives promptly to take my order. This could be a criminal hangout or a political hole for the types who throw bombs. What will they do if they decide I am a government spy? They could slip a drug into my drink. My sedated body bundled out the back never to be seen again. I am beginning to sweat a little.

The waiter returns with my coffee. He has a friendly looking face. I take in the posters on the walls: masked balls and parties. These are not criminals but bohemian students. I relax - students aren't inclined to dispose of unwelcome customers in shallow graves.

A Russian, who had been sitting near the bar, comes over and joins me. He could be my age or a few years older. The lines engraved in his face tell of a hard life. We exchange brief formalities. He appears to be considering some private joke. His face is amiable, with a small goatee beard and dark eyes. He exudes a certain tranquillity which is broken by spontaneous moments of self-contained glee. When he speaks, it is with a slow and considered voice. His accent is strong although the words are clear. He sells me some hashish which we begin to smoke.

Breaking a long silence the Russian introduces himself as Mikhail. We shake hands. I cannot remember if we'd already introduced ourselves when he first came to the table. Mikhail tells me that he's been living in France since the end of the war. Before that he lived in Zurich. Whilst the other Russian émigrés were preparing a world revolution, Mikhail spent his time seducing as many women as he could lay his hands on. After the war those women returned to their native lands. Swiss women, he remarks looking bewildered by the concept, were immune to his physical charms. Allowing a coin toss to select his destination, Mikhail left Zurich for Paris. He tells me that his seductions recommenced three miles out from the Zurich main station. Over time his perpetual pursuit of women lost some of its allure. He explains that he has now settled into a form of domestic stability with a German girl called Astrid and an American called Helen. All three of them share an apartment not too far from the La Closerie des Lilas on the rue d'Assas.

After talking and playing backgammon for an hour or so I realise that today I have achieved my talking to people quota. Feeling contented I decide to go home. Mikhail shakes my hand again and says he hopes I'll return soon.

Outside the café, the day is fading. I stand for a moment, propping myself up against the wall. I want to go home and lie in my bed. This desire is not yet so great that it has been able to countermand the inclination to remain leaning against the wall. Two young women walk by laughing. Are they laughing at me? My head feels heavy; I'm having difficulty holding it upright. Concentrating my will, I hold my head up and cast off from the wall. Advance! To bed!

Having traversed a few impossibly busy roads, and nearly being run over at least twice, I arrive at the end of my street. I have no idea how long it has taken me to walk the three kilometres between the café and my house, or indeed if I have only walked three kilometres, as I have undoubtedly done some drifting. At first I'd found it difficult to gauge the speed of automobiles and trams. Difficult, too, to anticipate the course of other pedestrians. Now I am growing used to it, so why go home?

The evening has arrived, darkening due to the time of year, and Paris is awakening. I can feel her power as she comes to life. Cobbles shine beneath the street lamps. Excitement sparks across the city. The Eiffel Tower and the Sacré-Cœur broadcast a silent reveille. At this hour dreams still have the chance to be realised. Hope is permitted to reside over reason.

On reaching the boulevard Saint Germain I can see the awnings of the Deux Magots. The terrace is already filling with customers. Flames from the braziers fight a battle with the wind. The scant amount of warmth these emit has enticed customers to sit outside. The Abbey of Saint-Germain-des-Prés towers in the night sky and looks on in beneficent toleration at the sinners congregating below. Two nuns leave the church wearing beautiful white butterfly hats and long dark habits. They are laughing, as the two by the Café Copenhagen had laughed.

I take a seat under the dark green awning and face the boulevard rather than the churchyard. Some of the other customers look at me askance. On arriving I'd been distracted by two ugly Chinese dogs. These statues so intrigued me that I forgot where I was and stood staring at them, blocking the doorway. The waiter comes to take my order. He exudes an indifference to my existence, developed from years of practice. Perhaps he ignores his reflection whilst shaving so as to keep his hand in. I order two orange juices, two grapefruit juices, a double espresso, and a glass of red wine – Côtes du Rhône if you have it.

'Would you like me to bring an extra chair, sir?' he asks.

'Only if I grow an extra arse,' I reply.

Almost directly across the road is the Brassiere Lipp. That's the kind of joint a stockbroker would eat in. I should cross over there and ask if they know Marty. However, I don't have any inclination to move, so I sit and stare. The first batch of evening diners are arriving; diplomats, politicians, journalists. They all bow stiffly to one another. A doorman holds the door open as the customers remove their hats and make their way inside. Ensconced in leather-backed chairs they will commence to stuff their bulbous faces with chunks of sausage, and pig grease. They will wash this down with over-sized jugs of frothy beer. Perhaps they'll swill from a bottle of champagne. Every day is a feast day at the Brassiere Lipp. When fully sated they will pick bits of flesh from their teeth before sauntering out into the night, slapping each other on the back as they go. Even from across this broad road I find them quite disagreeable. For some people there are never any hard times: they can always click their pudgy fingers to summon a waiter or servant.

Dismiss these thoughts! It's vital I think of something else and I must do it right now. I'm on the cusp - Dr Jekyll one second before his transformation to Mr Hyde. I picture a bridge, the Pont Neuf. A simple stone bridge, nothing more than a bridge. Now water, the Seine, flowing beneath it. Silence too, the bridge in silence and water flowing beneath it. Water slightly muddied. I hold the image and use it to block any other thought which tries to invade my head. I have learnt that by doing this I can control myself. If I fail, the resentment will grow in to a rage which will then consume me.

My equilibrium returns. I shouldn't be too resentful; after all I have decided to take my army captain's pension.

Previously it had been a point of pride with me that I would not profit from the war. I had also resolved I would not profit from my birth. That false pride lasted for too long. There are only so many times you can pick yourself up after weeping in the dirt before you have to change your way of life. Taking the pension was easy. Taking the trust fund was not. It meant contact with my family. I can't think too much about that right now. I re-summon the bridge. For a moment it is empty, and then it is crossed by those laughing girls from outside the Copenhagen. There is something about them, something I feel I am on the edge of grasping...

*

I wake early the next morning feeling refreshed. At the very least I normally wake up cursing a mild hangover. The hashish took away my desire for both wine and coffee and I slept as soundly as a corpse encased in an Egyptian sarcophagus.

Today I'll head up to Saint-Denis. If I have no luck there I'll follow that with a tour of fancy restaurants – taking a supply of bills in different denominations to bribe the staff.

Downstairs I share a morning coffee with Filatre. He'd been rummaging about in his office wearing a dressing gown. I hope he doesn't decide to take my rooms back so he can sleep in a proper bed. If he does, I suppose I could rent out his house. Then I guess I'd end up sleeping on a chaise longue in my office.

We are halfway through our second cups when Hervé arrives. I've never met Hervé in person before, our previous dealings having been conducted over the telephone. He's a shabby, paunchy man, sporting a torn pale-blue jacket. He wears a pair of grey flannel trousers which have seen better days, but probably not during Hervé's ownership of them. Instead of customary going-about-shoes he sports a pair of tennis shoes. His face and his shoulders slouch in the same way his moustache droops. He is most deferential, going so far as to touch his forelock on entering the room. That is a gesture I have not seen for many years.

'Pleased to meet you, Hervé.'

I reach out my hand to shake his. Hervé only has one arm, but judging from his grip it is as strong as two.

'You too, sir.'

His accent is pronounced and southern. Langue D'oc, he informs me.

'I have found something out about monsieur Gustave Marty and thought I should inform you right off.'

He takes off a shoulder bag and pulls from it a dog-eared, buff coloured folder. Next he produces a piece of paper with small but very precise handwriting.

'I copied this from a newspaper. It's not much, though I reckon it could be useful. It was dated slightly over a year ago.'

The message is a notice which reads: Maurice Kuo and Partners wish to make it known that monsieur Gustave Marty is no longer in their employ. We also wish to make it known that we have no forwarding address for the said Gustave Marty.

CHAPTER SEVEN

I cannot work out why Maurice Kuo and Partners would print a notice like that. They have paid good money to ask potential customers not to visit them. They're certain to have another broker there who could take over Marty's old clients – leeches like that usually come by the jar full.

'It looks to me,' says Hervé, 'as if they are distancing themselves from him.'

'Distancing?'

'Yes, sir. It's as if they are trying to say, "Monsieur Marty isn't here and we don't know where he is, so leave us alone, why don't you." They don't say when he stopped working for them.'

'And you think this implies something nefarious?'

'If that means crooked, then yes I do,' Hervé says.

'Did you find anything else out?'

'No, sir. That is also a little bit odd. I looked through all sorts; birth announcements, wedding announcements, death notices, and bankruptcy hearings – there are a lot of those nowadays. He isn't registered with the stock exchange or with any of the préfectures in central Paris. Foreigners require permits to work in France. Of course, I haven't got access to their historical records, so he might have been registered at one time.'

'Ah yes, I had to register. And I let the British Embassy know my address.'

'Quite so, sir. All foreigners should do this, else we can't tell what you are getting up to.'

I pay Hervé's fee and give him a decent tip. Maybe that's

what the forelock-touching is all about, generating a good tip. Filatre gestures toward the chess board. I would love to play but, for a change, I have work to do. I head upstairs to make some notes.

In my office I have a very large, very empty, filing cabinet. I'd spotted it outside a bric-a-brac store and paid them extra to deliver it for me. They earned their fee that day – they hadn't bargained on the stairs. Currently this cabinet contains a single folder with the address of my client and her brief description of monsieur Marty. I write out an index card and put Marty's name at the top. Then I write out 'known employers'. I put the name and address of Maurice Kuo and Partners under this title. Their office is on the boulevard Rivoli. A well-to-do address on a road which runs parallel to the river, passing the Hotel de Ville and the Musée du Louvre. I'll have to pay them a visit, forwarding address or no forwarding address.

Fifteen minutes of brisk walking sees me across the river and into central Paris. In certain states of mind a busy city can be quite intimidating. People bustle along intent on their business as if their courses have been preordained. They proceed with a determination which leaves me doubting my right to exist. Losing all sense of certainty I begin to roam aimlessly from street to street. I ought to take cover before I fall prey to the religious sects who hunt the crowds for lost souls like mine. I take refuge in a seedy café.

I order a glass of red. The waiter obliges, I feel a little guilty that he is working whilst I am shirking. Well, it would have been no good visiting Kuo and Partners in the state I'm in. When facing people who have no vested interest in your case, it is preferable to exude confidence and authority. They won't take heed of a man who ambles up looking bemused. I signal the waiter to bring more wine. I shall make him one of my three conversational targets for the day.

'Ever been in love?' I ask.

'Yes, sir, but that's really none of your business.'

'I thank you for your honesty. Honesty and candour. May

I buy you a drink?'

There are no other customers so he condescends to join me. He pours himself a glass of wine then insists on standing and drinking it while looking over at the door.

'My good sir, you are nowt but a disappointment.'

'I beg your pardon, sir?'

He looks slightly offended which rather pleases me.

'Before, when I asked if you were in love, you were both honest and blunt. "Good for you," I thought, "buy the man a drink". Now look at you. You don't want to drink with me or talk to me, yet you knew by accepting the drink you would be obliged to do those things. So you stand instead of sitting, you look at the door instead of at me. Well, fuck! Why not say, "no, sir, I do not want your sodding drink". Better still, "yes, sir, I will take the drink and consume it over there and if you don't like me doing so you can shove it up your arse!".'

'Very good, sir.'

He walks away leaving behind his glass of half-finished wine.

That conversation didn't go as well as I'd expected, yet I did find it satisfying. I'm now prepared to face Maurice Kuo and his gang of financial miscreants. If I weren't being hired to track down one of their kind I would quite happily arrange for all stockbrokers to disappear. The Black Hole of Calcutta isn't in use at the moment.

Back on the street I feel ready to deal with the city's challenges. I'm also a little drunk. I must get some food. I stop at a boulangerie and order some bread. I eat it dry. I walk merrily along the street and catch myself whistling Tipperary. Spotting another café I step inside and order a coffee. I settle down to read for an hour or two – no point arriving at Kuo's when he's itching to get to lunch.

Three o'clock finds me walking up the stairs outside the offices of Maurice Kuo and Partners. The overt grandness of the entrance rubs me up the wrong way. What right have these people to marble staircases, Doric columns and classical façades? The ostentatious waste of money, spent making this building look like a Greek brothel, is in poor taste in this age of poverty. Less than one mile from these steps there are children who have learnt to ignore the pains of hunger.

The lobby is chequered with black and white ceramic floor tiles. The effect is pleasing, like a chess board or a Moroccan courtyard. The rest is a vast desolate expanse, speckled with occasional chairs and coffee tables. Behind a reception counter sits a middle-aged woman and a more elderly man. They are gargoyles peering across a lifeless domain, motionless and silent. My appearance on the scene has not registered with them. Approaching the desk I look from one vacant face to the other. The man is wearing a black suit with a waistcoat and silver watch chain. His hair is a pepper grey, which matches his face rather well. He still hasn't moved. If he opens his mouth, will words or dust fall from the void? The woman, who does at least blink a few times, is wearing tweed. I am perturbed by her hat, which contains a long pheasant feather; it looks like the one Douglas Fairbanks was wearing in Robin Hood.

Standing in front of the counter I address the space between the two. I explain that I am here to see monsieur Kuo, and that, no, I do not have an appointment. The old man looks at the woman, who in turn looks at me. I put on what I imagine to be my charming smile. Neither of them look as if they are charmed, so I drop it. The old man catches my attention by coughing. For a moment he looks as if he is about to speak. All he does is remove a handkerchief from his pocket and then look at his shoes. I can tell they are unsure what to make of me; that is to say they have an inkling but aren't quite certain of the depth of my depravity. They are obviously aware that I am under the influence. My coffees at that last café transmuted into wine. Still, the boardrooms of Paris are filled with executives who consume more than their fair share at lunch.

In my favour I am dressed in an exceedingly fine linen suit with a natty waistcoat. This is accompanied by a shirt and tie, each of which is at the zenith of Parisian fashion. My shoes are polished as only an ex-soldier can polish - even under the dull light of their reception area they gleam. The receptionists are obviously astute enough to realise I am both very rich and disreputable; two conditions which make for a prized company client. Instead of asking me to leave, the old man stands up and beckons for me to follow him.

Travelling at the speed of a continental shelf, we make our way to the ante-chamber of monsieur Kuo's private office. During this overtly time-consuming voyage the old man tells me that his son had once worked here as an apprentice before being called up and then killed. I have no idea why he relayed that story to me. The information is trotted out as if he had been informing me that the banisters are made of mahogany. He brushes aside my sympathetic replies and offers no further details as to where or how his son died.

We arrive at the ante-chamber and the old man introduces me to Kuo's secretary. She greets me and invites me to sit anywhere I fancy. I take a seat near her desk as she slips into Kuo's office for a few minutes. Unlike the two downstairs, this woman is both attractive and lively. I'm not sure why he hired them but I have no doubts about this one.

She returns to the desk and watches me while pretending to work. I am obviously more interesting than paperwork. I wink at her; it buys me a salacious smile. She could easily pass for Louise Brooks - a perfect black bob and breasts straining to break free from her blouse. If only they could rent asunder that flimsy silken cage, even momentarily, I would die a happy man. I must look away; I feel like a sailor being lured by the song of the harpies, drawn despite fore-knowledge of the consequences. Am I really so feeble-minded that a beautiful woman, with positively perfect breasts, in a blouse a little too tight, who licks her lips and smiles seductively, can distract me from my work? Of course I am. If all I had were a photograph of her I'd be compelled to take it out and ogle it every ten minutes. What hope have I with the living, breathing version sat but a few feet away?

To distract myself from these unproductive thoughts I try to read one of the economic journals which have been deposited on a coffee table in front of me. I do this while pulling cross-eyed faces at the secretary. Gaining a satisfactory response, I proceed to one of my Chaplin impressions. I do believe I'm getting good at Chaplin. She laughs out loud, and the more she does, the more I pretend to read the journals.

Kuo, peering out of his office, looks annoyed. The secretary tries hard to contain her mirth while I nonchalantly replace the magazine. Kuo beckons me with a little wave of his hand. He hovers around, unsure as to what to do. He'd like to chastise his secretary as he can sense she hasn't been working. He can't do this until he has ascertained exactly who I am. If I am rich and want to invest, and his secretary has helped me pass the time pleasantly, which she has, then what better use of her time could there be? He is loitering at the doorway, not quite coming out and not quite going back in. He obviously can't make me out. If he really suspected that I'd become a valued client he'd already be at my side, pumping my hand and asking if I'd like anything to drink.

'Come this way please, monsieur Salazar.'

I wink again at the secretary, who giggles delightfully, before I get up to enter Kuo's lair.

Kuo has outfitted himself in the uniform of the French bourgeoisie; impeccable morning suit, jet black jacket and waistcoat; starched white shirt with brilliant white collar. His charcoal trousers look as if this is their first outing. His hair is a dark grey, greased back with Brilliantine, and not one strand is out of place. His hands are delicate; I doubt they have ever experienced a blister. Is his mother lurking somewhere in the office ready to straighten his little bow tie should the knot slacken? His every wish would be fulfilled if he could travel back through time to the Second Empire, and live under the auspices of Napoleon the Third. I imagine that each night he hangs himself up in the wardrobe whilst his wife makes a cuckold of him in the marital bed.

This office is huge. We have to walk the length of it to reach Kuo's domineering walnut desk, where neatly aligned leaves of paper have made homes for themselves. His chair, suitably large to match the desk and embellished with carvings, looks as uncomfortable as it is ornate. Being a man both slight and short, the chair makes him look slightly comical - a Jack in the land of the beanstalk. I yearn to look under the desk to see if his feet reach the ground.

CHAPTER EIGHT

Before Kuo can invite me to sit I have ensconced myself in the seat in front of his desk. I pull a cigarette from the case and start taping it on the silver lid. Kuo, noticing what I am up to, passes me an ashtray and says: 'Be my guest.'

'I have come, monsieur Kuo, to talk about monsieur Gustave Marty,' I say.

'Then you have wasted our time, for I shall no longer speak of him.'

He pats his lips with a dainty white handkerchief, then looks furtively from side to side.

'Are you ashamed at having had him in your employ?'

'No, sir! Anything monsieur Marty may have done he did in secret and of his own volition, completely against the principles of this enterprise. Our clients can place their fullest trust in myself and this partnership.'

'Monsieur Kuo, please keep calm; I don't give a shit about petty pilfering. I only want to know where I can find Marty.'

Kuo turns red with feigned indignation. I wonder if he has trained himself to do that whenever he hears a rude word.

'Don't blow a gasket, Kuo, we're not in a church and I'm sure you heard worse at the front. You were at the front, were you not?'

Men like Kuo never went near the trenches, so why not rub some patriotic crap into his eyes? He coughs and shuffles in his seat. I watch unblinkingly, as if expecting him to regale me with a soldier's tales of scavenged food and makeshift latrines. The true story would be one of connections used and strings being pulled.

'Erm, no, not the actual front. Of course I was ready to serve as a soldier. Unfortunately, I have incapacities which restrict my usefulness for active duty. I served my country, under difficult circumstances, at the Ministry for Finance. We often worked well into the night. We knew that the Ministry would be one of Big Bertha's targets as she rained death upon the city.'

I've made him squirm, which puts me at the advantage. I'd enjoy seeing him squirm some more but I am here for a different purpose and mustn't allow myself to be distracted. Kuo dabs his forehead with his handkerchief, then he offers me a scotch.

'You, monsieur Salazar, you did your bit at the front I suppose?'

I detect a trace of hope in his voice – hope that I may have been a conscientious objector perhaps. Or does he want me to provide some Boy's Own adventure stories which he can then use for himself?

'Yes, I was. I don't wear my ribbons as they remind me of those who died.' I pause to let my eyes rest upon his red Legion of Honour ribbon. 'I was awarded the Distinguished Services Order for jumping into a blast hole. Four Germans were about to execute six of my men. My six made it out, the Germans didn't.'

He sits enthralled like a school kid and, I admit, so am I. I've never described it that succinctly before. It does sound a bit Boy's Own. Previously I'd remember the moment of the German officer's death. Time seemed to stand still and he caught me with a look which cried out against the pointlessness of it all. I'd recall the way his blood flew across the chest of his sergeant. The sergeant, beginning to realise what was going on, received a bullet in the guts. The other two Germans, distracted by my arrival, were killed by the captive Englishmen. I had to apply a coup de grâce to the sergeant. There I was, stood in a pit, with four dead men, none of whom had reached their thirtieth year. A vortex of war with me at the centre wallowing in blood and dirt. I've lost count of the nights I've lain awake, full of dread, thinking of their children growing up without their father's love.

'Sir, I salute you!' Kuo says.

These days most of France finds war abhorrent, yet one stumbles across these islands of despair who still salute the war. Kuo stands, holding his glass high, then proceeds to down his drink in one noisy gulp. This is enacted with all the flourishing extravagance of a Russian cavalry officer. I am expecting the glass to be thrown into the fireplace at any moment. There is no throwing of glass, instead he sits down and pours us out another drink.

I feel like a real shit. I've used the deaths of those men for my own advantage. First I let that medal get pinned to my chest, now I drink toasts to their murder. I down my drink in silence. I take another and begin to brighten up. Kuo, it seems, has decided to get into the spirit of things by reciting some bawdy stories.

At some point in his youth, Kuo seduced a girl from the typing pool. This girl enjoyed making love outside. According to Kuo, he ravished her over every statue in the greater Parisian area. I try to look suitably impressed while feeling suitably repulsed. Now I have to reciprocate with a tale of my own.

I tell him about the hookers in Arras. The picture I paint is of seductresses in flimsy dresses and frilly underwear, giggling as they lead me upstairs. In reality the women were stout, middle-aged and wore frumpy patched-up dresses. But we were desperate, and so were they.

Kuo goes on and I let him ride this wave for a while before directing the subject back to Marty.

'So, monsieur Marty. Any ideas?'

'That man is a shit - pardon my English. I have no idea where he may be and I'm perfectly happy for it to remain that way. I know he got another position, with Lacman Brothers. He lost that under a cloud. I would not be in the least surprised to learn that he is working as a gigolo along the Riviera, or that he is languishing in jail for fraud. Nor too would it surprise me to hear that he has been left for dead in some Montmartre gutter; killed by a jealous husband.'

'A bit of a ladies' man was he?'

'Yes, and he made it obvious in the most vulgar ways. Don't misunderstand me, monsieur Salazar; you and I are men of the world and,' he looks both left and right before leaning forward to whisper, 'you know that I enjoy a dalliance as much as the next man.'

'But,' he says, returning to normal volume and pose, 'monsieur Marty was rapacious. I let him go due to irregularities in his conduct. It could have been because of the way he behaved with women. Mind you, he did have some decorum; he never once did anything untoward with a client and we were always able to recruit new secretaries.'

I thank Kuo for his time and leave him pouring himself another scotch. There won't be much work done in that office this afternoon - if work is something that ever goes on in there. No sooner have I closed the door when Kuo's secretary pounces on me. I'd forgotten all about her. I had resolved that, when I started my agency, I wouldn't embroil myself with the women I encounter. I'm feeling somewhat resolute right now, as her hand travels up my inside leg.

'Slow down, gorgeous.' I take her hand in mine. 'How about you and I go punish a bottle of wine?'

'Meet me at six-thirty at the Café Bourbon on the rue Cambon.'

I consider going straight home and forgetting all about The Café Bourbon. Is it my detective instincts or baser feelings which decide I should keep the rendezvous? I'll need to keep my mind on the task with her. For all I know she may be Marty's mistress ready to lead me a merry dance. Or she could be operating with a partner - the moment my trousers are down I'll be hit over the head and my wallet removed. There is also the distinct possibility that she is what she appears to be - a vamp. I walk about, growing sober, killing time before six-thirty. When we meet I'll cut out the flirting.

Seven o'clock; I'm on my third coffee, no sign of Kuo's secretary. I take out my pad to re-read my notes from the meeting with Kuo. I haven't made any notes. To rectify this I scribble out an account of our conversation. I jot down certain phrases; ladies' man; disreputable; fraud (within the law?). I'm not positive on that last point. He may have done something untoward but not actually illegal. I have the impression that Marty operates in that legal grey-area inhabited by politicians and advertising men. I look across the road at a large sign which declares 'Great Tasting Flavour' above a drink which tastes like piss.

Her arrival is heralded by a musky perfume. The atmosphere in the café transforms with her presence. I have become the subject of a hundred how-did-he-manage-to-get-a-girl-like-that glances. Most of the male clientèle are either looking at us now, or have been looking at us. This must be what it's like having dinner with Lillian Gish, only I guess we'd be somewhere classier where the people don't stare so openly. I feel like picking my nose and unleashing a loud fart just to confound them all. I decide to show decorum instead; I stand to greet her.

'I ordered champagne on the way over darling,' she says. She blows me a kiss and takes the seat opposite mine.

The waiter arrives promptly with the bottle then dallies. I watch him for a moment. He's had long enough to take in the view and I don't want the extra company.

'We've got your address, Charlie – we'll write you if we need anything.' He takes the hint.

She smiles at me over the bubbles from her glass. The drink has wetted her deep red lips. I yearn to lean over and lick them. The smell of her perfume mingles with the champagne and her foot starts to rub slowly up and down against my leg. Who am I that I must resist such temptations? I make no claims to sainthood and most certainly don't claim to be decent. I bite my lip to try and regain focus. I hope I'm not drooling too much.

'Did you know Marty?' I ask.

'Not half as well as he'd have liked.'

'Not your type?'

'Listen, darling, everyone is my type on the right day if they ask in the right way. His way of asking was taking - for that all you get is a slapped face and, if required, a knee in the vitals. Besides he was a real creep.'

'What sort of a creep?'

'Are there different sorts? I guess there are. I don't know. Suppose you had a twelve-year-old sister, you wouldn't want him to meet her. He tried it on with everyone but he really went for the younger girls. Guess it gave him more of a thrill, more of a chance to play the big man. I gave him the cold shoulder. When that didn't work I explained that my brother was likely to give him a good hiding if he didn't stop bugging me. To make sure he got the message, I arranged for Freddy, my brother, to pick me up a few times. He's as sweet as a kitten but he could probably lift a cart horse and toss it across the Seine, if he were ever so minded.'

'So, a regular kind of creep then,' I say.

I hope Freddy is out of town.

'That's about as nice as I'd ever be about him.'

She places her hand on my knee with serious intent.

'Look, I hope you don't think I am a creep too but-'

'You're not interested in me?'

'I am, very, that's the problem.'

'You've got a wife? I can't believe that's a deterrent.'

'No, I don't really have a good reason.'

'Ah! Don't worry, sweetie, I have some friends like that. If you ever get curious you know where to find me.'

The champagne wins back her attention. She takes a sip and then giggles as if the glass had whispered a joke.

'Can you remember anything else about Marty?'

'Sure, loads. First you might want to tell me why you're asking.'

I decide to be truthful and tell her I am a detective working on a case. This has the unfortunate side-effect of making me appear more attractive. I haven't regained control over my primal urges as she moves around the table to sit on the chair besides mine. She draws it up a little closer.

'We wouldn't want people to overhear our detective talk,' she whispers.

I am facing the daunting prospect of a nymphomaniac in a tight dress, sitting so close I can feel the heat of her breath. I'm finding it hard to keep my hands off her. I want to get up and shout 'everybody out!', then ravish her right here on the table. I'm shaking and find it hard to breathe properly. Whatever I do now, I've a feeling I'll regret it one way or the other.

I use some of the mental training I'd previously applied to my angry thoughts. I close my eyes and picture a green field, rolling meadows, butterflies fluttering, and cow bells jingling in the distance. It's beginning to work. I am able to block out her alluring smell and the sound of her deep sensual breathing. Opening my eyes to her smile and those large, dark, bedroom eyes, I have to pinch myself on the thigh to distract myself. I'm drowning in a sea of desire.

'Look, miss, you are sitting too close and it distracts me, please move back before I forget myself.'

She laughs and returns to her original seat and I give thanks for that. Like Wilde I can resist anything but temptation. I drink a beer as she sips at the champagne. She leans across the table to speak to me; I have to focus intently on her nose so as not to be drawn to the cleavage.

'There are a lot of people in this city looking for monsieur Gustave Marty.'

'Really?'

'He must have ripped off fifty or more while he was working with us; they weren't all little amounts either. Those people have families. You steal twenty thousand francs from some old bird and all of a sudden her son and grandson are interested. They couldn't give a hoot that she's been ripped off, but that money is their inheritance.'

'Did he actually steal?'

'Not legally. Legally they signed it all over to him. Legally they can all go to hell in a handcart. A couple of blokes came round looking for him once - they weren't seeking legal retribution.'

'That's fifty at your place with perhaps fifty more at the Lacman Brothers. Marty must have a tallied up a number of enemies.'

I can imagine my client being taken in by some sweet talking banker – especially as she knew him of old. I doubt she'll get any of it back even if we do find him.

'Have I been of assistance, monsieur Salazar?' She asks this with such a coquettish voice I'm not sure if she wants paying.

'A great help, thank you. By the way, I never got your name.'

'My name is Céline, and, if I may be excused, I'm going to find a man to screw. See you around kiddo.'

She winks, turns, and wiggles away. How many in this café will dream of her tonight? Her silhouette fills the café doorway and then moves into the street. I drop some cash on the table and make a dash for it. A girl like that could easily meet someone else in the time it takes to tie a shoe lace.

'About that man...' I say.

CHAPTER NINE

Nights without sleep can be joyous – provided you are kept awake by Céline and not insomnia. I steal away from her sleeping body at four o'clock. Meeting in the morning is rarely pleasing. I leave my card on her table so she won't think me a heel. Céline lives off the rue des Batignolles in the 17th arrondissement. It appears to be a cheerful place. I can easily imagine Édouard Manet creeping around in similar circumstances all those years ago. I wonder which house was his.

There is precious little to do at this hour except go home. I don't feel ready to go home. I could walk all the way down to the all-night cafés of Montparnasse. That would involve walking past my apartment, but I want something sooner. With a slight deviation my route could take me to Les Halles. Something must be open down there; the market operates on a different clock from the rest of us.

By the time I reach Les Halles I have descended enough hills to have reached the upper levels of hell. This hell is chilly and comprises of a series of cafés, all of which are shut. One of them has even left a light on to provide a moment of false hope. I light a cigarette and read a tatty poster advertising a flea circus. Behind me there's a bench with a man slumped over on it. He's wearing a nice suit and shoes. I stand closer to check he's breathing. I doubt he'll still be wearing those shoes when he wakes up.

There is a time to continue foolish pursuits and a time to head home. I have abandoned all prospect of a night cap and plod on towards the river. Not having travelled more than a few hundred metres I see two men walk around a corner up ahead. I quicken my stride to catch a glimpse of what they are up to. Part of the pleasure of a night time ramble lies in indulging your curiosity. I reach the corner and see them enter a café. What luck! And the drink will taste twice as sweet from my having given up on it.

I enter the café and nearly vomit. All eyes are upon me. The place stinks like an open sewer. Worse than an open sewer; this stench could only come from a covered cesspit. I retch a couple of times to the sound of laughter.

'Get him a cognac,' I hear someone shout.

A man with long slender fingers passes me a glass. I hold it to my nose, letting the drink's pungent aroma obscure the stench of the café. I look around the room still holding the glass beneath my nostrils. The place is packed, all men and all filthy.

'Were you expecting to find a bar packed full of young ladies?' someone calls.

I am a source of amusement for these strange people. They have given me a drink, in a clean glass, so I'll allow them a few minutes' fun at my expense before I leave.

'What's this place?' I ask.

'A café,' somebody replies.

'Don't you worry, mate, we won't eat you.' The guy speaking walks up to me and offers his hand. I shake it. 'This is our café. We have one rule, if you can stand it you can stay.'

'What is the smell? You can smell it?'

'The smell is us, mate, and no, I can't, not any more. My name is Louis and these are my workmates.' He gestures around the room and a few of the heads nod at me as I scan around. 'We operate the shit pumps.'

I finish my drink and order another so I can listen to the rest of his story with something to see me through. I don't want to stay too long as I fear I am getting used to the smell. Louis explains that he and the other men here empty the city's cess pits. They travel with a pump on a wagon and suck up the effluence. They'd be driven out if they tried to enter any other café. I down my second drink and bid them adieu. I must remember never to go there again.

Filatre is standing by his door ready to collar me as I enter the entrance hall. He's wearing a pair of flannel trousers with a white vest and dressing gown.

'Not managed to sleep?' I ask.

'I got a few hours in around eleven. I've been up reading since three.' The expression on his face changes as I approach. 'What's that smell? Have you trodden in something? Don't walk it all over the house man, take your shoes off.'

'The smell is me, not the shoes. Can't talk now, I need a wash.' I ought to bathe too but the public baths don't open 'til six. I can fill a bowl and soap myself down for now. I'll visit the baths when I wake up.

'If you aren't tired, come down after and have a game of chess. You can let me know what you've found out. Did you make it to Kuo and Partners?'

'I'll be down soon. A scrub with a cold wet flannel and carbolic soap is going to wake me up. I'll probably conk out around nine. When are we going to get hot water in here?'

'What do you need hot water for? You can boil a pan for shaving and the baths are less than half a kilometre away.'

'You get some coffee ready; I'll be down in twenty minutes.'

I undress in the corner of my apartment piling my clothes near an open window. I wash myself down with cold water and apply ample Eau de Cologne. Hopefully Filatre will have the coffee ready - he is the devil for forgetting and asking me to make it. Those clothes will have to go to the wash house in the morning. If they still smell after that I'll leave them for the rag pickers.

Filatre has set up the chess board. A steaming cup of coffee sits alongside – good man. He is puffing on his pipe, giving the area the enchanting aroma of a good club. I sit down and adjust the position of my knights – Filatre always places them pointing forward where I prefer to have them looking towards the rooks. I push my king's pawn forward two squares. If the last few games are anything to go by, we should be heading for the Evan's Gambit.

'So, how goes it, Monsieur the Detective?'

'Very well indeed. Kuo's secretary is a nymphomaniac and invited back me to her place. We went at it like a pair of professional wrestlers.'

'Then her husband came home and emptied a chamber pot over your head.'

'No, then I popped into a café occupied by cess pit cleaners. They spend the night working and then retreat to their café - they aren't allowed in any others. Nice chaps, but you really wouldn't invite them home for dinner.'

'What of Kuo himself - did you get anything out of him, or were you too distracted by the secretary?'

'You know me, Filatre, business first. I had a good interview with Kuo. He told me that they had let Marty go. The secretary told me more: he'd been ripping people off. Diddling them out of their savings. All this was technically legal. He then went to work for another brokerage called Lacman Brothers.'

'There are a lot of people involved in fraud these days.'

'Why do you think that is?'

'The government let people down with its financing of the war. Bonds which promised six percent were realised at four and a half. By the time they cashed them in, with inflation and currency devaluations, they had made a considerable loss. So, people either took their money and stuffed it under the mattress or they started looking for alternative schemes. Then there's all the tax avoidance. You know what we French are like; we'd rather spend two francs to get out of paying one franc in tax.'

'Marty must have been running something like that. Apparently people came looking for him and, by the sounds of it, were planning to beat the cash out of him.'

'That's probably why Kuo placed that notice in the press. People are fools when it comes to money - money and love. Are you going to go to the Lacmans' place?'

'I don't have anything else to go on, other than the Marty who's living in Saint-Denis.'

'Your old stomping ground. I don't suppose a trip up there will bring back any happy memories.'

'None at all. You know, there are times in your life which you know were bad then, years later, you start looking back on them fondly. I occasionally remember moments from the war and catch myself thinking, "it wasn't so bad". Despite the horror, the fear, the death, I can still think that on occasion. Saint-Denis has never evoked such feelings. If it ever comes to mind, I recall the pettiness, the nastiness, and the way the people fed upon each other. Do you know what my fondest memory of the place is?'

'Yes, you've mentioned it a few times. Something about it raining.'

'That's right, going out at night to stand in the rain. Watching the slurry running down the road while getting soaked. That is my fondest memory of the place. I remember getting home one morning and seeing a crowd of people out in the street. An old bloke from up the road had died of hypothermia. The gathering was to watch him get carted away. Most watched in silence. Someone shouted, "the old bastard won't be cold much longer - not where he's going". That prompted a wave of laughter, which I joined. We were all laughing and watching that man, who died of the cold, being carted away.'

'I think that's the fifth time I've heard the rain story. The dead man is a new one though.'

'Sorry, Filatre, I don't wish to bore you with reminiscences from the miserable quarters of my life.'

'Think nothing of it, old chum. Before we go on, I should remind you that this is Friday morning and we made a vow not to get maudlin on any day other than Sunday. So say something cheerful, or concentrate on the game.'

Filatre is being blunt, as we have learnt to be about such things. If it wasn't for this watchfulness, any moment could dissolve into self-pity.

'If you really don't want to go to Saint-Denis you do have the option of sending Hervé. I know you use him for paperwork, but he'll do a bit of snooping if the money is right. If I understand the situation correctly, all he needs to do is go up there and find out how old the fellow is and whether he hails from Belgium.'

'Do you think he could do that? That would be wizard. I hadn't thought of that. Oh, but getting other people to do my dirty work is exploitation. If I ask Hervé to do this, how can I distinguish myself from the factory boss who sends children to work down the mine?'

'I'm not sure it's the factory bosses who do that, but if the idea troubles you, pay him more. Think of a reasonable sum then double it. When he comes back give him a tip. Then the difference will be that you pay a living wage.'

The relief at not having to go back to Saint-Denis has left me feeling light-headed. I don't even care that Filatre has beaten me for the third consecutive game. Well, actually I do care - rather than engage him in a fourth game, I bid him goodnight.

Entering my apartment I can see my clothes piled up on the window sill. This is a sight all the more pleasing because I cannot smell them. The dawn has broken and light fills the room. I close the shutters in the bedroom and climb into bed.

A nagging sensation which I can't quiet fathom keeps me from falling asleep. I have an irritating brain itch which requires a very specific thought to reach down and scratch it. The whole thing makes the backs of my eyes hurt. Exasperated, I give up and turn on the bedside light – we may not have hot water but at least we have electricity. I pick up a book and read until my grip on the book loosens and my head starts nodding. I'm about to fall asleep when I realise what has been annoying me. The brain itch was that girl! One of the laughing girls from outside the Copenhagen, I have seen her before - she is Robert's kid sister.

Her name is Megan; she's a friend from my childhood. Our elder brothers, Alfred and Robert, were friends. Really I guess it was our parents who were friends, but that wasn't how Alfred put it - and Alfred always knew best. As snotty-nosed tykes, Megan and I were fobbed off on each other: Alfred didn't want to know me when Robert was around.

At first we played near to each other but not together. This was spiced by squabbles and territorial battles. Over time our games merged - we began hunting spiders or snails together. Then, one day, I found myself looking forward to her visits. I remember paying her the highest compliment I could, one she didn't seem to appreciate. I'd said: 'Megan, sometimes I can almost forget that you are a girl.'

As I grew older I spent years shut away at boarding school, then university, and our meetings became infrequent. When we did meet, rather than hunt spiders, we played tennis or croquet. It meant we could spend time together without any awkwardness. The last time I saw her must have been mid-1914. She wrote to me once at the Front. And now she is here - somewhere in Paris.

CHAPTER TEN

I wake to catch the last trace of light leaving the afternoon sky. My head is fuzzy from lack of sleep but I'm too excited to remain in bed. I will not visit the Lacman Brothers, I will go to the Café Copenhagen and search for Megan. There is no point tracking down a stranger for a stranger when there is someone I want to find for myself. Once I have found her I'll recommence my search for Marty: in fact this will be good practice.

I walk to the Copenhagen, observing every face hidden behind a scarf or under a hat. When you start looking at them in turn, you soon realise that there are far too many people in Paris. Keep the ones who smile at me, or are at least indifferent, the rest, the ones who snarl, should be sent to live in Peru.

Mikhail watches me enter the café then beckons for me to join him. He is partially concealed beneath a fog of hashish smoke, a micro-climate which, at this hour, affects only his table.

'Good to see you again,' he says. He gestures to the chair next to him with a casual wave of his hand.

'You too, Mikhail. Have you got the board?'

He reaches beneath his chair and produces a backgammon board. He also produces his smoking paraphernalia and commences rolling something for us to share. I don't mind, it's late afternoon and I was planning on spending a few hours here to see if Megan turned up.

'It is good to spend time with someone my own age,' Mikhail says while passing me the reefer. 'These students bring youth and beauty but they also bring too many of their follies. They talk about revolution and pester me for titbits about Lenin. Pah! I never liked the man when he was alive, why should I care about him now that he is dead? Trotsky, I did like. He was always ready to share a joke. Trotsky was also able to forget about politics and concentrate on the important thing in life – ladies, and how to seduce them. We had some good nights out in the Zurich Old Town. Today, it seems, it is wrong to like Trotsky; it's all Stalin, Stalin, Stalin.'

The dice rebound around the board as Lenin, Trotsky and Stalin are forgotten.

'Mikhail, the other day I saw someone.'

'Did you my friend? Was she amenable?'

'We didn't speak. I spotted her that's all.'

'Monsieur Salazar, you are shy! You must never be shy with a woman. A slap on the cheek is a small price to pay for what the others will do with you. I'm absolutely certain that this is what Jesus was referring to when...'

'It's not that. I didn't get a chance to speak. I think I know her from England. Megan Fitzwilliam - have you heard of her?'

'I don't believe so. Does she come in here? There was a time when I would have been able to describe every woman who ever entered this place right down to the colour and texture of her underwear. Now, I smoke and play board games. If I tried anything else, either Astrid or Helen, or more likely both, would hang me by the scrotum from the spire of Sainte-Chapelle.'

'Can you keep an eye out for me - I'll clear it with Astrid and Helen if you like. Megan is about five foot seven with black hair. Her nose is a little larger than it has any right to be. She has a tiny scar on her chin. When the mood takes her she can lose herself in laughter. I used to feed her jokes to see if she might actually explode.'

'If I see her, I promise, I'll let you know.'

'Oh, and Mikhail, if you decide to revert to your old ways with this one, I'll nail your scrotum straight to your forehead

- there won't be any messing about with the Sainte-Chapelle.'

I leave the café, having spent a couple of distracted hours with Mikhail, feeling guilty. Whatever I may or may not want to do I can't escape the fact that I've given my word to Marie Thérèse. I told her I would search for Marty and until I tell her otherwise that is what I ought to be doing; I'm back on the case. My days shall be spent in pursuit of Marty and my evenings spent in the Copenhagen, on the café terraces of Montparnasse, loitering outside the dance halls, in all the places where Megan might show up. Tomorrow I'll get Hervé to start asking around at the Prefectures to try and get an address for her. I could write to her parents and ask them to send me her address. Megan's mother always used to like me. Provided she hasn't heard the stories of my post-war exploits, she should send it to me.

I think I'll visit my client again. I forgot to ask her some pertinent questions; who is Gustave Marty? What does he enjoy doing? Does he have family? After all, an opera buff must visit the opera and a loving son must visit his parents. I'll go in the morning - I'm not exactly compos mentis at present.

Instead of walking around peering into people's windows, I decide to ride the Métro. It's not something I'd normally do for such a short distance but if Megan is in the area the chances are high that she'll be down here at some point. And although Paris is large enough, the expatriates tend to stick around here.

Whereas a walk opens up my mind, Métro journeys leave me thinking about rain. I get a vague notion of sheltering under a rock on a windswept Pennine hill. On that hill it is always raining. I'm never sure how I got there or what I'm doing there. The daydream is repetitive and dull, constructed by my subconscious to numb the sensation of subterranean rail travel. There can be no worse a method for getting from place to place. You are shut up in stinking, hot, airless, metal containers being unceremoniously dragged from station to station. There are plenty of windows with nothing to see other than the reflection of your own miserable face. No scenery breaks up the monotony or gives the journey some markers. Not wanting to look at the depressed faces around me, I gaze at the dirty grey floor. Why didn't I just walk home?

After five minutes of travel I start feeling as if I'm on that hill. I never get a proper fix on the sensation; all I get is a picture of a rock, the rain, and me. The process puts me into a trance. The other passengers seem to have entered trances too; are we all hiding from the Yorkshire rain? A jolt in the line brings me back from the hills of northern England. I look up and perform a quick scan around the carriage to make sure no buskers, with their accordions and God-awful renditions of Maurice Chevalier's Louise, are likely to interrupt me.

I notice her sitting a few seats further along the carriage from me. She must have gotten on at Montparnasse Bienvenüe or even Vavin. I've not been paying attention to my fellow citizens again. The Métro is not a café; I do not have to pay attention to them down here. Here we are not people with sparkling eyes and dreams for tomorrow. Here we are cattle being transported to market and resigned to our fearful destinies. These trivial thoughts flash through my brain, as I don't know how to act. This isn't the shyness Mikhail accused me of; this is a fascination. Finally I take a deep breath and let myself go.

'William FitzMegan!'

I walk towards her and she turns round.

'Well pluck a duck!' she says.

She stands and holds out her arms to embrace me. The train judders and we fall unceremoniously to the floor. She, I notice, is half-cut.

'Shall we get off and catch up?' she says.

'Yes, right now.'

I pretend to reach for the emergency cord and she grabs my arm.

'I still can't believe I've run into you like this,' she says.

'Yes,' I say, 'a real coincidence.' I won't tell her that I've been searching for her and hanging about in places she may happen to visit. Or that I was going to employ Hervé to track her down. If we hadn't met here today, it would have been tomorrow at the Copenhagen or the day after on the terrace of one of the Cafés in Montparnasse.

We get off at Saint-Sulpice and find ourselves right outside the conveniently placed Métro Café.

'In here?' I ask.

'No, it looks shabby.'

She loops her arm through mine and guides me towards boulevard Saint Germain.

'You know I'm nearly home, I normally get off at the next stop,' I say.

'Then we could get a bottle of whisky and go to your place, or would you prefer the Deux Magots?'

'The whisky idea is good, but I'm not sure that it's a good idea tonight.'

'Why not? Would it be embarrassing for you to have a woman in your apartment? Do you have one of those old crone concierges who hates you having guests? Or is there someone else there?' A crooked smile creeps across her drunken face.

'Christ, no! In fact I have very few friends and no concierge at all. I live above an office and mine is the only apartment there. It's just...'

'Yes?'

'Seeing you now, I'm not sure I'll be able to keep my hands off you.'

'Then don't,' she says.

We don't even buy the whisky.

*

Megan blows large smoke rings at the ceiling. I lie on my side admiring her profile. That nose is still a tad too large, but she's all the more beautiful for it.

'I'm so glad we bumped into each other,' I say.

'I've got a confession to make, Reggie. I thought I saw you the other day near the Café Copenhagen. I was a bit far gone so didn't react. Since then I've been drinking where I can see the Métro Station, waiting for you to pass by. Last night I followed you down and jumped on the carriage behind you. At the next stop I got out and got onto your carriage.'

For some reason we both find this hilariously funny and fall into a fit of laughter.

'I always had the most ridiculous pash for you, Reggie.'

'Really? I never thought about us that way before.' I hate the word 'pash'.

'I know - that's why it's taken us nearly thirty years to get into bed together.'

'I thought you might have married by now,' I say.

'Don't start on marriage. It's one of the reasons I left England. An unmarried woman on the wrong side of thirty is a family ailment. How about you, mister? Is it not a truth universally acknowledged that a single man of good fortune must be in want of a wife?'

'I seriously hate Jane Austen and I have never been in want of a wife. Willing women have always served me well.'

'Willing women like me?'

'They like me too. Actually, I've been through some bad times and went right off the rails for a while. I'm beginning to get on track again.'

'Tell me about it. The whole world got screwed up and now we go around as if it were all some aberration. You know, Reg,' she rolls on her side to fix me with her eyes, 'I'd like to keep on seeing you. We don't have to be lovers; we can be friends, like we used to be. I've lost a lot of people I love and I don't want to lose you again.'

We hold each other for a few moments. Long enough to fight back the tears. I light two cigarettes for us to share. For a while we lie in silence.

'I wish I could have been with you, could have held you. I wish I'd been your lover when we first met,' I say.

'I was five, you were six - our parents would not have approved.'

'When we were older, in our teens.'

'I told you, Reggie, I wanted to. I didn't seem to interest you in that way.'

'You're right; I was more interested in sport. It was only sometimes, in the night, I needed someone to hold me. I needed someone – it didn't have to be a lover, we could have lain side by side and read a book together.'

'Are we to be lovers now, or shall I fetch you a book?'

We make love again and talk until night comes. She falls asleep and I lie beside her, watching her sleeping.

A couple of days pass before we decide to resume our lives. Megan returns to her apartment and I go for a short walk. I have been on the case for a week and three of those days were spent in bed with Megan. Today I will visit my client and quiz her about Marty. Then I will go to the Lacman Brothers. Then this evening will be mine and I can enjoy it with a clear conscience.

*

I don't want to take the Métro to Marie's but it's too far to walk there and back and still have time for anything else. I'll walk for a mile or so and then go underground. This will give me a chance to think over what it is that I want to ask Marie before I slip into Métro stasis. I'm on the other side of the river when it occurs to me that I have not been thinking about the case at all. I had started out thinking about it before an image of Megan in a purple dress overtook those thoughts. I find myself picturing her removing her stockings.

I'm powerless to stop thoughts of her entering my mind at any given moment. They come and go as they please, like the wind through a pauper's coat. I'm going to have to learn to catch them as they arrive and store them up for the evening. There is no point walking any further, I'll take the Métro from here.

My client, Marie Thérèse, lives out in the 19th arrondissement on the rue Cavendish. This is working class Paris, rundown without being a slum. I've been there previously en route to the Parc des Buttes Chaumont. That park is one of the few in Paris where you can sit on the grass without an irate keeper appearing from the bushes to shake a stick at you. There you can relax, smoke a cigarette, lie down and watch the clouds pass overhead. The summer is the best time to visit. Isn't everywhere best in the summer?

I've ridden the Métro to the Gare de l'Est where I change for Laumière. While changing trains I realise that I have gone eight stops without thinking about rain. Rather than the bleak Pennine moorland, I've been thinking of Megan. I wasn't only thinking about her naked body either. I was remembering things we used to get up to as kids. She was the first girl I ever heard say 'shit'. Her language has always been quite colourful; in fact she could make be blush merely by swearing.

As new passengers get on the train I notice they are not wearing the casual suits of Saint-Germain-des-Pres. The men are in dark blue overalls and have large flat caps on. Some of them are wearing wooden clogs. The women have white aprons over tatty dresses. They've all gone in for large kiss curls in the centre of their foreheads. They sit in silence and eye me with suspicion. These workers are radicalised and I represent the bourgeois oppressors. I get off at Laumière with the feeling of having been held silently to account for my wealth. Come the revolution, they'll be pushing me up against the wall. What would I have to say in my defence? Even my having lived as a pauper, rejecting all the privileges of my position, could be seen as an extreme act of bourgeois decadence.

I meander around for a few minutes trying to get my bearings. There is something unsettling about this place – at every crossroads I expect to encounter a highwayman hanging from a gibbet. I spot the rue Cavendish up ahead, a narrow road lined with five-storey apartment blocks. I start to feel insignificant and out of sorts. The road runs North-South; the sun fails to make it to either side of the street. There are no wide boulevards for the working class. Still, it will be easier to barricade these narrow streets when the revolution does come.

I find Marie's apartment near the junction with the rue Armand Carrel. This is a sparse area with a couple of parked automobiles to break up the monotony of grey concrete. These machines are like the yellow crosses of the plague, spreading across the city as each area becomes infected with auto-madness. If you want to travel a short distance, cycle or walk; if you need to go further, get the train. Why would you want one of these frightful contraptions? Filatre owns one: an otherwise level-headed man and he still found a reason to go out and buy one. He took me for a spin once, never again. He transformed into a raving lunatic the moment his arse hit the leather seat. This man, who would go out of his way to help anybody he met, spent the entire time in the automobile honking at pregnant women who couldn't cross the road fast enough.

I ring the buzzer. Was it working class rebelliousness that gave Marie that air of defiance when she came to visit me? She answers the door wearing the same dress she had worn for our last meeting. I doubt it's a coincidence. She is a little more relaxed today, although she does not invite me inside. Instead we leave the building and walk to the rue Armand Carrel and a café called Les Gondoles.

CHAPTER ELEVEN

Les Gondoles is one of those practical cafés located in exactly the place where a café is required. To compensate for this excellent location, it is a drab and soulless place. The paint work is plain and in need of a going over; it hasn't reached crisis point, so will remain in its deteriorating state for at least another year. The chairs are a wooden miss-matched collection. No doubt they were purchased from a bric-a-brac store before the war - which war I wouldn't like to guess. The floor has a stickiness which tells of careless customers and a lacklustre cleaner.

The two other customers are engaged in the noble art of ignoring one another. One is sat, with his back to the bar, facing a bawdy circus poster hanging on the wall. The poster looks to have replaced a large mirror, the frame for which still remains. The other customer is standing at the bar with his back to the poster. Both men look to be around fifty years old. It would not surprise me to learn that they are brothers. The waiter is reading the racing form. The silence is reverential.

Outside the café there are three abandoned tables. Are they meant for customers or had a delivery man reached this point before losing heart? Whichever the case, we sit at one of them. Our feet nestle amongst cigarette butts on the pavement. I light a cigarette and watch a page from one of last week's newspapers as it rolls along the road. My chair has taken umbrage to my presence - in the space of five minutes it has made two unsuccessful attempts to unseat me.

'I have received some information about monsieur Marty,' I say, 'the address of a former employer. He used to work as a stockbroker on the boulevard Rivoli.'

'I told you he was a stockbroker,' she says. Marie looks at me for a moment and then at the grocery store across the road. Perhaps she is searching for a rag and bone man's horse. Perhaps she finds me too attractive and is trying not to give in to her desire. If that is the case she has resisted for too long; I'm spoken for now. I wonder if that is true. Megan never mentioned anything about me not sleeping with other women.

'Yes, you did,' I say, 'but you didn't give the name of any brokerage or dates when he may have worked at them.'

'I am not in the least interested in the man's work history. I only want to know where he is right now.'

'Of course you do. This is like mislaying your cigarette case: you retrace your footsteps until you happen upon it.'

'A slug like Gustave Marty will leave a trail of slime for you to follow, I'm sure.' She takes a sip of her orange juice, ice jostling against the glass. 'Let me know when you have located him please.'

'I certainly shall. By the way, a rather consumptive looking youth followed me the other day. Goes by the name of Stefan.'

'Stefan is infatuated with me. It's really rather dreary, although he does have his uses. I let him carry my shopping or do odd jobs around the apartment.'

'I gave him a damn good thrashing. Following a detective is like crossing the road without looking. You are liable to get hit.'

'That's because you are brute.'

She says this as a matter of fact, and, as a matter of fact, she may be right.

'Has he recovered?'

'You hurt his pride as much as his body. He resents it but will do nothing about it. He used his bruises to try to persuade me drop the case. You told him about Marty, didn't you?'

'I asked him about Marty – that's what I do, it's called investigating.'

'If Stefan knew anything about Marty, don't you think he would have told me?'

'I don't know Stefan from Tom the Baker's son. For all I know, and for all you know for that matter, Marty might have sent him to spy on you.'

'Monsieur Salazar, you are barking up the wrong tree. Stefan, for all his many faults, is not particularly devious. Besides, Marty has no reason to spy on me.'

'Perhaps if you could give me a little more information as to why you want to track him down, or the relationship you had with him, I wouldn't waste my time barking up these wrong trees.'

'You have the pertinent facts, monsieur Salazar – I want to find monsieur Marty. He has no reason to believe that I am alive and if he did he would not give that fact more than a passing thought.'

She folds her arms and leans back in her seat. There is something very appealing about her, also something repulsive. It isn't exactly physical; there is nothing repulsive about her appearance. It's her mannerisms; she draws you in only to spit you out again. 1 can understand how Stefan has fallen under her spell. The poor sap better get over it soon or he'll be finished.

'Can you tell me anything about Marty's family? What did his father do - was he a stockbroker too?'

'No, he was actually quite a nice man. He owned a couple of furniture shops in Namur. He was even mayor there once, before the war.'

'That should make him easy to trace.'

'You don't need to trace him - he's in Namur Cemetery.'

'What about Marty's mother?'

'That bitch, I'm pleased to say, lies besides her husband.'

'You two weren't friends?'

She replies with a brief, malformed, smile.

'When was the last time you saw Marty?'

'Around 1922. He'd already left Namur for the university in Brussels. I saw him because he was visiting his parents for Christmas. He was walking down the other side of the street with some girl he'd picked up. I haven't actually seen him since.'

'And you have been looking all this time?'

'No. I started looking about a year ago – not in a serious way.' She drains her drink with one long swallow. 'Then I saw your card and decided I would track him down properly. Will there be anything else, monsieur Salazar?'

She lights a cigarette and walks away without waiting for my reply. I watch her cross the road and enter her apartment building. She's out of place in this district; she would be out of place in any district.

Without much else to go on I really ought to get over to the Lacman Brothers place. I should also write to Marty's university and see if they have an address for him. A trip to Namur would be pretty pointless and I have a duty to keep my costs down - Marie doesn't look as if she has any spare cash.

To achieve your goals, without over-wearying yourself, you should aim to achieve one thing each day. To me that makes perfect sense. I shall call on the Lacman Brothers in the morning. At the moment I have a bottle of wine in my apartment and Megan is due to visit in a few hours. I'll buy a couple more bottles on the way home.

*

Before starting on the wine I should write that letter to the university; it will be all the better for having been written sober. I get out a pen and some writing paper then fuss around to find an envelope. During the short course of its composition the sunny day has become a rainy evening. Does this symbolise my chances of a successful reply? I imagine it does. Marty doesn't strike me as someone who'd be foolish enough to leave a forwarding address before doing a disappearing act. Having wasted twenty minutes and the price of a stamp, I can at least drink the wine happy in the knowledge that I have achieved two things today.

Megan arrives in a green dress with a little hat and a bottle of red. After finishing off the wine we head out into the night in the direction of Montparnasse. Perhaps it's the evening breeze, or Megan's perfume, or the wine we drank together, but I'm in the mood for cocktails.

*

Morning beats a relentless tattoo on my brain. With this throbbing head and a strong desire to sleep for a year in darkness, I get up. I loathe hangovers, I enjoy drinking, such is my burden. In spite of the pain I remain intent on visiting the offices of the Lacman Brothers this very morning; it's a way to convince myself that I can drink heavily and still work the next day. I think that notion caused me to stagger home to bed rather than spending the night at Megan's place.

'I shall go by God!' I declare to a spider on the ceiling. I sit up, a little too quickly. My head spins wildly; I try to hold back the vomit. This is worse than I thought. Why, oh why, did I start on those cocktails and why wasn't that enough? I might have gotten away with it if it hadn't been for that half-bottle of whisky.

I sit in the kitchen with coffee and orange juice. A Gitane glows delightfully between my fingers. I've taken the only course available to a man in my position; I paid a visit to the nearest café, where upon I consumed two whiskies in quick succession. After the initial protests from my gullet, which tried to close, they went down fine. I don't normally go in for hair of the dog. I can't help feeling that you are storing up all those hangovers for an almighty day of reckoning, one I doubt my head will survive.

Place Vendôme, home to the Lacman Brothers, is also home to Napoleon's column and the Ritz Hotel. Fashion houses and private banks huddle together, whores with their pimps, preying on the rich and vain. Rapaciousness poisons the air. Is there a city in the world which has luxury like this without countless slums as a counterpoint? For each rich sir or madam who totters forth from a Mercedes Benz, patting a Bichon Frise, there are fifty men out of work, fifty families without an income, and a hundred children going hungry. In this square there is no poverty, only ice-cold consumption and the blindness which allows people to pass one day to the next without tying a rope around their necks.

I walk past the Lacman Brothers a few times without noticing it. Their entrance is understated, as opposed to the marble luxuriance of Kuo and Partners. Here an anonymous stairway leads up to an unadorned dark-green wooden door. It has the feel of a gentleman's club, tucked away in Piccadilly or just off St. James's Square. Climbing the steps I have the feeling of being neither invited nor spurned, as if I'm walking towards eternal limbo.

A doorman stands sentry at the top of the stairs. He opens the door as I approach and then opens an interior door. The receptionist is young and attractive. She wears expensive looking clothes. My shoes resound on the stone floor causing her to turn and greet me with a brilliant white smile. I can't help but be suspicious; what is she there to distract me from? My money, no doubt.

'Good morning, sir.'

She smiles again. I smile back, a yellow smile tarnished by nicotine, red wine and coffee. My smile isn't something I usually think about.

'Good morning, mademoiselle. I'm trying to track down an old friend of mine.'

'How can I help you?'

'I think he works here.'

'What is his name?'

'Gustave Marty.'

She smiles once more and then lifts up a big ledger from which she reads one of the pages.

'There is no Gustave Marty working here, I'm afraid. Could he be with The Jackman Brothers? They are four doors down from us.'

'I am positive it was Lacman. It's been a while; he may have left. Do you keep a record of ex-employees?'

'I'll take a look for you.' She opens the dusty ledger once more. 'Ah yes, Marty, G, Sordine A, now du Pont, S.'

'What does all that mean?'

'It means he did work here and A. Sordine was his secretary. Then she left and S. du Pont took over. She still works here. Monsieur Marty left just over a year ago though.'

'Do you think I could see mademoiselle du Pont, she may know where I can get hold of Marty?'

The doorman coughs.

'You might want to check with monsieur Lacman, mademoiselle,' he says.

'Nonsense, Philippe, I'm in charge of this desk.' She sends the doorman a little frown before giving me another smile. 'If you could please give me your card, I'll see if mademoiselle du Pont will receive you.'

I hand her my personal card and hope she doesn't ask if Reginald is really a Belgian name. She tootles off towards a stairway with her heels echoing around the lobby. I'm about to start reading the ledger when the doorman coughs once more. I turn to face him.

'So, did you know Gustave Marty?'

'I did, sir, much better than I know you, I should fancy.'

'My name is Salazar.'

I hold out my hand for him to shake. The gesture is ignored.

'Sorry, old chap, is there some merde on my hand?'

'No need to take that tone, sir. I don't shake hands with a man unless I know what he's about. Monsieur Marty is entitled to his privacy wherever he may be. I don't see how he'll gain from your finding him.'

'Very well, old bean. You keep your hands in your pockets and shake your little chap instead.'

The young lady totters over from the stairs to her desk.

'Mademoiselle du Pont says she can spare you five minutes, monsieur Salazar.'

CHAPTER TWELVE

I'd expected mademoiselle du Pont to be young and attractive like Céline at Kuo's. Du Pont is getting on and has already worked past her prime. It happens a lot these days, people working past their prime.

'Monsieur Salazar, how may I help you?'

She holds out her hand for me to shake. It is a delicate hand and, in order to win her over, I bow and kiss it.

'I'm trying to locate an old pal of mine from Belgium - Gustave Marty. We lost touch when he moved to Paris. The last I heard of him he was working here and the young lady on reception informs me you were his secretary.'

'I'm afraid he hasn't worked here for at least a year now.'

She draws her hand away, with some reluctance I might add.

'Drat! Did he leave a forwarding address?' I smile a beatific smile, or so I like to think.

'He did live on rue Léon out by the Parc du Monceau. I know that he has since left there though, as we have had a letter returned to us.'

'What absolutely rotten luck. I'm only in Paris a week and I can't spend all that time trying to track old Gusty down. How about his previous secretary, do you have her contact details? They may still be in touch.'

'I doubt that very much, monsieur Salazar. She left because she and monsieur Marty had irreconcilable differences.'

'Really? Old Gusty always used to get on so well with the ladies. You got on with him well enough?'

'He was an extremely charming man,' she says.

'That is exactly how I would describe him - charming and witty. Do you think I could I have her address anyway? It is possible he may have contacted her.'

'I couldn't give you a lady's address just like that, monsieur Salazar, it would be indecorous.'

'Oh well, I'm sorry to have troubled you, mademoiselle du Pont.'

Indecorous! What a joke. These people are making money hand over fist. Every time someone comes here to invest a franc, somebody else goes without food.

I think I hate myself sometimes.

Down in the lobby I try my luck with the smiley receptionist.

'Excuse me, mademoiselle - mademoiselle du Pont couldn't find an address for madame Sordine. Do you have it?' I flash a choir-boy smile as proof my innocent intent.

'Oh yes, I'm sure we do.'

My smile is earning its keep today. She pulls out a different ledger from before and scans a few pages.

'Here we are. It's mademoiselle Sordine, by the way, not madame. Yes, that explains it, she changed her address not long after she left here. That will be why du Pont couldn't locate it. It's on rue Sévin Vincent, right out by Saint Cloud; I'll write it down for you.'

'Thanks, mademoiselle, you're a real doll.' I wink at her to show what a doll she is.

I leave the Lacman offices with a light step and a slight smirk. I'd gotten what I wanted and I'd used charm and guile rather than threats and insults to get it. Even the doorman's scowl as I depart brings me a little extra joy. What's more, Paris is sunny and there is no better place than Paris in the sunshine.

No reason to delay when I'm hot on the trail. I make straight for the Métro which takes me to within a mile of the rue Sévin Vincent. I emerge from the stinking people-sewer and saunter over a bridge into one of the richest areas of

Paris. Lampposts are adorned with baskets of flowers. People appear to be going about their business with a certain degree of self-satisfaction, wearing post-coital smiles, no shirts unpressed, no item unlaundered. Spend the day sniffing the inhabitants here and smell violets, lavender, vanilla, lemon balm, eau de cologne. A myriad smells, none of them human. These are the children of God and they are occupied in His good work.

The sun glints off of an automobile's windscreen. As I'm shielding my eyes somebody jostles past me. They do this even though the pavement is wide enough to sail two galleons side-by-side and I'm the only other person on it. Bastard. I feel like chasing them down and haranguing them. Or tipping one of these flower–baskets over their head. I kick out at a lamppost and continue on my way.

At first glance the streets are too clean. A closer look reveals the dog turds to the side of the pavement. Little pampered dogs who eat more in a day than half the residents of Paris. A little dog empties its bowels as its over-made-up mistress holds her nose in the air because shit is not something she should ever have to deal with. Once this business is over they will make their way to a Patisserie where the mistress will buy herself a macaroon.

I feel sick and have to close my eyes momentarily. This case has taken me to some unpleasant places, not all of them physical. I wonder if I oughtn't to chuck it all in. No, I'll finish this one and then I'll spend my time with Megan doing as we please. The nausea is worsening. I head for a little café and steal into a corner. If I don't look at anybody and nobody looks at me I may be able to sit this one out.

The waiter brings my order of coffee and orange juice. I stare at the wall and a poster for Laurel and Hardy's latest picture. I gaze at it until my eyes lose focus and I'm not looking at anything at all.

I'm a dilettante, and I hate it. I was a tramp and hated that too. I've hated everything I've ever been and I fear I'll hate everything I'll ever become. The world is corrupted by my touch. If I could find something even halfway decent, I'd take it and make it my life. Perhaps I need a small house with a large garden where I can make like Candide. I could live off the plot, growing potatoes and slowly older. This is all something I should talk over with Megan. Right now I need to regain control. All these mental aberrations serve to distract me from the very simple task I have set myself. I need to leave here, walk to mademoiselle Sordine's apartment, and get a statement from her.

I finish off my drinks and leave. I walk for five minutes, keeping my head down, before I find myself outside Sordine's apartment block. She lives in a nice old building which radiates seventeenth century finesse. I can picture d'Artagnan whistling up to the rooms above, attracting the attentions of some fair maid.

There is no reply when I press Sordine's buzzer. I must not start thinking. I keep my head down and walk back to the café. I ask the waiter for writing paper and another orange juice. I write out a note and attach my card to it. Ten minutes later I drop the card through Sordine's mailbox and make it back to the Métro station. There, finished, with no nervous breakdowns required.

I'm glad mademoiselle Sordine was not in. I wasn't in the right frame of mind to question her. The next time I come here I'll know what to expect and brace myself accordingly. After riding for two or three stops I can no longer stand being cooped up in the Metro. I get off and find myself somewhere in the 15th arrondissement.

If I follow the river north I'll pass by the Eiffel Tower and reach the source of the boulevard Saint Germain. This will give me a couple of hours of peaceful strolling. The sun breaks through the clouds as I begin my journey; what better omen could a voyager have? This place is semi-industrialised, semi-residential, with the river providing the industry. Beyond the river the rich suburbs cling to Paris's western border like leeches on a swimmer's arse. Here it's like walking the decks of the Marie Celeste - the streets are deserted. There is no mystery; everybody is at lunch. If you ever want to invade France, do it between twelve and two. There'll be nobody around to stop you.

*

Not sure where or what. Where or what or why. Only pain and discomfort. Is it my head? I reach to touch it. The pain is in my ribs and it sends shock waves across my body. My hand hurts too; no it's the fingers not the hand. It's the hand and the fingers. My leg, left, right, my right leg. My head is vibrating. I can't keep a hold of anything.

I'm fearfully cold. My left hand can move; the pain there is not so intense. Is this the same moment? I touch my eye as softly as I can and pull gently at the lashes. Something is binding them closed. I think it might be raining. I pull bloody gunk from the lashes until I have the eye open wide enough to see. I'm looking at nothing. The sky. The night has come and I'm lying down looking up at the sky. There is a little rain - I knew it. I must be looking for shooting stars. Why?

I'm freezing and hungry too. Are my eyes open? No, they have closed again. The pain in my head is the worst. There is a continual throbbing and a spinning sensation which disorientates me. When I move my body, even a fraction, my chest, my right leg, and my right hand all seethe with pain. The world is pain and cold. I can't hold on to a thought for more than a few seconds. I consider my location, I find I'm thinking about a song I heard a few days ago, then a snippet from a conversation I overheard in a café, then I realise I'm not thinking about now and snap back to considering my location. Where am I? A phrase from Gogol keeps running through my head: 'Spain is under the feathers of every chicken.'

One eye is open. I'm lying on a pile of coal. With some effort and considerable initiative I lift one of the lumps up for examination. From what I can hear I must be by the river. Water is lapping nearby and I can feel a slight swaying. The night is far too dark to make out much else. I can see metal ridges. This must be a coal barge. By jingo I hurt! I'm so thirsty too. My mouth is dry and cracking. My lips stick when I open my mouth slightly. Night-birds will land on my face and peck at my eyes. They will slowly peck away my chances of survival.

Mustering all my will, I lift myself up on to one arm. My body screams in protest. I must drink. Having risen slightly, I have a view of the barge. I've grown accustomed to the low light. I scan my immediate surroundings. A small puddle has formed in the coal about a foot away. Through torrents of pain I clamber and roll myself in its direction, then I collapse face first in the water. I turn my head slightly so as not to drown. After a few minutes recuperation I can take a drink.

This is where I shall die.

The barge is moored up against a wall. I stare at the wall, passing in and out of consciousness, without any concept of time. I can see metal rungs which form a ladder to safety. Despite seeing the ladder and knowing I have to climb it, I cannot move. My body is insubordinate to my brain's orders. I'm moving! I drag myself over inches of agony towards that first rung. Right leg and right hand are useless. I have a stubborn survival instinct – I just wish I didn't have to make use of it so often. Now my head spins while my body shakes uncontrollably. What I wouldn't give for a jug of water and an opium pipe.

One day I'll be sitting waiting for someone in an office or perhaps a twice delayed train. I'll suffer from boredom and pace up and down. When I do I must remember this moment and be thankful that I'm not here on this barge. Thinking causes my head to swim. Am I here, or am I waiting for a train? Is this a vivid memory or a dream? Is it even my dream? It is a dream. I wake up. I'm still on the barge. I must make it to that ladder.

The ladder is too high. Six metres, perhaps more. It may as well stretch to the moon. How can I hope to climb this? I reach up with my left hand as high as I can. The rung is a cold and rough rusted metal. In the centre the metal is smooth. I pull myself up and my left leg scrabbles around for a footing. I begin to stand. The movement of the barge leaves me feeling sick. The river is tranquil. It feels like tidal waves. I vomit over myself. I heave again - nothing comes out. Maintaining its grip on the ladder, my hand steadies me as I sway uneasily.

I climb onto the first rung. Once on the ladder I lose the swaying motion of the barge. My right hand has no strength in it. I put it behind the rungs to keep my balance as my left hand searches out the next rung up. I'm trembling uncontrollably and have an urge to let go; not only so that this may be over. Tortured and weeping, I force myself to continue. I have slime all over my face. On and on and on. Through repetition I reach the top. Now I must clamber up and over the wall. I throw my body forward so my chest and head are over the embankment while my legs are suspended over the river. I bend a leg up and try to push off from the ladder. I gain too much momentum; it takes me over the wall and off the other side. I fall nearly two metres to the pavement and release a wild scream into the night.

CHAPTER THIRTEEN

I open my eyes with difficulty. There is a general bustling noise and, so bright, the lights. I'm in a bed, a hospital perhaps. The pain has diminished, although it still lingers. My right leg is in plaster; I can bend and stretch my left one. I lift both arms up and look at my hands. The left one looks undamaged, while the right is bandaged and some fingers are in splints.

'Ah, you are awake.'

The nurse is slightly blurry, I can't seem to pinpoint her face. Her body obscures then reveals the bright lights in the ceiling. By squinting I can make out her features. A large hat wraps around her hair as it cascades down her back. Her dress is pale blue and she wears a large white apron. Emblazoned on the front is a stylised cross giving her the appearance of a crusader from a lesser known order of knights.

'Don't try to concentrate, it will hurt your head,' she says. 'Relax and get some sleep.'

'I don't want...'

'Never mind that now. You have suffered a serious blow to the head. Your leg is fractured. You have some broken fingers and a few cracked ribs. Judging by your scars I'd say you were used to hospitals. How did you get those marks on your back?'

'What?'

'Are you a self-flagellator?'

'No. Where am I?'

'The Henry Dunant Hospital.'

'Why aren't I on the ward? This is a room.'

'Wards are for the hoi-polloi.'
'How do you know that I'm not hoi-polloi?'
'You are a lord.'
'What makes you think that?'
'The passport in your jacket.'
'Oh yes. It's an honorary title, I don't use it.'
'But you are a lord?'
'My father is.'
'Try to sleep.'

*

I don't know where that nurse is. The pain armistice is over. My head is pounding like a bailiff on a debtor's door. Is this really a hospital? How did I get here? Where is Megan? I got these injuries through the nefarious agency of another. My best chance for an extended life is to get out of here without that other knowing where I have gone.

I can see a wardrobe on the far side of the room. My clothes must be in there. Wires and weights are holding my right leg in the air. With a bit of straining I double up my body and catch hold of my leg. I fiddle with one of the wires until it comes loose and then flop back down to the bed. I take a breath and then lift myself up again. I pull at the remaining wires until the weights fall from my leg and land with a dull clang on the floor. My leg is free, plastered to the hip but free. I swing my legs out over the bed and sit up. The spinning in my head starts up again; it's disorientating and not something I can get used to. I can't focus or look for too long at the same thing. The windows are shuttered; it must be night time. The walk to the wardrobe is interminable. I'm too weak and I need to eat. My clothes are here, all dirtied and bloodied. I pull my jacket on, over the hospital gown they have dressed me in. Before I can get my trousers on I need to rip off the right leg. Even with two good hands this would be difficult. I scan the room for something I can cut with. There is nothing so I hold them with the rest of my clothes. Now all I need to do is catch a taxicab.

I open the door a fraction of an inch and peer out. I can see a short corridor. There is nobody about and only a few lights are on. These lights, like the ones in my room, are electric. Further along I can see another door – another room? The corridor turns to the left. I find a large doorway which fronts on to another, longer corridor. The flickering of the lights shows that these are gas. They were keeping me in a section away from the main hospital. I don't believe all that lord business. They wanted me away from the rest so they could murder me.

This corridor stinks, a mixture of cabbage and sweat. You get this smell in the picture house when certain people sit next to you. Non-smokers, I would guess; the rest of us hide the cabbage smell beneath that of tobacco. Now there is a distinct whiff of vomit and urine. The combination stirs up memories of my stay in a Belgian hospital. I pass a set of double doors with glass in them. Looking through, I can see the back of a ward-sister's head and two rows of beds. The occupants all seem to be sleeping – I wish I could join them. Each step is a torture. Ribs feel as if they are cutting into my lungs. I have to swing my right leg out and round to go forward. When it comes to a halt it is always with a jolt of pain.

Gritting my teeth, I hobble along to the end of the corridor. Here I notice a door with a stairwell sign on it. There's also an unshuttered window and I can see outside. I'm about three storeys up. I lean my shoulder into the swing door and stagger into the stairwell. The steps conspire to do me harm as I stumble over each one of them. Giving up means death; this torture must be endured. The plaster stops my knee from bending and the banister is only on the right-hand side; my right hand is useless. I can picture the line of my fracture by the surges of pain which course through my leg.

I make it down to the ground floor, where I lean against a wall to recuperate. My body is fracturing into fissures of glowing pain. I repress the urge to cry. Perhaps if I called out, a nurse or a porter would come and take me to my room, back to my bed. Before I can open my mouth a small germ within me assumes command. It doesn't take any crap and thinks only of survival; I'm on my belly creeping towards the door. Whenever I pause I can hear people talking. The sound emanates from a fixed position somewhere down the corridor. In the trenches I would have ordered two snipers to triangulate on the sound, and then open fire. With a great deal of silent cursing I manage to crawl to the door, open it a slither, and peep through. It's a dimly lit corridor with a reception desk at the far end. I can make out two people up there. One looks like an orderly, the other is a shadow behind a desk.

There is a window on this floor, same as there was up on the third. If my leg wasn't in plaster this would be easy. I stay on the floor with the door slightly open. If anybody comes down the stairs behind me I should hear them from a few flights up. I watch the reception desk – they are the only ones likely to walk up here. They don't look like they're going anywhere. In a real hospital I could just walk up there, bid them goodnight, and leave. Or I could let them take care of me. If this were a real hospital I wouldn't have been hidden away in that room. I hope that window is open.

Getting back on my feet is difficult. I scramble around, grabbing hold of the door handle to stop myself falling.

This is it – if I don't make it out now I won't have the strength to try again. I pull the door open and slip into the corridor. I press myself against the wall and keep my head turned towards the people on the reception desk. I count to three then make straight for the window. I place the bundle of clothes on the window sill. Got to keep up the momentum. The window is stiff. I shove it hard and it screeches opens. I duck back through the doorway scared witless that the game is up. I stand there breathing hard and clenching my fist, as if I am in any shape to fight my way out of this. There is silence for a moment and then the talking recommences. They must be able to see my clothes by the window sill.

Laziness or inertia keeps them at the reception desk. Now that the window is open I should be able to get out easily enough. They ignored the open window and the pile of clothes, will they also ignore a man in pyjamas crawling out the window? I doubt it. I pull the door open and drag my leg over to the window. Without looking back I give the window another shove. This time it doesn't make much of a noise. I'm not sure how I'm going to do this. I can't angle my leg up enough to get it up over the ledge. Without this damnable plaster I'd be halfway down the boulevard by now. There isn't anything to hand that I can cut it off with and I don't have time to go looking. I lift myself up with my back to the open window and the cold night air. There isn't enough room for me to turn around now. I hold the sill in my hands and lean back. My head is outside and my back is parallel with the ground. The strain on my fingers is too great. My right hand can hardly hold on at all. Before I know what is happening I tumble out the window and land on my back. Surprisingly, this hardly hurts at all.

I fight the urge to remain lying where I am. I'm out of their grasp but I'm not safe. Getting up isn't easy: I flail around like an upturned beetle for a while, then grimace and groan as I use the wall to climb to my feet. The road is about twenty metres away. Between me and it there is a collection of rusted iron bed parts. There is no option for me now but to pick a route through it all and hope I don't get tetanus.

This is a side road; to escape I will need to get around to the main road at the front of the building. A few people are out walking, but they don't pay me much attention; I'm just another oddity out on the streets at night. I flag down a taxicab.

'Rue Challot, and quick,' I say.

'Are you OK?'

'No chit-chat, just drive.'

We spin through the city – the lights whirl and dance on

the window. People's faces appear in the darkness. The sounds of the night sweep over me like waves on a beach. A repetitive puffing noise plays over in my ears. I'm going to vomit. The roads keep on coming. Buildings lighted and dark pass by. The heat is intolerable. I jerk the window down and drink in vast gulps of cold air. We stop and I push a handful of notes at the driver. He comes round to open my door and helps me onto the pavement. I make it into the building and up to my bed.

*

Light streams through my window. Filatre stands at my bedside puffing on his pipe.

'What's happened to you, old chum?' he asks.

I answer but Filatre isn't there anymore. I can hear him talking somewhere in the distance.

'Oh my God! Reggie, what's happened to you?'

'Megan?'

'Yes, darling, it's me.'

'It hurts.'

I think Megan is arguing with someone. I think it might be a doctor. Filatre appears at my bedside again. He isn't holding his pipe anymore.

'The doctor wants you to go in, old chum. He's called the Henry Dunant Hospital, they filled him in.'

'Filled him in with what?'

'They think you tried to kill yourself.'

'What, how?'

'Jumping off a building, that's what they say.'

'Which building? I was in the river. Someone must have hit me.' I put a hand to the back of my head and run my fingers over a large lump. 'They must have coshed me then rolled me over the wall. I was lucky that barge was there.'

'Who are they?' Filatre asks.

'Lord knows. They didn't leave a calling card.'

'Were you robbed?'

'No I wasn't. It must have been...I don't know who.'

'Marty!' Megan is standing by the bed with the doctor. 'Marty must have done it.'

'How would he know me?'

'One moment, Reggie,' she turns to face the doctor. 'Look, doctor, he's going in and he's not a suicide case. Can't you give him something for the pain?'

The doctor must have been persuaded as he's sticking a shot of morphine in my arm.

'Can you recall anything else, old chum?' Filatre asks.

'Not much. I was walking by the river. I woke up on a coal barge in total pain.'

'Before all of that, what did you do yesterday?'

The drug is starting to work. I feel a tingling excitement passing through my body.

'Can you remember what you did yesterday?'

'Yes, I think I can. I went to Lacmans'. I say!' I reach for my jacket which has been slung on a nearby chair. Megan sees what I'm reaching for and passes it to me. My notebook is in the inside pocket. I can't quite concentrate or focus enough to read. I hand the book to Megan who skims through it.

'He went to Lacman Brothers and interviewed some staff. Then on to an ex-secretary of Marty's. She wasn't in. Did you do anything else?'

'I went for a walk near the river.'

'So,' Filatre says, 'is it possible somebody followed you from Lacmans' and then waited for an opportunity to do you in?'

'I can't think who could have done that. I can't think of anything much at all.'

'Perhaps we should leave it for a while,' Filatre says. 'There's not much we can do now and I'm certain that these questions are doing nothing to aid your recovery.'

*

I pass in and out of consciousness, aware of very little. I know the doctor gave me another shot. I may have received hundreds more. I could not say for how many days I have been lying in this bed. Nearly every time I have called her name, Megan has been there to answer.

I hear people talking, mentioning the name 'Lady Soames'. There is laughter and the clink of a pair of glasses. I wish they'd shut up and shove off.

'Who the hell is Lady Soames?' I say.

'Oh, so you are awake now. I am Lady Soames. I know it's been a long time but I can't believe you have forgotten all about me.'

A strange woman is standing in front of the sun-filled window. The bright light has transformed her into a cameo.

'Aunt Bess!'

'Little Reggie, always in trouble.'

She puts her hands to my cheeks and places a kiss on my forehead. The smell of her perfume transports me to my youth. I feel safe having her here.

'How did you...'

'Megan, of course.'

'I called her, Reggie, I had to,' Megan says.

'They need help to care for you, Reggie dear. O my little darling, I wish you could have called me before. I've missed you so terribly.'

'I couldn't. I mean, I just couldn't.'

'Your mother has never stopped worrying about you.'

'That's all she ever does, Aunt Bess, she worries. She worries and worries and sometimes she cries. She never actually does anything.'

'Some things are beyond a mother's control, Reggie.'

'Only if the mother wants it that way.'

'Her first duty is to her husband.'

'Until she has a child, then her first duty should be to them, or at least some sort of duty.'

'Let's not talk about it now, Reggie dear, I can see it aggrieves you.'

She's right; I do feel aggrieved. I picture the bridge with water flowing beneath. I hold on to the image until my feelings of resentment subside.

CHAPTER FOURTEEN

Easter bells are ringing. The churches are trying to outdo each other. Five days have passed since I was hit and my head is finally calming down. Thinking is possible for longer durations. The leg is still in plaster and my right hand is bandaged up. Someone has rigged a make-shift traction system and attached it to my leg. I guess the doc-tor did that. I must have seen it before without it having registered. Or it did register and I forgot all about it?

My memory is patchy. The notebook helps as I go over the day of the attack. If it were solely an incident of crime, without ulterior motive, then I was just plain unlucky. My prolonged existence will be better guaranteed if I assume that I was targeted. Whoever attacked me meant to murder to me. I was not an unfortunate victim of circumstance.

The attack might not have been related to events on the day it took place. No, that sort of thinking is no good; I'm ruling out coincidences. The attack must have been directly related to my visiting the Lacmans and asking questions. All of this adds up to one thing. I'm getting closer to Marty.

Someone from Lacmans' either followed me and then hit me, or they tipped off somebody else. Who? There was that miserable old sod at the door. A man from whom all life seems to have been drained away, leaving him sour and vindictive husk. Then there was the girl on reception, or Marty's last secretary. There could have been somebody else lurking in the shadows, but I'm going to stick to certainties.

The secretary doesn't feel right. She didn't really know

who I was. The receptionist was helpful, maybe she... no, it was the old man. He had that look about him, snidey and conspiratorial. He's the sort of person I can imagine striking a blow from behind, yet I can't quite visualise him actually doing it. He isn't agile enough. What's more, he would've had to have followed me straight away and I'm sure I looked back and saw him still at the door.

I run through the suspects again, returning as always to the three from Lacmans'. From the three I always filter down to the doorman. At one point I consider the kid, Stefan. He may have followed me for a few days before carrying out the attack. If it were him, wouldn't he have struck nearer my office? I can't see him following me all day then whacking me on the head. Stefan is the sort to use a penknife, not wield a cosh. Perhaps I ought to start wearing a thick jumper in case he does attack.

That old bastard, the doorman. Philippe. He must have done it. I'm going to make him wish he'd never lived. As soon as I'm able to get out of bed, I'm going to dash his brains out. No, I'm going to break each of his bones - one by one - and leave him on a railway track for a train to finish him off. He is going to feel all the pain I felt and so much more.

I write out a telegram for my client – letting her know I will be out of action for a while. After that I write out a note for someone who once passed as a friend of mine. I leave them on the side table together with a list of books I want to read. I may as well make the most of the next few weeks in bed.

Pain mingles with the pages from my books to feed my dreams. I sleep and wake according to a rhythm I'm too dull to detect. Conversations, real and imagined, float through my room. For a while I am one of Charlemagne's knights. An injured knight laid up in his tent listening to the battles being fought around him.

Days fluctuate from bliss to desperation. If I were inclined, I would make a note of my mood and how it relates to my doses of morphine. Doctors the world over would tremble as they devour my findings. However, I'm not so inclined: those doctors can tremble from the DTs instead.

In the middle of a dream, a villain appears in the bedroom doorway. His body casts a long shadow across the room to my bed. He taps a cosh in to the open palm of his left hand. He grins a twisted grin full of broken, black, teeth. His face, hideous and deformed, is my own. A scream dies in the dryness at the back of my throat. No sooner have I reached out a pointing arm than he's gone.

I become more aware of myself and my room. The pain is traceable to distinct areas of my body. For the last few days I have been reading The Three Musketeers. There's an hour's reading left in that book and then it's The Hunchback of Notre-Dame. After that I'll move to something modern and English. Aunt Bess has brought me Point Counter Point; I can read it and imagine the life I might have led.

Megan brings in my gramophone and places it near the bed. Getting up to change the records proves too much of a strain for me. When Filatre appears I make him serve as my Jazz-wallah, playing records according to my whims.

I could easily be persuaded to retire to my bed on a permanent basis. Bring me books, wine, opium, and women. What more has this world to offer?

*

After being laid up for three weeks, I'm out of traction and able to hobble around. I'm also starting to keep normal hours. I have breakfast in the morning and sleep mainly at night, a few naps excluded. Aunt Bess is staying nearby at the Hotel Welcome. I always thought she was the sort to stay at the Ritz. Apparently the Welcome makes her feel she is a part of the bohemian artistic set. She and Megan, as well as caring for me, have started going on trips. They go shopping and eating out together - I fear they are becoming friends. The doctor makes regular calls and I have a nurse who visits every day. Tomorrow she will be removing the plaster.

'Up and about, old chum? Fancy a game?'

Filatre stands in a fog of pipe smoke holding a chess board under one arm. He smiles apprehensively when I look at him. I bet that crafty fox has been learning some new openings.

'Why ever not?'

Filatre beats me without mercy three times in succession. I lose my bishops and knights like a polar explorer losing his toes. I have yet to regain the art of concentration.

'Let's not play another game today,' I say. 'My ego won't survive another beating.'

'As you wish.' Filatre takes a look at his pipe bowl and gives it a good scraping. Then: 'I say, you are being rather well looked after. You've had a nurse and the doctor over most days. Then there is Megan; that girl must love you some. The way she sits and watches you sleep or reads in the chair besides your bed. Not many young ladies nowadays would keep that up the way she has.'

'Yes, she has been smashing.'

'Your Aunt too, she seems to be a very nice lady.'

'She is really. Whenever I was with her I always felt that that was how it should have been with my mother.'

'I can imagine she is a very caring woman – there is a lot of compassion there.'

'I suppose there is.'

'She has a kindness in her smile and her nose wrinkles like a hamster's. You know...'

'You don't need my blessing, Filatre. If you did, you'd have it.'

Filatre blusters for a few minutes before giving in and quizzing me in detail about my aunt. He leaves when Megan returns with the nurse.

Megan sits and watches as the nurse cuts through the plaster. Underneath it lurks a pasty-looking stick where once a proud leg had lain. An unpleasant smell comes from the leg and, although repulsive, I find I have to keep sniffing at it.

This reminds me of the time one of my corporals had to have his leg amputated. The thing had gone gangrenous and it smelt similar to this. I think this might be why I can't stop sniffing it – I want to make sure it's not gangrenous.

'For God's sake, Reggie, will you stop doing that.'

Megan looks repulsed as I try to get my nose closer to my thigh. The nurse is starting to look like she might give lunch a miss too.

'Sorry girls, I have a morbid curiosity, that's all. The smell reminds me of gangrene.'

'I see,' the nurse says. 'Give me five minutes, monsieur Salazar.'

The nurse leaves and returns with some sponges and water. Without asking for permission she begins sponging my leg with carbolic soap. When she's finished I give it a final sniff. The old stench has gone and my leg now smells how a hospital should but so rarely does. The nurse leaves and is replaced a moment later by Filatre.

'I say, old chum, there is an unfortunate at the door. Says you asked to see him.'

'Did he give a name?'

'Said he was called Yoann.'

'Yoann! Send him up, I've been expecting him.'

'Are you sure that is a good idea, I mean...' Filatre makes an awkward gesture with his head towards Megan.

'I don't follow you.'

'Well, there might be fleas and lice but also... are you sure you want him seen?'

'That's true, I'd forgotten about that. Megan, Yoann is a chap I knew in Saint-Denis. He was very near a trench shell when it exploded. It stole part of his face. He wears a dirty little veil but you can see through it. The scarring is hideous and there are some holes. I got used to it but I do remember how other people reacted when they saw him.'

'If he is a friend of yours I'd like to meet him,' she says.

'I never said he was a friend. I never had any friends up there. He is one of the two drinking buddies I had.' I look

---

105

over at Filatre. 'Send him up.'

'I'll send him up, but I won't join you if you don't mind.'

Yoann enters the room; I hold back a gasp. I'd forgotten how ghastly his wounds were; I'd forgotten how low I'd sunk. This man would make a run of the mill tramp look like a prince. He'd need more than a few sponges and a bar of carbolic to take that smell away. The stench is quite sickening. Only a year ago I'd regularly sit next to him in a grubby café and I don't remember him smelling at all.

'Come in, Yoann, and take a seat.'

'Is that you, Reg? You actually do look like a lord laid up there in those posh pyjamas. Was all that guff actually true?'

'It actually was. Would you like a cigar? Megan, go and fetch us a couple of good cigars.'

I don't want a smoke but the smell will drown out Yoann's. Megan leaves us alone as she goes for the cigars. I know she'll need a bit of time to get over having seen Yoann so I don't expect her to return soon.

'How you doing, Yoann? Still smiling I see.'

'I never stop, Reg.'

'How's Emil?'

'Gone.'

'Where?' I catch Yoann's eye. 'Oh.'

'Stepped in front of the Rouen express. Makes me think you were right about him.'

'I only said all that to rile him. How about you, have you found any other drinking buddies?'

In the ten minutes he's been here I've managed to forget about the scar tissue. Yoann makes it easier somehow; he must have been quite something before the war.

'Are you kidding? A guy like me, I have to beat them off.'

I sit up on the bed so I can face him properly.

'Yoann, tell me quickly, was it him?'

'I don't think it was. I asked around and spoke to some of his neighbours. They know me, so they talked. This guy is from Belgium but not from Namur. He's a few years older than you said. I don't think Marty is his real name.'

'Thanks, Yoann. Here's some cash for your trouble.'

I push a few notes into his hand. He slips them into his jacket pocket.

'It was no trouble, Reg, but I'll take your money — it's thirsty work coming all the way down here.'

'If you ever need more you know where I am.'

Megan returns with three cigars already cut. She hands them out, taking one for herself.

'I might have known Reg would end up with a girl who smokes cigars.'

'Is there something wrong with that?' Megan asks, while striking a match on the sole of her boot.

'I'd rather live in a country where the women smoke cigars than one where the men go to war,' he says.

Yoann holds the smoke in his mouth. Rivulets escape from the holes in his cheek. With his veil and twisted face he looks like a cross between Valentino and Quasimodo. The cigars are doing their work by disguising his smell. Megan tries to prise out a few stories about our days in Saint-Denis together. Yoann spins her a few yarns based on the truth. I doubt there are many who could stomach those stories undiluted.

By three o'clock Yoann has gone and Megan has left to meet my aunt for tea. That suits me fine - I don't want tea, I want information with a little vengeance on the side.

Revolver holstered and walking cane in hand I wobble to the Métro station.

Being out in the crowd is unnerving; I'm jumping at shadows, convincing myself that someone is sneaking up behind me with a cosh. The trip to Lacman Brothers is short; paranoia making it feel much longer.

Place de Vendôme is large enough and busy enough for a man to hide right out in the open — he'd have to be a rather stupid man or not care too much about being caught. I take up a position on a café terrace and use a pair of field glasses to observe my target. The miserable little bastard is at his post. There is still an hour before they close and I guess he'll be among the last to leave. Since my last foray out of doors the weather has improved. The wind and rain which seemed to promise a prolonged winter have been replaced with warm sunshine. Spring is here and there's nothing sweeter than spring – except, of course, revenge.

Ninety minutes pass before the doorman relinquishes his post. Leaving a few coins on the café table I make my way as quickly and discreetly as I can across the square. Merging with the crowds on the street, I fall in a few yards behind him. We all make our way to the Métro. I'm glad it's the Métro and not an auto-bus; it'll make it easier to hide. We travel east, out to Belleville.

Once out of the Métro we flow in to the narrow residential streets. The crowds disperse until it's just him and me. Finally I have my chance and I grab it without hesitation.

'All right, buddy, you come with me.'

I stick the barrel of my revolver into his spine, hard enough for him to stumble forward.

'Who are you?'

'I'm the guy who's going to kill you if you don't turn down that alley.'

The alley is sheltered and we walk about halfway along it.

'Now tell me who it was,' I say.

'I know that voice... you were in the bank.'

'That's right, I was, and every little bit of pain I've felt since then is going to be inflicted upon you unless you start talking.'

'You've got the wrong man, mister. Whoever it was, it wasn't me.'

I push him towards the wall. He reaches out with his hands – not quickly enough. He hits the top of his head on the brick work.

'Turn around and look at me.'

He turns around; his forehead above his right eye is beginning to bleed.

'Whatever happened to you had nothing to do with me. I

did my best to help you.'

'Help? How?'

'All that prying after monsieur Marty, that's what set them on you.'

'Set who?'

The blood, made runny by sweat, starts flowing into his eye. I pass him a handkerchief which he holds to the wound.

'Them. She called them as soon as you left. They probably got to Sordine's place before you did. Then what happened?'

'Then... I'll ask the questions. I reckon it was you who made the call. It was you who set them on me and it is you who's going to pay.'

'Reckon what you will but it's happened before. Someone comes asking questions about monsieur Marty then they end up attacked and dumped somewhere. Always they give their card to mademoiselle Legrand on reception. Always she makes a call when they leave.'

'Always, how many times?'

'You are number three that I know of. It's possible there were more, but unlikely.'

'What do you get out of it?'

'Sod all. I don't want any part of it. Besides, I reckon monsieur Marty probably deserves whatever he gets.'

'And you were acting as if he were your pal when I asked about him before.'

'That was to put you off. Asking about monsieur Marty can be lethal – as you know.'

'So what have you got against him all of a sudden?'

'Marty was a real piece of work,' he says. 'I liked him at first; you always do with guys like that. It was the way he handled women, it wasn't proper. Then there's all the folk he stole from.'

'Stole?'

'Yeah, I call it stealing. They end up with nothing; he ends up with everything. Look, monsieur Salazar, you're not going to shoot me, so put that thing away, will you?'

I holster the gun. Either he is one hell of a liar, and I'm

not ruling that out, or he's telling the truth. Whichever it is doesn't matter now - I can't shoot him in cold blood.

'I've told you more or less all I know. If you can make it worth my while I can give you a little more.'

'What exactly?'

'Where she lives.'

'Who?'

'They must have hit you hard. Her! The girl who made the call and got you done over – mademoiselle Legrand.'

'So what do you want?'

'Two hundred francs. I'll give you her address and I won't mention our meeting to anyone.'

'Someone who sells a girl's address would sell anything.' I hand him the cash. 'Remember, if you double cross me, the next time we meet there'll be no talking, just a knife in your lung.'

I leave him in the alley counting his money like a prostitute. I'm shaking a little. That whole encounter went badly. If someone had seen us or he had screamed out I'd be a lot worse off than two hundred francs. With the Legrand girl I'm going to have to be colder. I can't confront her in the street or threaten her with a gun. I'll need to catch her off guard and use something else to make her talk.

CHAPTER FIFTEEN

I ride the Métro trying to formulate a plan. Instead I'm distracted by my aching leg. Without enough room to stretch it I have to stick it out in the aisle. I could go and sit in the seats for wounded veterans – after all I am wounded and I am a veteran. The only thing preventing me is the idea of another wounded veteran getting on and engaging me in conversation.

Mademoiselle Legrand lives in a small apartment block in Montparnasse. That part of town is populated by students and foreigners newly arrived in Paris. Pretty much the perfect selection; there'll be all sorts of people coming and going and they won't pay me the least bit of attention.

I get out of the Métro onto the boulevard Montparnasse and walk around for a while to stretch my leg. The evening is quite a pleasant one, ideal for spending time on a café terrace, sipping wine and watching the world decay around you. No time for that now, I have work to do.

I find the apartments without difficulty – this is one of the areas I like to walk around when I can't sleep. Some prophetic soul has even propped open the front door with an old broom. The doorman claimed not to know the number of Legrand's apartment. Lucky for me it is printed quite clearly on her mailbox; number six.

I walk up to Legrand's apartment on the second floor. I make no effort to blend in or hide. The only questions people are likely to ask me are: 'got a light?' or 'fancy a good time?' I reach Legrand's front door and stick my ear to the woodwork. The only thing I can hear is my breathing. Being a Friday night, she is probably out enjoying herself, spending the extra cash she earns from tipping off assassins. Most of the other inhabitants will be out at cafes, bars and dance halls and won't return until the early hours. I'd much rather be out there too, much better than lurking around a strange apartment block. Sometimes this job is plain creepy.

I feel exposed standing here. Apartments four and five are near the stairs, six is along a short corridor. I'm covered from the stairs but if somebody comes out of apartment four they'll be looking straight at me. If that happens I'll have to bluff it out; this is Paris and she is a very attractive girl - I bet she has men hanging around here all the time.

I try the door - locked. Behind me a window looks out over a courtyard, a bleak affair with washing lines and dustbins acting as the only highlights. Her bedroom must be at the end of the corridor on the other side of the wall. By climbing out of the hall window and edging along, I may be able to get in through her bedroom window. The evening is warm enough for people to leave their windows open, especially when they are this high up. Now that the sun is going down I can probably do this without anybody noticing.

I open the window and lean out to take a good look down. The drop onto the coal barge was probably the same height. If I land wrong though, with my leg in the shape it's in, I could lose it. Hit my head, and I'm done for. Who cares? I live in the age of the automobile; I take my life in my hands every time I cross the street. Fortune favours the brave, let it also look kindly upon this poor fool.

After clambering onto the window sill I take another look down. If I was very lucky I could walk away from that fall with only a few bruises. Do very lucky people fall from windows? My right leg is trembling. Why am I doing this?

I lower myself out the window. My feet scramble about until they find the ledge below. By turning them sideways I can fit the whole foot on the ledge. There is an upper ridge of about four inches. Enough to get a hold on - although it's at an awkward height - and my hands are gripping the ridge an inch or so below the height of my elbows. Moving is more difficult than I thought and the wind is stronger than I'd expected. After a few false starts I get into a slow rhythm which sees me about three-quarters of the way along. Now I need to change the position of my feet. Having them sideways was fine when I was standing still, now they are restricting my movement. I edge my feet around so the toes are touching the wall – movement will now be a lot easier; left, right and down.

A muscle, buried somewhere in my left hand, has locked up. To fix this I'll need to open and close my hand a few times, only I can't because my right hand is too weak to support my weight. What sort of an idiot climbs out onto a window ledge with a dodgy hand and a stiff leg?

By leaning back a few inches I can see the bedroom window. There is nothing to consider now - it's move or die. Ignoring all complaints from my body I edge myself further along. The window is closed! Shit and shit again. If it was my window I would have left it open. Nearly all the other apartments have their windows open. The bitch, she has done this on purpose.

I may be able to force the window. Gripping the ledge for all it's worth, my hands refuse to obey any other commands. Time is running out. My remaining hope is that I can inch my way back to the hall window. I turn my body slightly to cast a glance down at the courtyard. Right below me are some metal bins - I can see myself landing on them. My hand hurts so much now that those bins are inviting. If I took a step back, within an instant the pain in my hand would be gone. The drop doesn't look so far anymore, I could close my eyes and let go. I struggle to put these ideas out of my head. Some part of me, the part which wouldn't allow my hands to push the window, knows that a twenty foot drop onto metal bins isn't a matter of a few bruises. Already I'm moving again and am nearly at the hall window. What would happen if that window fell shut? I'd have to smash it. Will my hands let go then, or am I going to have to smash it with my head?

The window is open. I've lost all pretence of bravery; I'm almost crying as I fall into the corridor. I lie there, a dishevelled heap on the floor – my formative years were spent like this. I roll over and land by the door to Legrand's apartment. Although I'm back where I started, this time I'm grateful to be lying here and not among the dustbins. My body, perhaps fearful I might try some other foolish enterprise, refuses to move. I remain on the floor looking up at the ceiling. When I'm able to get up I'm going to forget about this girl; I'll go home and see to a bottle of whisky. No, I'll go via the Copenhagen and buy some hashish from Mikhail. I'll spend the rest of the evening in bed smoking and listening to Duke Ellington records. Why, I wonder, do I not spend every evening in bed smoking hashish and listening to Duke Ellington?

The cold of the floor overwhelms my inertia, forcing me to get up. As I rise I catch sight of something on the floor. She's left the bleeding key under the mat! I'd knocked it out of place when I rolled on to it. Barely suppressing a mad cackle, I open the front door. Not wanting to lock her out I put the key back under the mat and then go explore her apartment.

I fumble around in the dark, afraid that turning the lights on could give me away. My eyes adjust quite quickly and there is still some light coming in from outside. If I'm caught I could be headed for jail. That feels trivial compared with facing death out on the window ledge. Instead of being afraid I feel slightly naughty.

Legrand has a small apartment. A little way inside the hall is a kitchen with about enough room for one person to move around – so long as they don't try to breathe out at the same time. Inside the kitchen is a small charcoal fuelled oven. There are two cupboards which have been pushed together to form a long surface. I guess that's all you need from a kitchen. The hall opens into the living room. On the right is a door which leads the bedroom I saw from the ledge. The few pieces of furniture are modern and slick. The coffee table is made of metal tubes with a glass surface. An ashtray and packet of cigarettes lay on the table. The chairs look like an argument between metal and leather. Three of the walls are painted plain white, the fourth is a dark purple.

An incongruous piece in the corner of the room attracts my attention – a dust covered upholstered chair. The springs are going but it's comfortable. This chair is in the corner and faces the entrance to the living room; it will make the perfect place to sit and wait for her to come home. Before I can rest and wait I need to check the bedroom. For all I know she may be laying across the bed – naked. As that pleasant image pops into my mind it occurs to me that the doorman may have been lying. I don't remember anyone calling that receptionist mademoiselle Legrand when I was at the Lacman Brothers' place. Some other girl could be living here, and what will happen when she gets back?

I cast a quick glance around the room without seeing anything which might identify the owner. The bedroom gives her away. The smell of her perfume fills the room conjuring her image right down to the dimples in her cheeks. On the dressing table there are a couple of photographs. One of them sees her with an elderly couple. They must be her parents. She is glancing coyly at the camera while they beam proudly at her. Funny, she didn't seem all that shy when I met her. There are no naked bodies on or in the bed. The wardrobe is full of dresses, all for warm weather; she must have put her winter clothes into storage. The draws are filled with stockings and underwear. Going through a woman's underwear when she is not wearing it may appear pointless, but this is often the place they hide their handguns. Would it be better to hide out in this room, under the bed or in the wardrobe? No, there isn't enough space. Besides, I don't want to jump out on her; when she arrives I want to look established and at ease. That will give me the psychological edge I'm after.

Returning to the living room I take my place in the

comfortable chair. I can feel all my muscles begin to relax. Suddenly, and without warning, I begin a sneezing fit. Four or five sneezes follow one after the other in quick succession. Must be all the dust in the chair.

I hope she's alone when she gets back. If she has a man with her there could be a fight. Unholstering my revolver I place it in my jacket pocket, and then I place my hand in the pocket too. If she's invited a crowd over for a party I'll be right up the creek. Actually, a crowd couldn't fit in here. I need a piss.

The light is starting to fade. Some of it came from other apartments and they have either closed their shutters or turned out their lights. She might have gone to someone else's place. I wonder if she has some rich elderly gent who pays court to her at the weekends. Perhaps she has gone to spend the weekend on his estate in the country. My head lolls to one side.

I wake with a start. The room is filling with the clean pale light of the very early morning. I look at my watch - five o'clock. The building is silent. Is she back? What if there is someone in the bed with her? I creep slowly to the bedroom and push the door open a fraction to listen. After a moment or two I can hear her breathing. I crawl inside the room, but there is only one head above the blankets.

What should I do now? My fingers close around the handle of the gun. Perhaps I'll have to rough her up a bit. Wait! I don't want to rough up a woman. Over on the sideboard her parents are smiling at their sleeping daughter.

The front door is unlocked. I slip out and down the stairs. Whatever she is or does isn't going to change who I am. I shall not become a man who terrorises women. By entering her apartment I degraded myself; I must never allow that to happen again. In an hour or two I'll knock on her door and question her. I won't use force, but I will use persistence.

CHAPTER SIXTEEN

There are better ways to kill time than hanging about in a café, but they require a willing accomplice. At six-thirty I leave the cafe and walk back to Legrand's apartment. The streets are strewn with broken glass and rubbish. Some of this has been blown from overflowing bins, most has been dumped directly onto the street. There are a few patches of vomit and the occasional one of blood. Saturday morning in Montparnasse – slightly nicer than Sunday morning in Montparnasse.

The front door of the apartment block is still open. I climb the stairs to number six and knock on Legrand's door. No reply. My yawns are coming thick and fast. Three or four hours kip in a chair isn't enough for me anymore - I need a bed and at least eight hours straight. I knock louder. She calls out: 'I'm coming; give it a rest will you?' The door opens.

'Good-morning, mademoiselle. Salazar's the name; we met at the offices of the Lacman Brothers.'

Her face shows tiredness, surprise, and a touch of fear. She's done well to produce a combination like that at this hour.

'May I come in, mademoiselle?'

Without thinking she opens the door a little wider and I step through. She follows me to the living room, where, without invitation, I take up my seat in the dusty old chair - my chair.

'What do you want, monsieur Salazar?'

'Well, you're such a doll, I thought I'd pop over and invite you out to dinner.'

'At six-thirty in the morning!'

'It is early, isn't it? Too early for playing games. I want to know who you called and why.'

She ceases her pacing of the room to look at me. Our eyes lock for an instant before she turns away. She takes a step back and picks up a packet of cigarettes from the table. After lighting one she turns around to face me again.

'What are you talking about? I'm going to call the police.'

I doubt she will – unless she's had a telephone installed while she slept.

'Would you mind if I wait for them here? It's a bit chilly out this morning.'

I take one of my own cigarettes and light it. She moves towards the bedroom, stops, then takes a few steps towards the front door, and stops again. I feel guilty seeing her scared like this. I shan't leave though - her fear doesn't stem from my presence in the room; it comes from having been caught. She is an accessory to an attempted murder, and my murder at that.

Giving up trying to leave, she thumps down her cigarette in the ashtray before fumbling around for another. Her hand is shaking too much to light it. My body twitches but I resist the urge to stand up and light it for her.

'Someone beat me over the head and dumped me into the river to drown,' I say. 'I have a witness who names you as the instigator. The police could go through all the telephone records at the local exchange and find out who you called that day. It's all quite tedious and will involve a lot of time, lawyers, and jail. All for what? You end up doing a stretch and I don't get to question you.'

'If I talk I don't know what will happen to me.'

'We none of us know what will happen to us. Will it be worse than jail?'

'They may kill me.'

'They might - although they are a little slip-shod on that score. You talk to me and I may not let on where I heard it.'

So flow the tears - a ploy which doesn't work. I'm not

interested in her tears any more than I seek out her smiles.

'Take a deep breath and let's get this over with. Then I can go home and you can go back to bed. Who did you call?'

'I don't know.'

'I don't know is so terribly vague. Try to be a little more precise. Which numbers did you dial?'

'It was 74 84, a Paris number,' she says.

'Who did you speak to?'

'I don't know.'

'Come, come, mademoiselle Legrand, you can do better than this I'm sure.' I frown at her and try to cast myself as a friendly but disappointed schoolmaster.

'I don't know their names. It was a man.'

'That's better. What did you say to the man?'

'I told them someone had been asking about Marty. Then I described you and read the particulars from your card. I told them you were going to mademoiselle Sordine's and gave them her address.'

'Have you made calls like this before?'

'Yes, twice.'

'So, one day, for no particular reason, you decided that if anyone came to the office and asked about Marty you would call 74 84 and tell them all about it.'

'No, he asked me to do it.'

'And who is he?'

'Marty, of course!'

'Ah, my old friend, Gustave Marty. Was he the one who answered the telephone?'

'No, it wasn't him. The person sounded Parisian, Marty has got a slight accent.'

'How long ago did he ask you to do this? And why?'

'Soon after he left Lacmans' a lot of people started turning up looking for him. Most of them ranted and raved then stormed off after kicking the furniture. Some had to be removed by the police. A few weeks later a private detective turned up. Not long after that Marty met me. Should any more detectives come asking about him I was to call that

119

number. He gave me a thousand francs. A few weeks later another detective came by asking questions. I called that number and the detective fell under a train. I thought it was a coincidence but decided I wouldn't call again.

'It wasn't long before another detective came – from the same agency as the one who'd died. This time I didn't make the call. A week later this woman met me on the way home. She said I was in too far – I could either carry on helping, or they would fix me. Then she gave me two thousand francs. I've called the number twice since. One of those calls was for you.'

The big raindrop tears give way to the all-out remorse of someone who realises their actions have landed them in the shit. She sincerely regrets having been caught.

'When did you last meet Marty?'

'It was when he gave me the thousand. That was a little over a year ago now.'

'Where do you think he is now?'

'I have no idea. He made a lot of money at Lacmans'. I guess he has gone down south or back to Belgium.'

'South? Where? Why?'

'He told me once about a place down there. It's in the middle of nowhere but by train or automobile you can get to Toulouse in an hour or so, or the Riviera in a few hours. I reckon he might have other places but that's the one I'd go to if I was hiding and wanted to stay in France.'

'And what is this village called?'

'I don't know. I swear.'

I believe her. Perhaps I'm a sucker for those tears after all.

'Next time you have to call them I want you to call the number on my card instead. I'll come and keep you company until your telephone pal shows up with her threats and cash.'

I hand her a business card with my address and telephone number on it.

'I will have to call them too.'

'Up until today you could go into court and claim you were coerced. If you do it again, it will be for the money and for no other reason. They'll throw the book at you. They'll call you a siren and your photograph will appear in all the scandal sheets. The press will chew you up and spit you out. Your parents won't be able to look their neighbours in the eye again.'

'What about the person who hit you? What happens when they come looking for me?'

'You're a smart kid, figure that out for yourself. You may be better off going to the police. The flics might be able to round them up and you won't have to fear them anymore. Maybe you could move to Bordeaux or Marseille and get a job down there.'

If she's lucky I'll get to them first and they won't be going after anyone ever again. Now she's giving me a look as if I got her into this mess. I had better get out of here fast – I can feel myself getting angry. She can stand there giving me that accusing look, when it was her who signed my death warrant. I leave before I throw her out that closed bedroom window.

As I reach the hallway something she said strikes me as odd. 'One more question,' I say. 'When I called at your office, how did you know I was a detective?'

'You were asking after Marty and didn't look like you wanted to kill him,' she says.

I find an alley almost opposite the entrance to Legrand's apartment building. I wait in there and light a cigarette. She will spend a few minutes getting over the shock of my visit and a few more panicking. Her devious mind will eventually settle on the obvious solution – go and dial the number and give them the address from my business card. The second she makes the call I'll get back to my place and start preparing for visitors. I still entertain some half-baked ideas about people's inherent good so I wait; perhaps she won't make the call.

Fifteen minutes later I follow her to a café on the corner. I don't go in – I don't have to, it's the one I went in earlier. She heads straight for the telephone booth and I head straight for the Métro.

First things first, I fill in Filatre. He's been pottering around in his dressing gown and I don't want him about when my guests arrive. I arrange for Filatre to go to the nearest café and keep André company. If there's any news I will telephone him. Filatre calls his char lady and tells her to take the day off, with pay. He looks at me as he says this and I don't miss the point.

Now that I have the place to myself I set about making it welcoming. I'm hoping there is only one of them but I have to plan for more. Upstairs I get out my weaponry and then put on two pullovers as a protection against knives. Every detective should own a pair of hand-cuffs – I'll put that on my shopping list. In the meantime I have some rope which I leave on the filing cabinet. The rope is strong and thin so there'll be no chance of escape.

The window from my office provides a good view up and down the road. A thug who whacks you on the head may not fancy walking up to the front door and asking you to turn around for a moment. My guess is that he'll loiter around outside and wait for an opportunity. I could try the same thing I did with Stefan, although that is a risk. If I'm spotted lurking down the stairwell it will turn into a bloody fight. Or they will scarper and try their luck another day. There is nobody on the street at the moment.

I take some wire and start laying a few traps around the office and stairwell. If they aren't careful they might trip over one of these. For the hell of it I also put a few pans above the doors in true Billy Bunter fashion. They won't cause any harm but they will make a hell of a racket. I telephone Filatre at the café and warn him not to come up-stairs until I give him the all clear. I then tell him I'm going to be walking by in five minutes. He will sit on the terrace and if anybody is following me he will scratch his head. He may not notice anyone on the first sweep so I'll walk to the tobacconists at the end of the road then head back past the café. If he scratches his head this time I'll duck in for a quick coffee and he can pass André a message describing my pursuer.

Forewarned is forearmed. It's also rather scary. Somebody out there is going to try and kill me. Not only have they already done away with two of my kind but they nearly did for me. I walk with my hands in my jacket pockets. The left is clenching my revolver; the right is wearing a knuckle duster. Expressing nonchalance while holding a gun is harder than you'd think; the only way I can carry on the act is to whistle and the only tune which comes to mind: Louise. I hate that tune - it has burrowed into my brain like a well-trained maggot. I try to force it out by considering The Mooche. Just as I reach the wah-wah trumpets I find myself singing 'every little breeze seems to whisper Louise', as if whistling it wasn't bad enough.

Filatre has not had a sudden attack of head lice so I continue to the tobacconist. On a normal visit I'd equip myself with one or perhaps two packets of Gitanes. Imagining this could be my last tobacco purchase, I go for three packets and two packets of American Chesterfields for Megan. Feeling generous I buy Filatre a packet of Dutch shag.

There are plenty of people milling about at this end of town. The tobacconist is on the corner of the boulevard Saint Germain. If anyone coshed me here they'd be in cuffs before I hit the floor. I'd still be hitting the floor though.

I spot Filatre from a long way off. He is scratching his head like a bemused Orangutan. When I arranged these signals I should have worked out another one for 'message received and understood'. If we'd done that Filatre could have stopped scratching himself by now and those ladies passing by wouldn't be giving him such strange looks. He stops when he sees I'm entering the café. How is it I managed to pick up a tail without noticing? Perhaps, in my efforts to look casual, I didn't look about me as much as I usually do. André comes over to take my order.

'Monsieur Filatre has filled me in with what you two are up to. I wouldn't care if somebody did want to hit you on the head, but when you were laid up my takings went down.'

André leaves and returns with a hot cup of coffee.

'A man in a brown suit. He is hatless, with dark black hair. Around one metre sixty tall. Not thin, but not too fat either.'

André is shrewd enough to leave after giving me the information. It's difficult for me to scan the street from inside the café. Filatre is still out on the terrace; I may have to get a light off him. He pretends not to know me as I ask for a light.

'Where?'

'The vespasienne behind me, other side of road.'

Two can play at that game. I leave the café and retrace my route to the rue Challot. Then, instead of turning left and heading the office I turn into the neighbouring street and take refuge in the vespasienne there. I wonder what old emperor Vespasian would think if he knew the people of Paris named their pissoirs after him?

This lookout comes with the concentrated stench of urine. There are tiny ventilation holes in the metal screen which allow me to look down the road. If I stay here too long people will think I'm seeking a different kind of action. Who cares? This might save my life.

I see him! He knows I came up this street and I'm sure he knows I'm in here. Even so, he hasn't seen me so he can't be certain. He walks up the road, pausing now and then to look around. That's right, sunbeam, come and take a good look at Salazar in the toilet. I pull out my revolver in readiness and move around the central pillar. The posters on this one warn of the dangers of venereal disease – I prefer the ones advertising Lux biscuits.

Before he has a chance to move his head around the metal screen I step out and cosh him with my gun. He goes down. If we were near the river I would be tempted to throw him in. Being a helpful fellow I pick him up and rest him over my shoulder. The walk to the office takes less than five minutes. One person spots me with my unlikely burden. I raise my hat and smile, then make a drinking gesture. They won't believe it but it gives them an excuse not to get involved.

I haul his body up to the office and tie him to a chair. I give Filatre a call to let him know I have caught my fish. I advise him to go and watch a Western or three before coming back.

CHAPTER SEVENTEEN

While my new friend is sleeping I go through the pockets of his jacket. His wallet is in there, with a few bits and pieces to identify him. In one of the pockets is an old fashioned blackjack – made of leather and, from the feel of it, filled with lead. I was lucky my skull wasn't crushed, assuming this is the same one he hit me with. The blackjack goes on my desk alongside my knuckle-duster and razor. There is nothing like a cut-throat razor when you're lost for words. During the war the Americans would boast about their safety razors – that's all very well if you only use them for shaving.

The man tied to the chair makes a few groaning noises. His head is beginning to move, although it's lolling, and he looks like he may go to sleep. I crouch down next to him.

'Wake up, pal. You've got a bit of explaining to do.'

Through the grogginess he must be getting an idea of where he is – or where he isn't. I don't suppose he thought much beyond killing me. He's stalling now; I can tell by his breathing that he knows the game's up.

I never tortured any of my captives during the war. They got a bit of rough treatment from my sergeants, but what's a black eye or two between friends? For all of its horrors and for all the bullets and shells that come your way, you can't take war personally. When somebody follows you, hits you over the head, and throws you in the river to drown – that, you can take personally. This fellow here, Pascal Blanchart, is going to find out what that means.

I have bound his arms, legs and torso to the chair.

Grabbing the hair, I pull his head back and stuff an old sock into his mouth. He starts to struggle without getting very far. Now that he is unable to, he looks as if he is trying to talk. I pour myself a whisky and, after taking a swig, I throw the remainder in his eyes. He flinches and his eyes turn red. Tears stream down his face. From what I remember of having whisky thrown in my face he won't be able to see very well for a few minutes now. If I can convince him early on that I'm going to break him bit by bit then I probably won't have to. I slip the knuckle duster onto my right hand.

I aim my punches around his torso, causing some serious bruising and, I suppose, a few cracked ribs. To finish, I land one blow to the side of his face. Not as heavy as the ones to his ribs; I don't want to break his jaw. When I replace the duster on the desk I make sure he gets an eyeful of the razor.

'Now then, young fellow, you might like to tell me first off what your name is.'

I walk over and remove the sock from his mouth. He chokes and spits on the floor.

'Stop hitting me, you son of a bitch.'

I think about putting the sock back and beating him again. I don't – if I start hitting him again there's a chance I'll puncture a lung and then he won't be able to talk.

'So who are you?'

'Blanchart, Pascal Blanchart. You have my wallet on the desk you can check in there.'

'Who sent you here?'

'My boss.'

I clasp my hands on to each side of his face and leave them there. I crouch down so we are almost nose to nose.

'Try to anticipate what I want, Pascal. "My boss" doesn't help me very much. What colour shoes was your boss wearing when you saw him last?'

'Colour? Brown, I think.'

'There now, a boss with brown shoes. How can we narrow this down any further? What colour eyes does he have?'

127

'Brown.'

'Eyes to match his shoes, very natty. You're doing well, Pascal. Now think hard – what is your boss's name, and where does he live?'

'I can't tell you that!'

The sock is in his mouth again before he has the chance to say more. I take the blackjack from the table and strike him across the shins of his right leg. His body tightens with the pain. By the time he has calmed down I'm on the other side and strike him across the left leg. I replace the blackjack on the table and then remove the sock.

'Please! Please...'

'Can you remember the question or do you need me to remind you?'

'He'll kill me!'

'You can't kill a dead man, Pascal, and the way things are going I can't see you leaving here alive.'

Before he can reply the sock goes back. This time I have to pinch his nose and force it in. I lay the chair down so that Pascal is lying on his side. I then walk around behind him and pace up and down for a bit. I'm not sure what to do next. I don't really want to kill him. That is to say I do want to kill him, but I will not. Pacing around where he can't see me will give him time to think about the hopelessness of his position.

There have been nights over the last few weeks when I have fantasized about this moment. I dreamt of smashing in the face of the man who tried to kill me. I would break his fingers, then his arms, and then his legs. When he was about done in from the pain I'd smash his head in and leave him, dead in a dark alley. The victim in those daydreams was always an evil entity – the vile force who tried to finish me off. My brutality is an act of retribution, justified and exonerated. This guy in the chair is a man, trying to cover up his fear. Now I have beaten him I feel no sense of justice - I feel sickened. I'll have to change tack. The next round will be purely psychological. The violence I have already inflicted may have been enough.

'I'm going to give you a second chance, Pascal.'

I lift the chair up again.

'When I pull that sock out of your mouth you will start talking. If you don't answer my questions I'm going to take you to that window and drop you to the street below. You might just survive the fall - providing you can dodge the metal railings.'

I take a step towards him.

'Nod your head if you are going to talk, or shake it if you want me to drop you out the window.'

He nods his head. Lucky really, with a weakened arm and leg I'm not too certain I could have lifted him up to the window.

I pull the sock from his mouth. He spits a globule of cotton onto the floor. Before he has the time to vocalise the hatred in his eyes I ask him again: 'Who do you work for and where are you based?'

'Antoni Girondé,' he says. 'Montmartre.'

'Where in Montmartre?'

He looks down at the sodden glob of cotton. Something about the way he turned his head enrages me. I leap forward and grab him by the lapels on his jacket. In one flowing movement I lift him and the chair and toss them towards the window. He travels half a metre before crashing down and hitting his head on a desk leg.

He's a pathetic sight. I move towards him and hear him make a spluttering noise. He turns his head towards me. Blood dribbles from a fresh cut on his forehead.

'We work out of this house in Montmartre. It's a real shit hole, but one of the downstairs rooms is all right for us to meet.'

I heave the chair back to the upright. The hatred in his eyes has been replaced with fear. I've finally gotten through to him that, while he is strapped to that chair, I'm more dangerous than Girondé.

The adrenaline is causing my knees to tremble. I take a

seat myself and light a cigarette. Before I say anything more I want to make sure I'm feeling calm, that my voice is calm. If he senses any nervousness on my part the game will be up. I'll either have to throw him out the window or let him go and I don't want to do either.

'And?' I ask.

'Girondé has a café he uses. People can telephone him there. He comes to the house to give us our orders. Somebody called to let him know I'd failed to kill you the first time. He sent me again as a last chance.

'And what were you going to do this time?'

'I was going to kill you and make it look like a mugging,' he says.

His head hangs down; I think he is trying not to cry. Why do I feel sympathy for him?

'Well, Pascal, here's what I'm going to do. I'm going to take you upstairs and put you in my wardrobe. Then I'm going to pay a visit to your boss. If all goes well I will return and release you. If all goes badly you will have nothing but the smell of your own shit to contemplate until you finally die of thirst.'

He looks up with a start. 'There's something else you need to know,' he says.

'I thought there might be.' His mind is focused by the prospect of dying in my wardrobe.

'There are lookouts. To get into the house without being seen you will need to go around the back. You will see a narrow passage. Walk along there until you get to the back wall of the building – you'll see a small grey gate in the wall. The building is falling down. Half the floorboards are rotten so watch how you go. If you go upstairs, test each step. We don't go up there anymore – someone fell through and broke his leg last time anyone tried.'

'This Girondé... what is he like? What does he do?'

'He is a nasty scar-faced brute from the South. Now that he has marked your card, you are a dead man. It won't matter what happens to me now – he'd kill ten of me if he thought there was a little money in it.'

'He won't be so keen to kill me when he realises there is no money in it.'

'You can't tell. He acts on whims,' Pascal says.

'Aside from killing detectives, what does our man do?'

'Anything and everything. He has a fat finger in every pie. Runs girls, sells drugs, steals, and runs gambling joints. If you owe money, he will lend. If you can't afford to repay him, he mutilates you. He doesn't kill debtors – deformities are a greater deterrent than headstones.'

'So what's he doing in a ramshackle Montmartre house?'

'Montmartre's where the action is. The house was deserted so we took it. We can talk there without being overheard.'

'Thanks, Pascal.'

The sock goes back in his mouth. Throwing him out the window would have been easier than lugging him and the chair up these stairs. Leaving him in the dark of my wardrobe, I head out to Montmartre.

The Métro ride is dull; when my leg is better I'm going to give up the Métro altogether. In fact I'm going to fix my bicycle and start using that instead.

The streets are busy with Saturday afternoon crowds. The artists have moved away to Montparnasse but the area's reputation remains. This is where the city's visiting dignitaries and rich tourists come to see the real Paris. And the show is put on for them here. Nightclubs with half-naked dancing girls, Josephine Baker in her skirt of bananas, Bricktop in her nightclub beguiling the Prince of Wales. Chorus lines of can-can girls high-kicking it at the Moulin Rouge. Where the painters once lived, you'll now find the gangsters; pimps, drug pedlars, pickpockets and muggers. I don't get up this way often and I do remember why.

Like the tourists I'm here to see the real Paris. First I think I'll take in the sights. I have a very loose agenda – I'd like to see the Lapin Agile where Picasso used to drink, then Montmartre's vineyard, and oh yes, that house with the murderous dog who ordered my death. The lookouts won't have any idea who I am – I'll be another tourist wondering about, lighting a cigarette, and passing by.

These long tree-lined stairways, which cut up the Montmartre hills, might look beautiful in photographs but they are playing merry hell with my leg. After limping around for half an hour I stop for coffee, followed by a glass of wine. Sparrows chirp and dart after each other. Music flows from an open window accompanied by a woman's laughter. From here it's two streets to the murderer's den.

There are two thugs standing in the street with their hands in their pockets and caps riding on the back of their heads. There is no point walking up that road pretending to be lost. Anyone who had any business being there would postpone it and come back when those two had gone to bed. It might be interesting to see how they act if I do stroll past them. On the other – more sensible – hand there's no point tipping them off. I double back and take a different route round to the passage.

There are no hoodlums standing around the back of the house. I would have placed at least one goon to watch the entrance to the alley. The passage way is very narrow, running between two dilapidated buildings. If I'm to be ambushed, this is the place for it. I take my gun out; nobody is going to buy the lost tourist line here. The middle of the alley is almost pitch back – the sun isn't stupid enough to send its beams down this way. No point dawdling. I run the final few metres, coming out into an area behind the backyards of the two rows of houses.

I can see the rear of their house through the broken gate. The windows are hidden behind layers of grime. There are two sets on the ground floor. One window on the far left is broken. From the other set comes a flickering yellow glow which indicates candles burning. The gap between the broken gate and the wall is wide enough for me to squeeze through. I get into the yard and climb down on to my belly and crawl towards the candle-lit window.

There are voices inside – at least three. The words are indistinct but the tone is jovial. I creep over to the broken window. From here I can only be seen if there is someone in this room. I take a look through the break. There are bits of broken furniture, some piled up high and some scattered around the room – one false move and I'll send a tower of chairs crashing to the ground. Here, too, is the source of the city's dust. Mounds of it are piled up over every object in the room. Getting about in there is going to be difficult.

My hand fits through the break and, with a few heavy yanks, I open the window. The sound of raucous laughter comes from the other room. I climb in through the open window. The dust is pervasive, getting up my nose and in my eyes. I want to sneeze and cough. Tying my handkerchief over my mouth I take a look around. There are places for me to hide in here – and tracks in the dust to give me away. I creep towards the door. My movement is slow and I test each step before I put any weight down. The door is hanging off its hinges and rocking slightly in the draught.

There are at least three distinct voices coming from the other room. I don't reckon on a fourth, shy, gangster in there. Sounds as if they are playing cards. Glad they are having fun while their pal is out trying to kill me. Or would be trying to kill me, if he weren't bound and gagged in my wardrobe.

Girondé must be a slob. Instead of having his men play cards he ought to send them to a hardware store. The gap where the door is hanging is large enough for me to crawl through. I could open it, but why take the risk? Before I go any further I lie still and listen. There is no sound of movement from the other room. My plan is to get to the room above theirs so I can listen to them without being visible.

If they catch me halfway through the door, I'm dead. I couldn't make it easier for them if I stuck my head in a guillotine. They won't know who I am, of course. I will have to bluff it. That should keep me alive for an extra twenty minutes. No doubt, as a payback, I will be made to suffer a little more before I die. Forget bluffing -- I'll go down fighting. I take out my knife and hold it between my teeth.

My jacket catches on the door as I'm part of the way through. If they open their door now, it's rest in peace, Salazar. I fish around with one hand and break off a jagged spur of wood. Once freed, I clamber quickly into the hall. No point lying down to crawl now; if I'm on my feet I can fight. Before making tracks to the stairs I listen at their door. I can hear them clearly but understand little. They are speaking a mixture of Parisian and criminal slang.

The stairs look treacherous. A huge hole halfway up must be where the guy who broke his leg fell through. Some of the stairs look too rotten to try. The banister is spindly and weak; I think it's being held together by cobwebs. To rush here would be fatal – to delay could be fatal. Not a great choice, but I opt for the slow route. I tuck my knife in its scabbard. I ascend using a technique my brother taught me – stand as close to the wall as possible and put your weight down gradually.

I suppress a yelp as my foot goes through one of the steps near the top. My heart is beating loud enough to be heard by those goons out on the street. That step has taken a patch of skin off my shin. Blood seeps onto my trousers. I lean against the wall and untie the handkerchief from my mouth then wrap it around the cut to stop it bleeding. A door downstairs opens. The voices are louder. I draw my revolver and point it down the stairs. A man passes; I see the crown of his head. If he turns around now I'll have to shoot and then I'll be stuck up here. He opens the front door, and I jump the last couple of steps to the top. The man starts pissing just outside the door – at least they are civilised enough to go outside.

CHAPTER EIGHTEEN

The floor upstairs is every bit as perilous as the staircase. Some of the holes are obscured by fallen debris. The floor reeks like an old bird cage. Pigeons have made a home in one of the rooms, coming and going as they please through a broken window. I thought birds weren't supposed to crap in their nests. Maybe they live next door and use this place as their lavatory.

The man who went for a piss is coming back. I use his return to take a few bold steps towards the room above theirs. This room is as inviting as the others with one added delight – floor to ceiling cobwebs. I can hear the men clearly through the holes in the floor. This means they can hear me too. I sit against the wall and try not to move. I risk a cigarette, thankful I purchased so many.

For an hour I sit and listen to the men downstairs talking in their gobbledygook language. Occasionally somebody leaves and returns a few minutes later. They must be taking it in turns to water the garden. At some indeterminable point my fear is replaced by boredom.

After a further twenty minutes I hear the door to the house open. Someone calls out from the hallway. I hear scurrying in the room below. The door below me opens and someone says, 'Boss.'

Using the disturbance as cover I get down on my belly and put an eye to one of the holes. I can see four people. One of them is large – Girondé? He is wearing a fedora which obscures his face. Someone brings him a chair.

'Where is that fool, Pascal?' he asks.

'Still out,' one of the three replies.

'I told him to kill the man, not court him and marry him: why must he take so long? Pascal is losing his touch. You,' he jabs a finger towards a skinny, hatless, man who is fiddling with a slender knife. 'Go and find out what has happened.'

The skinny man departs.

'Toni,' says one of the two men standing in front of Girondé. 'What'll we do if Pascal fails? Should we give up on the man?'

'I will kill the man myself,' Girondé says. 'Then I will kill Pascal. Toni Girondé does not fail.'

'I know but...'

'You do not know! I will go down there and cut this Salazar's throat. I will cut his wife's throat and I will cut his children's throats.'

'That would bring a lot of heat. Couldn't we keep the money and tell Legrand to go screw herself?'

'You are a simpleton. If we do that, what happens next? Who will want to come to me? I am a company with two assets; fear and reputation.'

That conniving bitch, Legrand. I knew there was something wrong about her. But what does she get out of killing me? Until I walked into the Lacman building we were complete strangers. Ten minutes later she starts forking out money to have me killed. Is it the way I wear my hat? It doesn't make sense – unless she and Marty are lovers.

There was no evidence of Marty at her apartment. They may have another place together somewhere. I'll deal with Legrand when I get out of here; in the meantime, fatso down there needs sorting out.

I can't let Girondé keep coming for me until he succeeds. Then there is Megan and Filatre to consider. No, Girondé will have to die and the sooner the better. Perhaps with Girondé out of the way the other guy will take over. Then he could do what he said – keep Legrand's cash and forget about the killing.

The men are still talking and Girondé is drinking a glass of wine. I creep to the wall and pull out my knife. Girondé arrived alone; he may leave alone too. Or he might send the other two away and spend a few moments alone in his safe haven below. When he gets up to leave I could get downstairs and stab him in the lung. I've done it before and, if you get the angle right, they die almost silently. Only bubbling blood and gasps for air are to be heard. His overcoat doesn't look any thicker than a standard issue German trench coat.

Then I'll deal with Pascal. Nobody else knows I'm here; only he could link me to Girondé's killing. I'll have to suffocate him. Then I'll dump his body in the river. If the flics even bother investigating these deaths they'll look for rival gangsters.

I crawl out of the bedroom on my belly with my knife held between my teeth. The best place to get at them will be via the other room downstairs. I listen out for a few moments at the top of the staircase. Then I stand up and make my way down, trying to put my feet in the prints I made coming up.

As I pass the door to their room I imagine kicking it open and gunning them all down. The element of surprise would be so great I could kill them all easily. Instead, I stand in the dusty room with all the piled up furniture and make like a hat stand. The knife feels easy in my hand. I picture the actions I'll need to perform when killing Girondé. Three or four fast strides; my left arm goes around his neck; my right brings the knife up quick and hard. Blood will gurgle in his mouth. For a moment he'll struggle. I'll hold him as he dies and then leave his body in the hallway. If I keep my gun tucked into my trousers I can use it if the others come out to see the show.

I wait for them to make their move. My pulse pounds in my jugular. The rhythm is steady and strong. Entranced by the beat my mind begins to drift. Killing is easy – too easy – and some days it seems that everybody's at it. I can't sleep at night because of the deaths which come to haunt me. Germans from the trench, the one I shot as we were running across no man's land. There was another; I was with the snipers and I picked him off as he lit a cigarette. I went on a raiding party and I took one out in the same fashion that I'm planning to take out Girondé. There were others too, and some I will never know about. The times I threw a grenade, or sat with a mortar crew and spent an hour barraging a trench. I heard screams and I must have taken lives. They were all wartime deaths. Then there was Saint-Denis, down by the river. I often see his eyes as they looked in that instant I hit him with the rock. Do I really want to add to this roll-call? Will my life's achievements be the sum of a series of acts of violence? On my deathbed – if I'm given such a luxury as a bed – will I say: I killed people, most of whom deserved it?

I need to stop thinking this way. Gironde won't even blink as he sticks it to me. Like he said, he'll slaughter me, my wife, and my children. I don't have a wife or children but Gironde doesn't know that. He is a man who'd creep into a kid's bedroom and slit their throat. Meanwhile, I'm stepping down when I ought to be stepping up. If Gironde leaves this building without my knife in his belly, then we're all in trouble.

This is all fat man gangster talk. He's trying to impress his Apache goons. The bit about my wife and kids is to step them going for him. He's right when he says fear and reputation are all he's got. If they fear him enough he remains in charge. If they don't, he's gone.

Am I no better than a greasy hoodlum? Do I need to create a reputation based on fear? In my dreams I drown in the blood I've spilt. Each death is another nightmare waiting to haunt me. The idea of war repulses me and yet I contemplate my own killing spree like the most sadistic of generals. I have the opportunity to give the order to go over the top or I can give the order to lay down arms.

I can't kill Girondé, then Pascal, and the other two if they get in the way. I know I can do it, physically. I know that once I set on this course you can be sure they will all die. A gangster's children are no less deserving of a father than the German children I've orphaned. And then, with them all dead, will I go and play chess with Filatre and kiss Megan's lips? Someone sneezes and it brings me back from my contemplation. I must break the spell violence has cast upon me. I shan't go home tonight with blood on my hands. My mind is made up. Girondé can live, even if that means I have to leave my beloved Paris.

I climb out of the window and force my way past the broken grey gate. The alley feels as if it is closing in on me as I dash through it. I run to the Métro station and jump into a carriage heading south. There isn't much for it now; I have only one way out.

Once off the train I make for a café and call Filatre – he's still at André's café. I tell him to make use of his house in the suburbs and not to return to the office until I say. I then call Megan and give her similar instructions. Luckily she had been planning to visit a friend in Dijon for the weekend. I have a house call to make before I can go home.

Today has been good, weather-wise. Megan and I should have spent this Saturday evening lounging around sipping cocktails. I should be with her now, dancing at the Copenhagen and smoking with Mikhail, or doing whatever it is people do in Dijon. Of all the things I could be doing on a Saturday night I'm standing in an alleyway, down in Montparnasse, smoking a cigarette and looking over at a seedy apartment block. The door is open and I could slip in easily. There are a few too many people around for my liking. When it quietens down I'll cross over and pay mademoiselle Legrand a visit.

Being a Saturday night the comings and goings are getting boisterous. People come and whistle up at windows from which others shout down to the street. Small packs dance along the road. Bottles crash somewhere unseen, ready to cause Sunday morning punctures. Figuring I'd have to spend the night and half the morning waiting for a quiet time, I cross the road.

A young woman bumps into me in the doorway. She smiles seductively; I smile too and check my wallet is still there. There are a few people sitting on the stairs drinking wine and smoking. They part, letting me pass, paying me as little regard as they might a cat. There is light escaping from under Legrand's front door. The key is not beneath the mat. I try the handle and the door opens. If I'd sent some gangsters out to kill a man in the morning I would lock my door at night. I can hear her in the living room singing to herself.

'Evening, mademoiselle, planning a vacation?'

She turns with a start; my gun is trained on her belly.

'You better sit down – why not use that chair in the corner?'

I nod towards the old chair. I take a metallic tubular seat and sit facing her.

'What do you want? I told you all I knew this morning,' she says.

'Sure, you told me all right. Then I went up to Montmartre and made friends with Girondé. He tells a different story – one where you do the paying. The way I see it, you're going down for two murders and one attempted murder. If there are any more I'm sure the flics will enjoy beating the details out of Girondé's crew.'

'You've got it all wrong -'

'I followed you to the café this morning. I saw you make the call, then I went home and waited for a visitor who turned up as expected. I persuaded him to tell me all about the shabby house up in Montmartre. Then I went and met Girondé and his gang.'

Her face pales and she sinks further into the chair.

'So tell me, mademoiselle Legrand, how long have you and Marty been lovers?'

'We aren't lovers.'

'From where I'm sitting you look like a sweet kid – so why

do I have the urge to throw you out the window?'

I grab her arm and yank her from the chair. She struggles and I put one hand over her mouth and carry her over to the window. With the other hand I flick the latch and push the window open. If it worked on Pascal it ought to work on her.

'You are either going to talk to me or you are going to commit suicide.'

'You wouldn't dare!'

I push her half way out the window and make like I'm going to lift her the rest of the way. She struggles in my arms, fighting to get back into the apartment. Her aloofness has gone. Sweat is running down the back of her neck. Her breathing is fast and erratic.

'Stop! Stop!' she says.

I pull her back inside, turn her around, and then give her a shove towards the centre of the room. She takes a few steps back before regaining her balance. For a moment she stands there and looks as if she might come at me. Then she collapses into one of her chrome chairs and buries her face in her hands.

'Time to spill it, sister,' I say. I take a few strides over to where she's sitting and place a foot on the arm of the chair. She looks up at me, white faced and forlorn. I lean in closer. 'I'm waiting.'

'We were lovers for a week or so. Then he left. I got over it quick – it wasn't anything serious. Then people started turning up looking for him. Well I knew Girondé, so I told Marty that I'd deal with it. He pays me a fee each month and then a large sum each time I have to make a call. I pay Girondé out of that.'

'So where does Marty live?'

She looks away. I take her chin in my hand and force her face back to the front. She fixes me with an evil look, wishing me a thousand deaths but knowing none of them would come soon enough to help her. I release her chin, take out a cigarette and light it. 'So where does he live?'

'I don't know exactly – down south in a village called Vaour. There can't be more than twenty people live there, I'm sure.'

I grab her arm and drag her into the bedroom. From there I take up the picture of her with her parents. Removing the picture I throw the frame onto the bed.

'First thing we are going to do is ring your folks. You better give me the number, as I'll be doing the dialling. Then we will call Girondé – tell him there has been a mistake and you are cancelling the contract – you will pay him anyway. Then I will go. If anything should happen to me then this photograph will be sent to the police along with my case notes. Even a Parisian flic will be able to build a case from that. I'll give you twenty-four hours to leave town.'

I don't have much else to threaten her with – but if she keeps the photograph on her bedside table she must think highly of her folks. When I look in her eyes I can see her measuring the angles, trying to work out an escape route. She agrees to my demands. What else could she do?

I march her down to the telephone in the café on the corner. First, I call her parents – an old woman answers and I hand Legrand the telephone. For two minutes I listen to her tell her mother about the weather and how well she is doing in her job. I write their number on the back of the photograph. Then she calls Girondé. I listen in and there is some arguing on the other side. The problem that end - they have already dispatched two people to kill me. I know where one of them is so I'd better keep a look out for the other; must be the fidgety guy with the knife. Legrand argues and they agree to recall them, but with no guarantees. That'll have to be enough. I nod and she agrees with Girondé. I'd love to turn her in, but right now that would be too big a risk. She scurries off the moment I release her arm. I doubt she'll drag her escape out over the entire twenty-four hours. I head for the Métro.

Somewhere on my street, a man is waiting for me; waiting for the chance to stick his knife in my back. He doesn't know what I look like, which gives me a chance. I walk on the opposite side of the road from my apartment. Trying to appear disinterested, I peer into all the dark doorways and stairwells. I walk on past the apartment without seeing a soul. There's no way Girondé could have gotten word to recall him already. Two houses down I hear a cough. I spin round to look but there's nobody there. I know a spot further up the road where I can hide out and keep an eye on the apartment. Forty minutes pass before an auto drives up and pauses outside my place. A shadowy figure approaches the driver's window and then gets in the auto. They speed away and I push off from my spot to have a word with Pascal.

CHAPTER NINETEEN

The traps! They completely slipped my mind. That would be a treat for Megan: me lying at the bottom of the stairs with a broken neck and Pascal dead from starvation in the wardrobe. Maybe he wouldn't be dead; Megan will be back on Monday morning. I'm certain a grown man can survive for three days without food. How long can he last without water? None of this matters as I'm not at the bottom of the stairs and all the tripwires have now been cut.

Thankfully, Pascal has not soiled himself in my wardrobe. He looks like an overgrown puppy, jumping up and down in his chair making whining noises and looking at me with his big brown eyes. I drag the chair out into the room and make a show of checking my revolver is loaded. If Pascal is anything like me he'll have spent the last few hours imagining all the things he is going to do to me, none of them nice.

'There are two or three ways we can do this,' I say. 'More if we include torture. I could hit you on the head and dump your unconscious body out into the street. I could throw you in the river – I know what you're thinking, but I'd make sure there was nothing between you and the water. Or I could take out your gag and release you here. You could get up and walk outside without making a fuss. That way I won't have any awkward explaining to do, and you won't have a fractured skull or lungs filled with slurry.'

Being caught and tied up will have hurt his pride. At this moment he'd probably sell his sister to avenge himself on me. He'd probably sell his sister for a pack of American cigarettes – if she's anything like him that's a good deal. I'd better sleep with the gun under my pillow from now on.

Pascal nods his head to signify agreement. He splutters as I pull the sock from his mouth. The spluttering is followed by obscenities. The sock goes back in. He struggles frantically with the ropes as if blind rage could loosen them. And what if you do loosen them, Pascal? I'll shoot you in the guts before you even realise you're free.

I give the chair a kick which topples it over. Pascal continues his struggle like a keen but inept Houdini. Not wanting to interrupt a man so engrossed in his work, I sit on the bed and light a cigarette. Closing my eyes I can imagine that there's a badger snuffling around the room, rather than a man tied to a chair with a sock in his mouth.

With the cigarette finished I haul Pascal back to the upright and remove the sock. This time he has the sense to stay silent. I keep the revolver trained on his back as I free his legs and arms. He tries to stand but collapses on the floor instead. Well, he won't come at me until the circulation returns, by which time he will be back in Montmartre and Girondé can take care of him.

I grab him by the shoulders and pull him to his feet. He explains what he'll do when we next meet. Without going in to all the various intricate details, he plans to cut out my liver and eat it. I allow him to go on like this for six or seven seconds before I shove him into the door frame. By releasing him all I'm doing is delaying the day when I'll have to kill him. Or the day he kills me.

From the doorway I frogmarch him to the top of the stairs. One push and he'll tumble down; all I'd have to do is finish the job if he survives. But that way I'll never be rid of him.

'You can see the door – use it once and you'll live. Use it twice and you'll die.'

I sit on the top step and watch him leave – a wild animal released into the jungle. Thoughts fire through my head, warning me I've made a fatal mistake.

He slams the door behind him and I dart to the living

room window. Pascal looks briefly at the house before staggering off into the night. I remain at the window smoking a cigarette. People pass by underneath, alone or in small groups. The sound of men singing echoes from one of the side streets – making the most this Saturday night.

In case I'd forgotten, my eyes are reminding me; I've been awake for twenty hours and that was on the back of three hours' sleep. They are starting to sting and refusing to remain open. I go to the bedroom and lie on the bed in my shirt and trousers. The gun under the pillow is uncomfortable so I place it on the bedside table. The moonlight decorates my room with expressionist shadows. Exhausted, my mind is re-running scenes form Nosferatu. I'd much rather it had picked The Jazz Singer - I could have sung along.

*

Why didn't I kill Girondé? If ever a man deserved a knife in the ribs it was him. Perhaps I'm off the hook; or perhaps not, there will always be someone in his sights. They ought to hand out medals for killing men like him. Not that I'd have hung around to collect mine.

And Pascal, what will he do now? He's probably in some Montmartre dive trying to get a gun especially for me. Perhaps he'll round up one or two pals and make a party of it. If he tries that then Girondé might get wind of it and stop him. I'm putting a lot of stock in Girondé - a man who kills for profit.

If Pascal hasn't made an attempt on my life in the next twenty-four hours then there's a chance he won't come at all, unless I accidentally happen across him in a dark alley. The next few hours will be the most dangerous.

The light grows dimmer. The shadows lose their shape and take over my room by creeping up the walls and crossing the ceiling. The German officer I'd killed keeps coming in to my head, interspersed with images of Girondé. Blood drips from his mouth. His eyes are black voids filled with the stars which used to shine over No Man's Land. I can hear the sound of the artillery letting go a barrage from way behind the German lines. A snake with a dagger between its teeth is winding along the trench.

I've had nights like this before – so many of them in Saint-Denis and a fair few in London – they never end well. I ought to get up and stick my head in a basin of cold water. After that I should grab a bottle of whisky and start hitting it until it hits me back. That way I can spend the night unconscious and not have to endure these dead faces.

Five minutes later I'm asleep. Five minutes after that I'm awake. I change into my night clothes, knowing I should stick my head in that water, but I'm too tired to try. A few minutes later I'm asleep once more. Was it Namur where the fortresses were? I wake again and see the room is dark. Outside a dog is calling out to his tethered comrades. They reply and pass his message on across the city. I'm sweating and rolling about, feeling heavy from fatigue. My body is rebelling against its very being.

I have to piss. With eyes half-closed I stagger across to the chamber pot. I stand there, looking at my reflection in the window. Not a glimpse of humour in that face. Afterwards I fumble my way back to the bed. The sheets are tinged with dampness from the cold and my sweat. Already I feel the need to piss again.

Not wishing to witness my misery, the moon has taken cover behind a cloud. The room is condemned to the darkness. Thoughts beat against my skull like the wings of an eagle trapped in a cage.

How long ago was it I heard that man, one of the night's stragglers, singing in the street outside? The song had been faint, growing louder as he made his way along. Occasionally he stopped to belch or perhaps pick himself up. Maybe he stood to admire himself – king of the empty street. There were a few minutes when the noise remained at a certain level; he must have been using the pissoir. He passed by under my window and then his song grew faint. All that time

I held a picture of the man in my head. I could see him as he progressed along the road. For those few minutes he was a friend who held at bay my demon mind.

*

Awake, I stare out of the window at the sky. Stars fade as the sky turns a pale grey then blue. Noises enter my room, the clanging of bells, the occasional auto, footsteps and children shouting. The sounds are no longer human, no longer recognisable. All I hear is a distant hum. This must be Sunday. I don't recall anything else before sky blackens and the stars return slowly to their posts.

My stomach starts to cramp and I double up on the bed. There are people in the apartment; I can hear them walking around in the office. Somebody is in the kitchen. They have an accomplice out on the street outside, sitting in a big auto and gunning the engine. Any minute now they will burst through the door and fill me with lead. Have I been poisoned?

Marty must be laughing out loud. Right at this exact minute he is laughing and sipping wine with a beautiful woman tending to his every perversity. Why do you want him, Marie? Let lying dogs sleep. All those people he conned... I ought to get wise. Ha! I'll visit each one and tell them I'll track down Marty, for a small fee. Oh God! Is Marty tracking me down, sending hoodlums from Marseille to get me? I'm not hard to find; my number's in the book, give me a call.

The pain in my gut subsides. I dare not move. My ears strain, trying to pick out every sound the night has to offer. The people in the apartment are silent and the man out in the auto has turned off the engine. If only I could creep to the window and take a quick look outside. I remain perfectly still and drift off to sleep.

I suffer from a propensity to turn in on myself, like a clockwork mechanism where the cogs have worked loose and grate against one another. Spectres metamorphose from the shadows and lure me to the darkness, not with promises of joy, and I go - a beaten dog following its master.

These last few months I have been free of it – I'd hoped free for good. The agency gave me a focus, and Megan has now given me hope. This is as bad as any of those times I'd been lost in Saint-Denis. Back then, a week could pass as I lay on my cot staring at the ceiling. These are the dues I have to pay the cosmos.

That is bad thinking. I fell into that trap before. The downward spiral can be so persuasive. There was a night, alone in a park long after the keeper had locked the gates, where I'd realised that I was in control. Earlier that day I'd seriously considered jumping in the river. I'd gotten so close I could almost taste the water. At the bridge I turned and ran and kept on running until I collapsed with exhaustion behind a hedge in a park. Then I'd fallen asleep. In the early hours of the morning I climbed the park wall and jumped to the pavement below. On the way down a sign across the road caught my eye: Salazar, importers of wine. In that moment, I resolved not to kill myself – instead, I would transform myself.

*

I sleep for a few hours then awaken, dripping in sweat, afraid that a demon is sitting on my chest. With the lights on I search the room for the creature who'd been trying to steal my breath. I start talking, but to whom? Rocks of pain grow in my stomach. I pace the room until a pressure in my head forces me to lie on the bed, holding it, and begging for mercy. I sleep once more.

*

I'm awake again, unsure how long I've slept. I can't motivate myself to move. I am lost. That night in the park I'd pledged against suicide; now I'm falling off the wagon. A voice says, 'why not now, why not bring it to a close?'

I could open the window and step into the void. The thought of those spiked railings stops me. I do have the revolver. No! I will not kill again, not me, not nobody. I take the gun and remove the bullets. I fall asleep clutching them in my hand.

CHAPTER TWENTY

There are voices – indistinguishable – out in the hallway. A knock comes at the door. I turn my head to look in that direction. I make no further attempt to open the door. Have they come for me now that I'm too feeble to defend myself?

A voice permeates the fog... Megan! Why doesn't she come in? I don't want her to see me weakened like this. Before she arrives I'll get up and pretend to be drinking coffee. I cannot move; perhaps I can blink - I think not. My eyes are wide open, staring through the semi-darkness, burning in their sockets. Will she come? The voices fall silent.

They are back. I will myself to sit up, without success. A key clicks in the lock and the voices grow louder. Megan and Filatre - my friends! I try to cry out but my voice is dry and hollow.

'Turn on the light.'

'Christ, it stinks in here.'

'You check in the kitchen.'

The electric light on the bedroom wall flicks to life. I raise a hand in defence against its blinding glare.

Megan calls out: 'He's in here.' I lower my arm and see Filatre entering the bedroom. He loiters in the doorway as Megan comes over to me.

'My darling, are you OK?' she asks.

She crouches down next to the bed and puts her hand on my forehead.

'All been a bit worried, old chum,' says Filatre from the

doorway. He lights his pipe and starts making those familiar putting noises. A moment later the smell of the smoke overrides the smell of me. Filatre continues, 'We weren't sure what was happening after you told us to stay away.'

The reassuring smell of Filatre's pipe continues to infuse the room. Megan opens the window and a welcome blanket of cold air wraps itself around me.

Megan addresses Filatre: 'It's OK; I'll take care of him.'

'I know you will, my dear. Let me know if you need anything, I'll be downstairs. See you later, old chum.'

Filatre ambles off, silhouetted by the living room light. I hear the front door open and then close, followed by the sound of creaking stairs. The sounds fade. Megan is stroking my hair and holding me.

'Are you all right? You look deathly pale,' she says.

'I don't know, Megan. These black spells come and I drift away.'

She holds my face in her hands and looks at me so close that our noses brush gently against each other.

'I love you,' she says. 'Hold on to that thought and don't ever let go of it.' She stares into my eyes as if projecting her love there. Then she says: 'You look like you need some coffee. Do you think you can get dressed, or do you want to drink it in here?'

'I'll give it a go, if not I can always drink in the nude. You make it, I'll join you in the kitchen.'

She leaves the room and I climb out of bed. My limbs feel weak. I pull on a pair of trousers that were hanging over a chair, then pick a shirt up off the floor. Halfway dressed I take a look out of the open window. Jumping would have been horrible, for Megan as well as for me. I amble through the kitchen, mumbling as I go.

In the toilet I look at my unshaven, pallid face in the mirror. There is more than one day's growth on my chin. Sweat has dirtied me up. At least it's not as ingrained as it was in the old days. I wash, then shave, before the smell of coffee mixed with the fumes from one of Megan's cigarettes enters the room. We have achieved a husk of normality.

While drying my face I begin salivating uncontrollably. One whiff of food and my body abandons all decorum. Aromas from the kitchen torment me. For the last few days I've been starving myself, an unintended consequence of the depression. I must eat. I enter the kitchen carrying my shirt. Megan is toasting some country bread. I cut a few slices off the loaf and eat them as they are. With my mouth still bulging from the bread I search in the cupboard and find some pickles.

Megan brings over the coffee as I sate my hunger on gherkins. After a swig of coffee I button up my shirt. I'm presented with jam and toast. I don't have the stomach for it. The belief that my hunger cannot have been so easily satisfied keeps me eating.

'So,' Megan says.

'So,' I echo.

'What has this all been about?'

'I don't think I know.'

'I think I do,' she says. 'I think something in you is broken and we've got to fix it. Deep in your subconscious there is a conflict, a repressed idea, and it's fighting to get out.'

'You sound like you've been reading Freud,' I say.

'Everybody has read Freud. Old ladies on the bus talk about their super-ego as if it were a new dance. They claim it's causing their grandchildren to come down with mal du siècle. Reading Freud is easy; working out what it all means is another story. I'm not sure I buy any of it. So you and I will talk it out, as my own grandmother might have said.'

'I don't have mal du siècle,' I say. 'Whatever I have normally comes and goes.'

I smile wanly and hope it isn't too pathetic. I feel sick from the pickles, although the coffee combats the rising nausea.

'I get the uneasy sensation of falling,' I say. 'After every fall it's impossible to climb all the way back up again. I'm always losing a few inches.'

153

'And have you always felt like that - as long as you can remember?'

'I think so, although I do have a primal memory of happiness. That could be a trick of the mind to torment me further – my very own paradise lost. I had these feelings a lot at university. I never had them at all during the war. That was the longest period I ever went without them.'

'Not during the war, but as a child? Do you remember them as a child?'

'No, the fears I'm talking about are intangible. As a child I feared being pulled from the bed and beaten. The scars on my back are witness to the tangibility of that fear. For a few weeks each summer we went to stay with Aunt Bess in Norfolk. Alfred and I could waste hours skimming stones across a pond. I even remember saying to Alfie, "Some kids' lives are like this all the time. They don't get the beating, or the prodding, or the name calling".

'During the last week of the holiday I'd start to wet the bed. My Aunt put it down to a nervous disposition. She would say things like: "Don't worry, my love, you'll be home soon and then you can sleep in your own bed." I'd have killed not to have had to return to my own bed.'

Megan's eyes take on a deeper beauty behind her tears. Mine just cloud my vision. She has been gently rubbing my back as I spoke. We aren't going to get through this without some very real pain. I don't find it cathartic. Each moment hurts - which is why I rarely dwell upon it.

'I wish I could have been there to have comforted you,' Megan says.

'There wasn't anything you could have done. Besides, I would have been mean to you. I hid a lot of myself behind a veneer of nastiness. When I think of myself then I was so twisted up that everything I did or said was a contradiction. All I wanted was someone to be close to me, but there was no way I would have let anyone get close.'

'Some would say that stems from of a fear of getting hurt.'

'A psychiatrist might say that if they didn't have any real

answers.'

'So what is the real answer, Reggie?'

'I think it was more protective. If I let someone get close to me there was a chance my curse would rub off on them.'

'You were being gallant?'

'Maybe, but I doubt it.'

'So if we are ever going to get close we need to work this out.'

Megan pulls a notepad and a pencil out of her bag and gets ready to start taking notes. I find it disconcerting - one minute I'm talking to my girlfriend, the next I'm talking to a psychiatrist.

'When did it start?'

'Today is Monday, isn't it?'

I'd been aware of days and nights passing but hadn't stopped to count them. Megan nods.

'It began late on Saturday. I'd released Pascal and was waiting in case he decided to return.'

'Who is Pascal?'

How much should I tell her? Does she need to know about the secretary in Montparnasse, or my planning to kill Girondé in Montmartre? I may as well fill her in and see how it goes.

Megan asks for further details as I try to recount everything, beginning with the moment I followed the doorman from Lacmans'. When I get to the part about Pascal she asks exactly what he looks like – sensible as she may encounter him hanging about and can tip me off.

'Let's go back to that house in Montmartre, I want to get something clear,' she says. 'You were planning to put a knife in Girondé because you thought he may harm me as well as you. Then, as you were visualising the act, you had a change of heart. I find that hard to understand. You've killed people before, you had the knife ready, and you were confident you could do it. You didn't do it because you have nightmares about the Germans you killed. Is that right?'

'That's as good a summary as any,' I reply.

155

'But it doesn't ring true. There must be something else.'

'There was nothing else. I had a sudden flash of past nightmares and I didn't want to add to them.'

'What I'm getting at, Reggie, is this: it wasn't the thought of nightmares that stopped you... it was the reasons for the nightmares.'

'This could go round for a while – the reason for the nightmare is the killing.'

'No, the reason for the nightmares is regret. You may not have regretted killing those Germans at the time – after all they were about to kill your men. But later, after the war, you started to have the nightmares. You've told me that you think about their children – if they had children. You imagined their wives receiving the telegram. They were normal people who got sucked into the war and were killed for it. Then there is Alfred.'

'I didn't kill Alfred, the Germans did.'

'The war did. He was killed because he was at war. And so were all the other dead men you saw. My brother was put in to a wheelchair and will never be able to stand unaided. Men walk about with missing limbs, missing eyes, scarred faces, all because of the war. You see them every day on the street and feel guilty because you took part in it. I think this guilt is contributing towards your depression.'

I let Megan's words sink in. I want to tell her that she's wrong, but it doesn't feel wrong. Not once, in all the times I have seen that officer since his death, have I ever thought: you deserved to die. I have never said it because it is not true. He happened to be in the wrong place at the wrong time and so did I.

'When you let Pascal go, what were you thinking?'

'I'd already decided not to kill Girondé; it would have been unfair to kill Pascal. At least not in cold blood. If he'd tried to jump me I would probably have shot him and told the flics he was a burglar. No doubt they have him on file.'

'After he left, you sat on the bed and waited in case he returned.'

'Yes, although I was exhausted. I'd had hardly any sleep for nearly twenty-four hours. I started conking out.'

'Lack of sleep wouldn't have helped. What were you planning to do if Pascal came back?'

'There was a distinct lack of a plan. I had my gun nearby. The first time I was waiting for him I had the whole thing set up. Filatre went to the café to act as a spotter. In the apartment I set out trip wires and a few other things in readiness for a sneak attack.'

'After you let him go, you sat on the bed waiting until you fell asleep?'

'Pretty much.'

'Hmm.'

'What does that mean?'

'It means I have an idea which hasn't formulated yet. Can you make us some coffee?'

I put the pot on the stove and clear away the plates. Performing these simple chores makes me feel better. My stomach is over full. Despite having been in bed for over forty-eight hours I could do with a decent sleep. I serve up two espressos and retake my seat.

'This is what I think, Reggie. At the gangster's house your subconscious rebelled against more killing. You took the hint and left. When you released Pascal you knew that he might come back. You couldn't think of a way to deal with that threat without recourse to killing. This led to a deeper crisis which caused your body and mind to shut down.'

'Well put. Shall I pack my bags now?'

'There won't be any need for that. I doubt Pascal will turn up again.'

'I meant so you can take me to the funny farm.'

CHAPTER TWENTY-ONE

We burn a few cigarettes sitting in silence. Not a strained silence or an interrogation ploy. I'm beginning to relax, allowing my mind to go blank; to forget about Marty, the gangsters, and the city outside. The tiredness has momentarily passed and I've reached one of the lower levels of contentment.

What Megan has said makes sense. I'd never wanted to be a soldier, but the war caught me at a time when words like duty and empire meant something. I signed up like I was buying a new pair of shoes. Those were the days.

I thought I'd changed my life by becoming Salazar. All I changed was my address and my tailor. I didn't go deep enough, so the nightmares simply took the Métro to St Saint-Germain-des-Prés and hooked up with me again.

'When I was young I used to burn candles and stare at my reflection in a mirror,' Megan says. 'Someone told me if you did that for long enough you could see the dead.'

She giggles.

'Megan, from now on there can be no lies between us.'

'I wasn't lying, Reg; I used to do that a lot when I was a teenager. We were all interested in the occult in those days. We'd read Yeats's poems and imagine joining the Golden Dawn.'

'That's all yesterday, I'm talking about the future. We can take on the world so long as we can trust each other. If we've got that, then the rest can go to the devil.'

'We can try.'

'We must. Nothing in this life is worth a damn. We can walk away from it or we can face it and if we face it we'll be making us count.'

Megan smiles. Is she thinking of what I've said, or of those dead people in the mirror?

'Are you inviting me to join your detective agency?' she asks.

'I wasn't. In fact I'm thinking of chucking it in. Look at us – we're drinking coffee and smoking cigarettes like anyone else. We go to cafés and walk in the park. We queue outside picture houses and watch the movies.

'On Saturday I was in some flea-pit in Montmartre. There was a knife in my hand. I was afraid – as you should be – that I might get caught. But I knew the danger in the house wasn't them, it was me. Every action had been planned out. If I had to fight in the main room I would make this move or that counter move. If it went into the hall I would position myself here and force them back. They were dead men breathing their last.'

My heart's beginning to pick up pace and my hands have started sweating. Please let this be the result of too much coffee. I open my mouth to continue, yet other words fall from my tongue.

'When a man stamps on a flower he should be held to account. We rip and tear each other like taunted beasts. Fables are written to justify our acts. We know we are destined for hell – we are living it. Every heartbeat is a tribute to the god of war. Please let it end.'

'Calm down, Reggie, we've been over this. We can end it all now, right this moment. We do not have to keep death in our lives. I will make a list, number one; no killing.'

Megan jots this down in her notebook.

'Should that read: Thou shalt not kill,' I say. I manage a quick smile. I was on my way over the edge again and she's pulled me back. 'That means no killing at all – not even animals.'

'Don't be silly, Reg. Wait a minute... I've noticed you don't eat meat.'

'Not since the early 20s. I'd been on the pipe all weekend and went for a stroll, still feeling groggy. It was raining, but not enough to turn back. Water was dripping off my hat and I had my head down. I became obsessed with the idea of lamb chops. I would have walked to Wales if it meant getting some. I knew of a butcher's shop not far from my apartment. I thought I'd buy some and get my valet to cook them up – yeah, I still had a valet then.

'Straight away the stench of blood and the sight of strung up bodies hit me. Then I had what the magistrate called "an unfortunate episode". My good war record and better connections got me off without charge but I still feel that repulsion when I pass a butcher's.'

'This is going to be hard, but if it will stop you doing anything silly, I'll come along for the ride.'

'That's why I was thinking of chucking the agency. If I'm not going to kill, I'm going to be vulnerable.'

'I won't pretend that isn't true, although Gandhi is facing down the entire British Empire without having a gun tucked in his loin cloth.'

'He's got a few million Indians standing behind him.'

'I know you, Reggie. I know you are a brave and smart man. From now on that's what you are going to have to rely on. You can give up being a detective if you want to. The problem isn't money, it's boredom. You need the action. I know you fancy yourself as the cerebral type who can spend all day rearranging books, but that isn't true anymore. You'd do it for a few months and then go out one night and find trouble. What you need is something to occupy you physically and mentally.'

'Oh, but you do that, Megan.'

'If I were all you needed we'd be fine. Today we have to be serious. You need something to stop you going off the rails when I'm not around. I lost you once and I don't want to lose you again.'

I grab her hand and hold her tight. We both of us are

fighting not to cry. I draw her close: 'I'll never leave you again.'

We kiss and the kiss is our sadness, our joy. The kiss is our finding each other. We hold each other for at least ten minutes before reluctantly letting go. Neither of us wants to speak because our words will bring us back to the world.

'Three days have passed since I was up in Montmartre and the gang haven't killed me. They must have taken Legrand's pay-off, else I'd be dead by now. And Legrand spilt the beans about Marty's village.'

'Marty's village? What village?'

We go down to the office where I keep a map of France. We fold it out over my desk. Ash falls from Megan's cigarette and burns a hole in it. She puts it out quickly. So long as Vaour isn't a secret island in the English Channel, we'll be okay. Megan's enthusiasm rubs off on me. For the time being I'll forget about quitting and I'll play this out.

'First time I saw Legrand she fed me a few scraps so I'd think she was helpful. She said that Marty had spoken of a village - an hour from Toulouse and a couple of hours from the Riviera. That reduces it to a few thousand square kilometres.'

'Less, if you think about it,' Megan says. 'If it were an hour east or west from Toulouse it would be too near or far from the Riviera Coast. So it must be north or south. If it were an hour south it would be in the Pyrenees. They rarely have roads on those mountains and when they do they are more suited to donkeys than automobiles. So let's start by looking an hour north.'

We scour the map together, getting in each other's way, for about fifteen minutes. Then we decide to do shifts. Megan, being methodical, produces a pencil which she uses to shade the map as she examines it. After each grid we swap over.

'You know, Reggie, I think in some ways, this is all a bit sinister.'

'In what ways?'

'We're looking at a map so you can track someone down for a woman with unknown motives. That makes this work intrusive and unpleasant.'

'I don't care about other people's motives. One way or another, Marty was behind the attack on me. I want to find him so I can chuck him in the Seine or the Garonne or the Loire or any other bloody river.'

'Just so long as you don't end up on the guillotine. I still think it's sinister. Maybe your work is sinister, in the way a miner's work is dirty. I guess that's it. Do you really want to chuck him in the river?'

'I do, but I won't. I'm going to stick to what we said. In fact my gun, knife, knuckle duster, and spare knife can stay here. I'll travel unarmed and think peaceable thoughts.'

The names on the map merge into one another: Cabanés, Cuq, and En Périé. Do people live in these places? At some point in the near future I'm going to be in one them. I'll be walking around on some speck from the map. I'll find Marty and reveal his location to Marie. Then I'll sit back and wait for trade to come my way.

What trade? I've been in this business for seven months and this is my third case. Nobody comes to me because nobody's heard of me. I spread a few cards out in cafés at the beginning. Since then I've done nothing. When I return from catching Marty I'll place advertisements in all the newspapers.

'Here it is,' Megan says.

She points at another name on the map - one that reads Vaour. I take my pen and draw a circle around it. I look at the map and the series of towns between here and there. I can see myself sat in a train compartment for eight hours. Then eight hours back. I can think of other things I'd rather spend sixteen hours doing – like washing down a pissoir. Keep the train, I'll fix my bicycle and ride down there.

'I'll head down on Friday. I want to get my bicycle together and I'll need some gear.'

'You are going to cycle there?'

'Yes.'

'Why? It will take days.'

'Because I want to. From now on I'm doing things my way.'

'Are you going to become a hedonist too?'

'I wasted years indulging in drink and drugs. I did things because I thought people wanted me too. Then I did whatever came into my head and to hell with anybody who got in my way. After that I collapsed and ended up suicidal. Then one morning I realised my life needed to change – I took my army pension and trust fund and set up this agency. If I can't work the way I want, then what's the point? As you said - I don't need the money. All I need is to occupy my mind.'

'Occupied minds - probably all any of us need.'

'I don't think so highly of the others.'

I bring all the parts of my bicycle into the office and reassemble them as we talk. We go to bed an hour later, leaving the bicycle nearly complete. I'll finish it in the morning and spend the rest of the day cycling around Paris.

*

My first trip is out to Legrand's apartment. The 'For Rent' sign won't be there long; property is scarce these days. Satisfied that she is gone I ride to a camping shop near the Place de Bastille.

The shop is up a side alley. I walk in, unaware that the whole place is a trap for the unwary. I want to purchase some saddle bags and a water flask – the sort you might take if you were off to discover the source of some virulent river. Within minutes I've been persuaded to buy a pair of short trousers with lots of pockets. Next I find myself agreeing to buy a penknife to keep in one of those pockets along with a compass for another one. Afraid I may buy the entire shop, I grab the salesman by his lapels and tell him that if he opens his mouth again I will leave without buying a thing. He begins to protest so I put everything down in a pile and turn to go. He scrambles after me, carrying it all, and silently beckoning me towards the cashier.

At home I park the bicycle in the hallway. Before I reach the last flight of stairs to the apartment I hear Megan singing. The song is Louise. I stand and listen and, for the first time, I'm filled with love for the song. I am filled with love for her.

The following days are spent cycling while the evenings are spent poring over the map. My leg is holding out. At times it gets stiff, forcing me to get off and walk around. I'll use those moments to grab something to eat. To cater for the times I won't be able to find any suitable food, I have stocked up on dates, dried fruit and nuts.

I'm planning to stay in hotels along the way and, should I need repairs, to use local garages and forges. I'll wrap a few inner tubes around my neck and shoulders and trust to luck for a pump. One spare set of clothes will go in the panniers, along with an army wash kit purchased from a very expensive gentleman's retailers. This is a strange parody of the one I'd used during the war; I remember a particularly flamboyant lieutenant who served under me had had a kit like this – same items as mine, only made from more expensive metals.

The most direct route comes out at around 600 kilometres. I want to take in Orléans, Bourges and Clemont-Ferrand, which means there will be some extra kilometres thrown in. The detour might not add a lot to the time as the roads between those places should be in a better state of repair. I'm reckoning on seventy-five miles a day with the arrival some time on day six - on the seventh day I shall rest.

I know I can do it but as I hear the satisfying pop of Megan opening some wine I feel sick. I've never cycled that far in one go before and my leg is not as strong as it could be. What the hell. We drink the bottle dry and laugh. My gear, all piled up in the corner of the apartment, taunts me whenever my gaze falls in that direction. An-other two bottles have gone and I'm talking about going via Bordeaux,

---

perhaps detouring down a bit further for a peek at a Pyrenean peak.

Morning comes and the seconds beat time against my skull like elephants stamping on hazelnuts. I have reached an age where each hangover is worse than the last. Brushing my teeth I retch into the basin, not quite throwing up. I leave the bathroom feeling abused. I stand swaying slightly in the kitchen trying to remember what I was looking for. The world is moving in different, competing directions. For brief moments I feel all right, the rest of the time I'm deathly.

Megan appears bleary-eyed in a black silk kimono. She smiles, burps, and takes some orange juice back to the bedroom with her. She looks beautifully dishevelled. Despite my condition I follow her to the bed.

A moment of passion followed by a few hours' sleep and I'm in a condition to face the world. Even the drizzle, which was in the air during the morning, has gone, leaving a dry windless afternoon. I force down ten tablespoons of sugar dissolved in a glass of water. This should give me some much needed energy. After giving Megan a goodbye kiss I go downstairs. Filatre is standing in the hallway smoking his pipe.

'Afternoon, old chum. It's nearly two o'clock. You must be in Orléans by now.'

'Very good. I'll be there presently and when I wake up tomorrow morning I'll be on track again.'

I get on my bicycle and, as I pedal away, I hear Filatre shout 'Hat!' which I guess is his translation of 'Chapeau!'

CHAPTER TWENTY-TWO

Two hours of cycling and Paris is a just a memory. So too is the sun and the calm. The wind, which started up a mile or so ago, introduces me to its wicked sister, rain. I stop to put on some oilskins: Megan gave them to me as I was about to leave. I look like a trawler-man making a desperate bid for freedom from the sea.

The wind forces rain into every gap in my clothing. I endure another hour before finding a place to eat; dried dates have kept me going until this point. The place is a roadside bistro, the sort of joint you might take your wife – to discuss the divorce. I flop down at a table and order boiled potatoes, peas, carrots and orange juice. I follow this with a couple of espressos, a large glass of water and another orange juice. They serve me in silence, no questions as to why I want vegetables without meat, or why I don't want butter or what I'm doing here. I am, after all, an Englishman, fitted out like a trawler-man, riding a bicycle through a foul storm - what further explanations are required?

My smoke on cycle trips is a pipe loaded with Saint-Cloud tobacco. I smoke this while lingering over a cognac and staring out of the window. The wind and rain beat at the doors, walls and windows, demanding that I return to suffer further humiliations at their hand.

My clothes have been placed in front of a small stove. For decency's sake I've kept my trousers and vest on. I'd love to call it a night and kip here but I haven't travelled far enough. It's time to get going. My socks are now warm and dry.

Everything else is warm and damp. I may rot away long before I reach Vaour.

You feel at one with the landscape when you have to ride in rain-sodden clothes. I feel like a peat bog on wheels. Any dry patches have been dampened by sweat. I keep on like a mule or a pack horse counting down the days before the knacker's yard. My thoughts are limited to the next pedal stroke. Occasionally I consider changing into dry clothes, then I decide to wait a minute or two in case the rain starts up again.

I arrive in Orléans, hardly noticing the changing landscape. Fields, cows and trees are replaced by houses, people and noise. I don't let myself get distracted: my energy has been drained to the extent that I can't afford an unnecessary blink of the eyes. I'm focused on reaching my destination for the day – a bed.

Until now I've been shutting out complaints from my body. Little things, long suppressed, are bringing themselves to my attention. I am hungry, ravenously hungry. My back is aching. I make myself promises to keep going - first a coffee, hot black and sweet; some bread and jam, strawberry jam; a soak in a hot bath; a bed, any bed. I'm desperate now and my back is seizing up. I could lie down on the pavement and sleep here. Let them try to move me. I sit up straight in the saddle, taking my hands off the handlebars and stretching my back.

A short distance up the road I can see the canvas awnings of the Hotel Bristol. The hotel overlooks the Loire as it meanders through the city like a casual tourist on a sightseeing tour. I cycle straight up to the front door. The staff are dressed in a golden livery. At first they're not sure what to do with my dirty wet bike so I help them out.

'Don't be an arse, man, take it out back,' I say. 'Have the bags brought to my room and have the chain cleaned and oiled – get someone who knows what they are doing. I want hot coffee, with bread and strawberry jam, bring that to my room too.'

I take my key and follow a bellhop across the lobby. A few other guests are milling about in evening wear. On reaching the elevator I'm intercepted by an old duffer with a large Clemenceau moustache.

'My goodness, sir, you look as if you've swum the Sénégal River.'

'Nothing so easy, sir,' I say. 'Cycled down from Paris through a storm, en route for Toulouse.'

'Good man. Idleness is a curse. So many of your age would have pulled up in an automobile sounding those blasted dreadful horns. Much better to see a man in full health, having given battle to the elements, who is prepared to pay for his efforts with his own sweat. Good man and good journey to you.'

I squelch up to my room and give the bellhop a generous tip. I tell him I want that coffee and bread within five minutes. I take off my clothes and throw them on the floor; I put on the large dressing gown which is draped over my bed. The lad reappears with my drink. I tell him to take my wet clothes and launder them for the morning. Another lad arrives with my bike kit. I tip him too, and start cutting up the bread. I know I'm behaving like an upper class twit. Still, I'm getting what I want and am far too tired to give a damn about much else.

The following days are spent the same way as the first – long hours in the saddle and nights flopped in a hotel bed. I long for hills or mountains, anything to break the vast expanses of borderless fields. My future stretches out along straight roads which disappear into hazy horizons. Avenues of plane trees provide a welcome relief from the sun. I can't think of anything beyond the next mile. I drink sugary coffee whenever I spot a café. I go through the same routines in different hotels. My legs feel stronger each day. The hills grow steeper to compensate for this extra strength. At times I come to a standstill on the side of the road. I curse myself for being weak and pedal off again, like a stubborn child, over the hills and under the sun.

You learn things about yourself when the going gets tough. I'm learning that my imagination is seriously lacking - I'd previously thought it fruitful and inspired. When I'd been sitting over the map and planned this route, not once did I imagine bringing up acid and bits of bile as I crawl over yet another hill. Three times I've had to crap in a field like a common foot soldier. Obscenities sally forth from my grimacing mouth. Spittle clings to my chin. Each summit is a minor victory which sees my war against the landscape turn in my favour. I might not be winning but I'm no longer losing.

Saint-Antonin-Noble-Val is what passes for a town down here; it may not be much but it's the closest place to Vaour with any sort of a hotel. I've arrived six days after leaving Paris. I'll need a few more to recover. The cycling wasn't bad; it's leaving Paris I need to recover from. The heat here is almost as overpowering as the stench. Sewage flows in the street – or will flow if it ever rains. Until that day comes it sits at the side of the road and welcomes visitors to the town. People are walking around in clogs oblivious to the effluence. There is one hotel which passes muster, at least I doubt I'll find a better one. I check in and pay for a week in advance; I'm not being flash, the cost wouldn't cover a day in a Parisian flea pit.

On my ride down, apart from losing a few pounds through sweat and mucus, I formulated a single plan. You only need one if it's good - I could use three or four. My plan: pose as an Englishman on a cycling and sketching holiday. I have been pretending to speak virtually no French, although I always pluck the right word from the air when stuck. The pretence is made easier as the southern French they speak here is almost unintelligible.

My bicycle has been taken to the hotel stable. I'm sure they have a man out there who's trying to groom the tail. On my last city stop in Clermont-Ferrand I purchased some decent sketch books and pencils. Not only will these pass as props they will allow me to sit in one place and watch for hours on end without raising suspicion. I might carry it on in Paris for stakeouts. Although that won't work so well at night.

The hotel has a toilet - the toilet from your nightmares, if your nightmares lean that way. On my first visit to the little room I almost vomited straight into the hole. I had obviously arrived shortly after someone who eats festering rats and who'd recently divested himself of them. But I've been in worse and I have a pisspot in my room where I can pass the wine.

The bed is uncomfortable, being harder than the floor and twice as itchy. Having said that, I arrived and sunk into it and didn't wake again for sixteen hours. Had it been a comfortable bed I may never have woken. After sleeping I spend ten minutes checking myself for lice. There are none but when a bed makes you scratch like that you have to check. Time to examine my less immediate surroundings.

Ah, the stench, the streets! You can't escape either. Nor can I escape the eyes upon me. They are there; behind shutters, standing on street corners, sitting in cafés. I ignore these gazes and leave myself open to the opportunity which each corner portends. In Paris the adventure and mystery can last until dawn. Here, in Antonin, it lasts thirty minutes by which time I've examined every nook and cranny. I've seen everything this night is going to offer - which is darkness. Still, I enjoy the calm, the warm, and a glass or two of Pastiche in the café overlooking the tiny space which masquerades as the main square. The drink might help me sleep. Today is Saturday. I'll rest until Monday before I go to Vaour; if there is anything there it won't be open on a Sunday.

During Sunday I have nothing to do other than repeat my activity of the night before. I walk the streets, keeping to the shade cast by the high buildings along these narrow cobbled streets. To think, once, Paris was like this. These streets are as they were all those hundreds of years ago. Littered with the dung of a variety of beasts – I'm no ex-pert and haven't examined it all closely but I can make out, human, horse and goat. There must be some pig, donkey and dog in there too. Looking up at the blue sky and bright orange sun I fully expect someone to empty the contents of their chamber pot from one of those overhanging windows.

The streets are busy with people in dark clothing. They are hurrying to the call of the church bells. Children with their hair combed down watch their fathers steal a few last drags on their cigarettes. Young girls, confident - having had their weekly wash - make eyes at the passing boys. Their cleanliness and godliness drives me out beyond the edge of the town. Here I discover a river. I sit and watch the water flow, look at the mountains, and begin to practice my sketching.

People who encounter me think I am an eccentric English man with war damage. The more they think this the more I play up to it by being both scatterbrained and kind. I have the advantage in being able to understand what they are saying while they believe I'm ignorant of their comments.

By late Sunday afternoon I find my legs are twitching like a pair of frisky ponies. Having no appointments for the day I cycle out to Vaour. This will be a reconnaissance to get the lay of the land. The ride is almost entirely uphill. I cycle through Vaour a couple of times without stopping. I should say I cycled through Vaour a couple of times without noticing. The place is tiny; I wonder why Marty bought a house here. Was all this planned out years ago? Something must have gone wrong – no one would steal a sack full of money and then run away to a village that doesn't have a shop.

Monday - I set off with Vaour firmly in my sights. The morning is cool and the ride pleasant. The hills don't feel as steep as they did yesterday. Luckily I noticed that Vaour does have some medieval ruins which can act as my alibi - people would grow suspicious if I stopped to sketch the village pump.

In Vaour the buildings are spread out along the road

which dissects the village. The church and mayor's office face each other across this road. Somewhere there's a small school and somewhere else there must be a small café. The only surprise is a shack with a petrol pump. I stop near the cloth-capped attendant. He is sitting on a small wooden chair, smouldering cigarette hanging from the corner of his mouth, as he sleeps in the sun. If you switched his bottle of wine for a brown ale and replaced the sun with rain we could be somewhere in Yorkshire enjoying the same scene.

I'm about to wake him and ask where I can get some water when I spot that small café. Being set slightly off from the road it is not placed to attract passing trade. With this glorious sunshine, every café in Paris would be empty; all their customers would be sitting at the pavement tables. Here folk want to get out of the sun; they probably work the fields most of the day.

I cycle up to the door before dismounting. I want information as well as a drink. I doubt that the people inside will open up and start gassing to a stranger. Besides that, why would an English tourist be interested in Gustave Marty? I stand my bike up against the café wall and enter. Normally I would head straight for a table and wait for the waiter. Today I stand in the doorway and remove my cap revealing a head of sweaty hair. With trousers still tucked into my socks and my artist's satchel over my shoulders, I walk straight to the bar. On my way over I make a point of nodding my head and saying, 'Hello there, lovely morning,' in English, to one of the customers.

CHAPTER TWENTY-THREE

The café is small and dark. As I enter a chair screeches on the stone floor and someone coughs up a large amount of phlegm. There are around eight people in the café; it's hard to tell exactly as my eyes haven't adjusted from the bright sun outside. The patron greets me with a smile, which maybe a grimace. The look on his face is similar to the one I have been getting from all the locals when they realise they will have to speak to me. It's a look of horror and confusion, as if I'm a dastardly moustache-twirling villain preparing to defile them with my mispronounced vocabulary.

I ask for some red wine. The patron's smile is now assuredly a grimace. I say, 'Um', and scratch my head. Then, as if remembering some old school French, I say, 'Vin rouge, please.' I am met with the same incomprehension. Perhaps he suspects that vin rouge is an English phrase meaning something other than red wine. He is not prepared to risk showing me a bottle of wine in case that isn't what I seek. Reaching a stand-off I resort to a mime act which I have been perfecting these last few days.

I act out having a bottle between my legs whilst I tug on the corkscrew. This involves a lot of effort – the cork is a stubborn one – it then comes out with me making a popping sound. I pour myself a healthy snifter, down the glass quickly and pour another, then another. Now I start acting a little tipsy - I have to concentrate as I pour my next glass. The locals are watching and some are laughing. I decide to milk it and make out I can see two bottles and keep going for the wrong one. By the time I finish the patron has poured me a large glass of red wine.

Having broken the ice I decide to establish my reason for being here.

'The building is old?' I ask, in French.

'Here is, yes,' says the patron. The hopeful expression on his face pleading with me to understand his answer.

I shake my head and say: 'No, non, no. The road, the rue.' I point at the door and grin. I'd love to say, 'The ruins of the Templar stronghold. It's the only thing in this miserable village worth mentioning.' Instead I glance from blank face to blank face hoping one of them will put me out of my misery.

The patron seeks help from an old fellow who's sitting at the bar drinking a milky liqueur. I suspect he nurses that pastiche for most of the morning so he ought to be sober.

'Help me, Hugo. He is talking about some building in the road,' the patron says.

'Perhaps he means the garage,' Hugo says.

The patron turns to me: 'The garage?'

'No, near the garage. The building.'

'The church?'

'No, near the garage, not the church.'

'The Mayor's office?'

'No, no, look...'

I take a wine bottle and place it to the side of the bar. 'The garage,' I say. Three other customers come over to watch. I decide to play up to them. I take off my tie and lay it along the bar. 'The road.'

A few of them mumble out a 'yes'.

I place my empty glass next to the bottle. 'The church.'

'Yes, the church.'

Their agreement becomes assertive as they begin to recognise the map I'm making. I could have taken out my pencil and drawn one - I am hoping this will be a more profitable route.

'And this,' I point to the other side of the bottle-garage

where I'd seen the ruins. I look around hopefully, picking out Hugo for particular attention.

Hugo shrugs: 'Nothing there.'

'No, not nothing; broken,' I say.

'Ah! He means the ruins.' The voice comes from one of the customers standing behind me.

'Ah!' Hugo and the patron echo.

'Yes, they are old. Templar buildings,' says the patron.

'Templar,' I repeat as if learning the word.

Believing my cover is established I bid them all a good day. I leave, take my bicycle, and head over to the Templar ruins. Here I shall endure the punishment I have set myself - a couple of hours sketching in the sun with no shade.

There is no doubting my lack of sketching talent. Occasionally I'm hit by moments of inspiration where I can take out my notepad and sketch something recognisable. Deprived of those moments of inspiration, and I only have one or two a year, my drawings resemble my intentions in the way mountains resemble lakes. In short I have the artistic ability of a talented five-year-old.

At one time there would have been ample shade here. That would have been around the time the bits of rubble on the floor had formed a building. It is now eleven-thirty and already the sun is a formidable opponent. Drinking that wine has not helped. I produce my pencil and start to sketch. I have two lines which were supposed to represent the route in to this area from the road. The lines almost resemble the stem of a bottle, so I go with that. A bottle of wine. I draw a label and then stick a cork in it. I am proud of this bottle, although if it was real, and made of glass, it would topple over, the wine would leak from several places and anyone trying to hold it would be sure to cut their fingers.

I sit and stare at the road in front of me and then over to the left. The life of a detective - all thrills and lascivious women. The garage attendant is still asleep on his chair. I wonder, though, if he is asleep; perhaps he has been shot? The sun and the wine are getting the better of me. If I put my bag out here and my jacket there – yes, that just about does the trick.

I sleep for around three hours in all. My face is resentful at not having been covered. I need a drink; probably a couple of gallons of water. Back to the café.

The patron is wiping the tables. He does this so expertly that when he has finished it doesn't look as if they have been wiped at all. The café is nearly empty, even Hugo, whom I suspect no longer has a job to go to, has left. There are two customers, I don't recognise them from earlier but they could have been there. I bid them a jovial, over pronounced, 'Bonjour'.

The patron smiles at me and lifts up a bottle of wine. 'You like?' he says in English.

'I do, my old son, but it doesn't like me too much today.' I've strayed beyond his linguistic comprehension so I say, 'Non, thank you.'

I ask for 'rain' and pretend to hold out a glass. He catches on and fetches me a jug of water. It is cloudy and lukewarm. After three hours lying in the sun this is actually appealing. I drink a few glasses in quick succession.

The patron laughs then goes back to wiping the counter. I consider sketching in the café, inspired by a romantic idea of a young artist sketching away with a pencil in one hand, pad in the other, and a cigarette smouldering in the corner of the mouth. Before I have pulled the pencil from the pocket I remember: I am not an artist nor am I young any longer. On the bright side, I do have some cigarettes. And where did that bottle of wine go?

Damn! Damn! Damn! Halfway through my second glass of wine I realise that I can't start questioning these people because I can't speak effing French. What a near-sighted imbecile I am. I could stand up, wave them all goodbye, and declare that I'm going to start an intensive Berlitz course. How long would I have to leave it before I came back and started quizzing them? Shit!

I leave the cafe feeling like a prize idiot. An unsuspecting stone receives a good hard kick sending it skittling along the dusty path. The stone ricochets off other stones before coming to a standstill against a rock. A gecko scurries across the wall where my bike is leaning. I'm hot, tired, stiff, and achy, and I don't want to cycle back to Saint-Antonin.

The road crawls under me. Baked dirt and loose rocks conspire to crush my spirit. I thought the cobbles of Paris were bad until I reached the country roads. For miles at a stretch I feel more like a tight-rope walker than a cyclist, riding on the ridges between large pot holes. I fail to muster any enthusiasm for the journey. I'll call Megan when I get to Saint-Antonin and let her know what an arse I've been. Maybe she'll come up with a few ideas.

Despite aching and feeling as if my tyres have been glued to the road, it takes me as long to get to Saint-Antonin as it took me to reach Vaour in the morning. It felt a whole lot longer. At least the hotel, with its medieval toilet and beds designed by the Marquis de Sade, has a telephone.

A young swarthy-looking boy is lying on the reception desk. I recognise him as one of the proprietor's spawn. On seeing me he stops scratching his groin and turns his head in my direction. I order a vermouth and ask to use the telephone. He rolls off the desk and disappears out the front door.

I'm beginning to wonder if he hasn't simply run off to find a private place where he can continue his scratching. Fed up with waiting I'm about to go and use the telephone when he appears in the doorway with my drink. There is ice floating around in it – I guess he spent a while tracking that down. I give him a decent tip for his effort.

I've never ordered vermouth before; I meant to ask for pastiche but the word 'vermouth' jumped out of my mouth. Actually it tastes quite nice. I call Megan. This process involves talking to at least four different operators. No longer so concerned about blowing my cover I speak in French to them and then English when I'm finally put through to Megan.

After a lot of miss-you-kiss-kiss and me filling her in: 'Reggie, you silly sod, what did you do that for?'

'Being smart, I guess. What shall I do now?'

I describe the town to her: 'A bit of nothing that grips the road like a drowning man grabbing for a rope. They do have a café, small and not as bad as it could be. The wine is rough at first but softens as you get to know it. There is a garage, though I didn't see any autos. A church and the mayor's office. All in all, it's the kind of village which will get wiped out when the plague returns.'

'What did they say at the mayor's office?'

'What did they say? I didn't go in to the mayor's office.'

'Marty is an alien. I know they like the Belgians here but they are still foreign and they do still have to register with the local authorities.'

I'd been a fool in not visiting the mayor's office today. That can be rectified come the morning. The remainder of our conversation has nothing to do with the case. I leave the telephone booth with an erection.

One thing I'll say for the south – tabbouleh, couscous with mint and vegetables. In Paris I spend half an hour explaining I don't want meat for them to serve up boiled potatoes – for all three courses. Then there is the evening sun; cruel and moody all day, becoming sympathetic in the evening. The wine here is rough, ready, and plentiful. If I could float Paris onto the river Yonne and sail it down here - at least for the winter - I'd be a happy man.

I get up early and ride to Vaour. The sun is like a guard dog sleeping peacefully in the sky. I am not fooled. That dog can bite; I'm still suffering from yesterday. I'm a weather communist; the sun's heat should be distributed evenly across the globe. Perhaps we could have a little more in the summer and little less in the winter. The rain, too, must fall evenly. A little snow, a few blustery days, all evenly distributed between the nations.

I have no intention of approaching the mayor's office until at least nine-thirty. Even at that hour I'm willing to lay even money that it won't be open. Freewheeling into the village I pull up outside the office to double check. This is the sort of place where it might only open once a week. Or once a fortnight. A notice by the door reads: open Tuesday and Wednesday, ten-thirty till twelve. Well, it's Tuesday. I have two hours to kill.

Given that I have now read the opening hours on the mayor's office door I have availed myself of all the free entertainment on offer. I don't fancy the café today. If I could go in quietly and order a drink in French I would. Right now it's too early and I'm too stiff and tired to be playing the English buffoon. The garage attendant is wearing a string vest and blue trousers. He's awake and sweeping the forecourt. A cigarette dangles from his lip. Perhaps it's the same cigarette he had there yesterday. What inspires him to get up each morning? That garage can't be making much; I haven't seen an automobile in all the time I've been here. Does he go there to escape his family? Perhaps there was a tree on the site, where he'd meet his lover. She had to go away and they swore to meet again, beneath the tree, one year later. The years pass - he cuts down the tree and sells it for firewood. Then he builds a garage, still waiting. Years later a fancy Daimler pulls up. She's in the passenger seat applying her make-up. He catches her eye as he wipes the windscreen. Now he rises each day and sweeps the forecourt, buys some wine, and sleeps in the sun. He's still waiting, but no longer for her.

CHAPTER TWENTY-FOUR

After two hours of pacing, and a short nap leaning against a wall, I'm ready for officialdom. At least there is some shade on this side of the building. I am alone; everyone else must be planning to conduct their business tomorrow. The door is locked. I check my watch – ten thirty-two. I check the opening time – ten thirty. Have I lost a day or two somewhere along the way? I can't have; I was here yesterday, and the day before everybody was off to church. It is quite definitely Tuesday and it is between ten thirty and twelve.

Ten forty-five: I hear a slight noise followed by the distinct sound of footsteps. Some cheeky so-and-so has opened the door on the quiet; if they try to make out it was open all along I'll swing for them.

The lobby is cool and dark. The floor is made up of large flagstones; someone went to a lot of expense making this floor, then the centuries took their toll. My eyes are struggling to adjust from the bright sun outside; there is probably some trick the locals have developed when they come in out of the sun. I can hear the sound of footsteps echoing from a hallway. The reception area is staffed by a man who is sleeping with his legs up on the desk. I'm tempted to pull up a chair and sleep alongside him. Instead I take a seat, then slap my hand hard down on the desk. He wakes with a start. I brush my hand on my trouser. 'Got the little blighter,' I say.

The man reaches for a pair of spectacles, fumbling them

onto his nose. Next he produces a handkerchief which, without ceremony, he uses to blow his bespectacled nose. He is about to open the hanky and inspect the contents when I cough. He puts it back in his pocket and inspects me instead.

'You were saying?'

Not a bad gambit. The man is not particularly tall; say one metre sixty, although it is hard to measure his height while he is sitting. He seems to be one of those pernickety men who always take a moment to brush invisible dust from their jackets. The cuffs of his once-white shirt are a little worn and the left one's stained with black ink. His bow-tie is tied loosely and hangs away from his neck. The time spent sleeping and working in this dark lobby has given him a pallor unusual for the town. He speaks with the local accent.

'You were going to look it up for me,' I say.

I speak in French, not English. Here's hoping I don't run into him in the café.

'I was indeed, sir, but what was it again?'

'Ah, you wise old dog,' I say and tap the side of my nose. 'Holding out for more are we?'

'I am not sure to what you are referring.'

I have played this gambit out and the fellow looks genuinely confused. Now is the time to play it straight.

'I'm going to give you fifty francs. You are going to show me a list of everyone living in the area. You are also going to remember if any outsiders are living here.'

'Was I? Not so sure I was, but I will.' He smiles and scratches the back of his head. 'For one hundred.'

I should have started with twenty but the days are too short to waste them haggling. I count out a hundred francs so he can see I have the money. I give him fifty and tell him he can have the rest when I get what I want. He stands up and walks over to some dusty drawers. I wonder if he'd walk faster if I'd threatened to bust his head open. He returns with a ledger which arouses my suspicion - it looks like the one Legrand used.

After sneezing at me a few times and then drawing his handkerchief, the man opens up the ledger. He looks reverentially at the pages, before I turn the book around so I can read it.

'That is a list of everyone living in the area,' he says. 'There are only three outsiders living here and I don't need a book to tell you who they are. There's the Matusi couple – Italians. I wonder why we don't turn the country over to them.' He looks to see if I'm going to encourage him in an anti-Italian diatribe. I don't. 'They have been living here since 1912. Then there is monsieur Dubois. He has had a place here for about five years. He's been living in it full-time for around a year now. Keeps himself to himself. I would be willing to bet the other fifty in your pocket that he's the one you want.'

I take out the fifty and give it to him. He goes on: 'Dubois lives in a farmhouse about three kilometres out from the village. Follow the road towards Campagnac. He isn't proper foreign though - he's from Paris.'

He gives me detailed directions and even draws a map. Now that I have woken him up he probably feels he should be doing something.

'I must say, you speak a lot better French than they give you credit for,' he says.

'Who?'

'The folk in the café.'

'No, I don't. I hardly speak a word of it, and we never met.'

'Quite right, sir, you never said a word and this is a dream.'

His legs re-occupy their former space on the desk and he slouches in the chair. I leave him to his work.

I know the road towards Campagnac as I cycled some way along it on Sunday. There's about a mile between the last house of the village and the turning to the Dubois farm. I can see farm buildings in the distance. I feel a certain amount of nervousness. I used to feel like this in the early mornings, in the moments before sunrise, on the days when we were going over the top. Then it wasn't about life or death; it was about how you'd die. I never once went over with any expectations of returning. This time I expect to return triumphant. The road out of Vaour is a quirky affair with a liberal scattering of pot-holes and mounds. I've gotten used to riding on these roads over the last few days. All you have to do is remember to proceed with caution. If you forget that simple rule the road will remind you – by bouncing you up a few inches and then sending the saddle straight up into your balls. I have had two such reminders and I don't wish for a third.

The road towards the farmhouse is a different breed. This one is narrow with a deep ditch on one side and a thorny bush on the other. In case you happen to have a good sense of balance, and aren't likely to fall into the bush or ditch, the road is covered in small rocks. Ride too slowly and you will fall into spiky arms. Ride too fast and the wheels fire the stones up at your shins. I push the bike along the road to the farm, giving the stones a good kicking along the way.

The outbuildings are falling down around the chickens which scuttle across the yard. The courtyard itself wants serious attention, although it's in keeping with other places I have seen about here. Nearer the house is an automobile, a Citroën like Filatre's, covered with old rugs and canvas. A pump stands on its own about four metres from the kitchen door. The property must have its own spring – a valuable asset in these parts. The house itself looks to be in a good state of repair, to my untrained eyes at least.

Enough of the sight-seeing. The time has come to meet monsieur Gustave Marty. After placing my bike carefully against the wall of the farmhouse I call out 'Hello?' May as well play the English tourist again. I walk up to the kitchen door, knock, and call out. No response. I place my ear to the door. Nothing. I take my water bottle from my bike to act as a prop before going walkabout.

The front of the farmhouse overlooks a large garden which merges into rolling hills stretching up to a forest. Not another building in sight. Deer frolic in the distance. You could go crazy holed up in a place like this.

The lawn has been mown and kept like an English garden with flower beds along the front of the house. A crumpled man sits sleeping in a deckchair. If he were younger I'd say the man was Marty. This guy looks to be in his fifties. His skin is tanned, no doubt from sleeping out under the sun. His hair shows a lot of grey. He could be Marty's older brother – Marie never mentioned him having one.

'Bonjour,' I say, loud enough to wake him, or so I thought. I repeat with more volume and edge a little closer. His chest is moving; at least he isn't dead.

'Excuse me.' This time I say it while standing right next to him.

I can hear his heavy breathing and an occasional whistling from his nose. He's dribbling slightly on to an expensive linen suit. Underneath that he has on what looks to be a silk shirt. The shirt is a mistake – it's showing up all his sleepy sweat. A little table beside the chair holds a bottle of London gin and siphon of tonic water. Besides them; a knife; half a lemon; a glass with a lemon slice wedged at the bottom.

The man wakes and rubs his eyes. He moves his head to one side and rubs his neck.

'What? Who the hell are you?'

I hold up my flask and say, 'Drinky water?'

Waking properly now, he turns in his seat to get a better look at me. I get a better look at him too. His right hand is patting against his thigh like an errant jazz drummer on cocaine. He spends a moment or two stretching his limbs. He must have been asleep for a fair while. Once the stretching is over he takes a pair of silver rimmed spectacles out of his jacket and puts them on. His face is inexpressive - I wouldn't want to play him at cards. I wouldn't want to play him at anything. I'd like to smack him over the head and throw him in the Seine to see how he likes it. Then again, he might not be Marty.

'You are English?' he asks in English with a Birmingham

accent.

'I am indeed; Nickson's the name – Harry Nickson. You are the first person I've encountered who can actually speak my language since I arrived in the South.'

I proffer my hand which he shakes. He has a weakened grip which I have the impression had once been strong.

'That, sir, is because you are in France. In France we speak French. I lived in Birmingham, in England, for two years and nobody there spoke to me in French. I had to learn English. The name of the country offers a good clue as to the language the people will speak.'

'Quite so, but if one spent all one's time learning the languages of every country one might visit one might never leave school.'

He humphs and climbs slowly out of the deckchair. His arms shake and his legs look wobbly. If that were me I'd lay off the gin. Once up he walks off towards the house. Seeing that I have remained near the chair he turns and calls out, 'Come then.'

We walk all the way around the house to the kitchen door. Along the way he pauses to inspect things, a bit of the wall; a flower; the drain pipes. I doubt these things provide the slightest interest – he's having difficulty walking and doesn't want to own up to it.

'Yours, sir?' He indicates my bicycle with a nod in its general direction.

'Yes, rode down from Paris on that blighter. If it wasn't for the channel I'd have ridden from London.'

He turns toward me. From behind a slight film his eyes seem to shine. 'I adore cycling,' he says. 'I can't do it myself these days. Each summer I travel down to the mountains and spend the day waiting for The Tour to go by.'

'I first saw it myself in 1912,' I say. 'The spectacle inspired me to take it up. My parents had taken us to the Alps for some summer hiking. Seeing a cluster of people gathered at a roadside halfway up a mountain my brother and I ran over to find out what was happening. I think I was expecting to see a dead body. What we did see was Eugène Christophe; we didn't know who he was, so an old fellow filled us in. I stood and gawped at him open-mouthed. The road was not much more than a rubble track and deadly steep. Here was this man, on a bicycle, covered in dirt with sweat streaks down his face, mastering the mountain. What really did for me were the stragglers. The ones who just keep going. They looked as if they had stolen their bikes to escape the mortuary. In that battle they fought against themselves I saw something - it was something I knew I had to do for myself. I got my first bike within a week of returning home. It's not a sport we follow too much in my homeland, not like you French.'

'French! I am Belgian!'

I know you are, you lying little blighter, but you registered here as a Frenchman.

'So you must have been proud to see De Waele go on to win last year's tour,' I say.

'I was indeed. I always feel the years when a Belgian wins are the special years. Have you ever been to Belgium?'

'Yes, but not under the best of conditions.'

'I see, of course. For that I thank you. Look, why don't you rest here for a while? If you have nowhere else to be I could use some company. I could even have the spare room laid out. My maid will be here soon and she'll conjure us up some grub.'

He leads me inside to the kitchen where he produces a few dusty bottles of beer from a cupboard. After twenty minutes of talking about the Tour de France I find myself growing to like the fake Dubois.

CHAPTER TWENTY-FIVE

We sit at the kitchen table drinking beer and talking. Outside, the sun turns nasty and starts burning up anything in sight. The shutters are part closed and the light in here is dappled and gentle. I feel at ease listening to Dubois and sipping his beer. If he isn't Marty I might invite him up to Paris. If he isn't Marty, then I'm a Dutchman.

At one point Dubois gets up and leads me on a tour of the house. There's not a lot to it. Downstairs next to the kitchen there's a drawing room – every home should have one. This one is stiff and formal like a dead general. Dubois points to a large carpet hanging on the wall and says it's from Flanders and expensive. I guess he stuck it on the wall to stop people wiping their feet on it. Two wide cream-coloured couches sit facing each other like overweight duellists. Seconding the couch on the left is an armchair which has been padded to the point of near bursting. The other couch has chosen a tall vase to side with it. One wall has a huge painting of an exceedingly ugly child standing next to an even uglier dog. It may have been painted three hundred years ago, or the kid's parents got him up in that garb to draw attention away from his bulbous eyes and minuscule forehead. Dubois misinterprets my silence for awe and whispers, 'This is my Versailles room.'

The rest of the tour goes by in a haze as I'm haunted by an image of the ugly dog wearing the child's face. It keeps calling me Mama. I need a drink – I tell Dubois this but I don't tell him why. We return to the kitchen.

After an hour of talking about any-and-everything the maid arrives. She enters the kitchen with the casual air of a woman entering her own domain. Seeing me she stiffens and assumes a formal posture. She managed to achieve this with a few gestures which demonstrate that she has been in service a long time. Service or not, she is the lady of the house. Her entrance was not that of a servant, even a familiar, long-standing servant. That was the entrance of a wife. She didn't head towards the larder or the sink she made straight for Dubois. Her whole body moved as one who is about to bend and kiss her husband on the head.

'Fix us some food, Nathalie. I warn you though; monsieur Nickson here says he eats nothing from animals. He is like some visiting Eastern guru.'

Dubois grins at me as Nathalie rolls her eyes to the ceiling. He said all this in French so he thinks I haven't understood him.

'I have asked her to fix us some grub,' he says. Then he goes to the cupboard where the beer is kept. 'I have ice delivered – it allows me to chill some wine.'

The wine is in a silver bucket, the ice almost melted. The bottle is covered in dew so it should be nice and cold. Nathalie walks over to a larder and returns with a basket of vegetables. She rolls up her sleeves and begins chopping and scraping as Dubois and I sip the cool white wine. I feel a tiny bit guilty watching her work like that – hasn't Dubois got some other room we can drink in?

We remain at the table. Before her arrival we'd been lost in talk and now Nathalie's presence has made us self-conscious. Perhaps he doesn't like talking English in front of her. With nothing else to do I gaze around the kitchen. The room is divided into two separate areas. One section is the working kitchen. The part we are in is the eating area. If you know the person living here isn't actually a farmer then what you see is what you might expect to find. There are some Japanese prints on the wall. The table has formal high-backed chairs as seats. Place mats are a delicate shade of turquoise. Nothing objectionable, nothing to remember, no sense of personality or ownership – the bland uniformity of bourgeoisie taste, or a man trying to hide is identity.

Nathalie is chopping vegetables to the right of a huge stone basin. To her side is the cooking area. This consists of two brickwork arches painted white. They hold wood supplies and also some pans. Above them is a long red-tiled surface. There, over a hole where the fire sits, is a large cooking pot. She already has some wood burning.

Our silence comes to an end with Dubois informing me that he detests city life. Long ago he used to live in Paris – to hear him you would think it were decades rather than a year. I guess time passes slowly here.

He begins describing his old journey to work. Thinking I'm from England, and not too familiar with Paris, he goes into enough detail to allow me to place his house within a hundred metres. I know he is talking about the commute from his home in rue Léon to the Lacman Brothers' office. He has given away enough of himself for me to be quite certain that he is Gustave Marty. I guess a man in hiding is cursed with a desperation to unload his every trivial thought and feeling. I wonder if Nathalie knows his true identity. She brings me over some salad and chunks of bread. Marty has the same food as mine only it's littered with bits of flesh. She puts the plates down and tells Marty we can have some vegetable stew later – it will simmer in the pot and we should help ourselves.

'This is the life, my friend.' Marty smiles and dabs his lips with a napkin.

Nathalie comes over and kisses Marty on the forehead. 'I'm leaving now, my dear. I'll come around again tomorrow afternoon.' She turns to me. 'Goodnight, monsieur Nickson.'

I raise my hat and smile at her.

When she has gone: 'That is a most informal maid you have, Dubois.'

'She is more than a maid, a little less than a wife.'

'A little less?'

'She spends the night at her home in the village. I have often asked her to move in here but she says it would be undignified. That does not mean we don't take occasional naps together in the afternoon.'

'Why not marry her?'

'I'm not the marrying kind. I value my freedom too highly.'

Freedom not to reveal your real name on a marriage certificate. Perhaps Nathalie doesn't know who he really is.

'The freedom to sleep alone at night?' I say.

'No, that is freedom's price. I grew weary of the city and its confines. I moved down here in search of the simple life. I was lucky. I cashed in all my American stocks before the crash and I was never foolish enough to buy French bonds. I'd been planning to spend my days hunting and fishing. Then, about a month or so after my arrival, I was diagnosed with Parkinson's disease. That put pay to most of my plans. I have found since then that my greatest pleasure is to sit in the garden and watch the sun pass overhead. We have become great friends, the sun and I. At night it's sleep I desire, not women. I shan't deny it would be nice to have someone's arms around me while I sleep.'

'I'm sorry to hear that – about the disease.'

'I suppose in some way I am reconciled to it. At least I'm reconciled to this life. It's more sedate than I'd planned but it isn't bad. Maybe I'll marry Nathalie someday; I have a horrible vision of myself passing away in bed and nobody noticing. But let's not get too maudlin. How about another glass?'

We change the subject and talk for a while longer.

'Time for my bed, Mr Nickson. Sad to say, but I rarely remain up past seven these days. You make yourself at home – I've shown you your room, go to it when you will. I'll bid you goodnight and don't worry, I'll fish you out some nightclothes. They'll be a bit too small for you but they'll do, I'm sure.'

The chilled white wine has long since gone. I pour myself a glass of rough red and light a cigarette. For a time I hear creaking and the occasional cough before the house grows silent. Marty must be asleep or at least trying to sleep. The time has come for me to go through his drawers. I can't help feeling a little despicable - rummaging through his personal belongings and violating the trust of my host. I finger the bump on the back of my head, which still hurts slightly when I press it, and continue with my task.

There is little of interest in the kitchen so I move on to the Versailles room. The darkness, with shadows cast by a candle I'm holding, makes this room quite creepy. There is a small trunk on the far side of one of the couches. The thing has been locked. I get out my penknife and start picking at the lock with one of the blade attachments. Aged thirteen, I would have had this open in a few minutes. Aged thirty-four, in a darkened room, it takes me ten. What sort of a man puts cushions in a locked trunk? I squeeze them in case something is hidden inside of them. There is – duck feathers. I empty everything out of the trunk by turning it upside down. The inside is made up of slatted wood. There is no lining to hide anything behind. He really does keep four cushions under lock and key. Perhaps it gives him a thrill, when there are guests over, to know that he has cushions held captive in the drawing room.

The ceiling creaks and I hear Marty cough. I freeze, holding one of the cushions and looking up at the ceiling. His bedroom must be directly above this room. Don't come downstairs now, Marty, get back into bed. I can hear him walking around, then silence. The silence lasts around two minutes and is broken by the unmistakable sound of piss hitting an empty chamber pot. The torrent stops and the floorboards sound off before the bedsprings groan. I stick the cushions back in the trunk, listening out all the time until I hear him snoring.

In the hallway, near the front door, is a bureau. In any other house I would say it was a strange place to have one.

The drawers are unlocked. I pull out a bundle of bills and letters. They are all addressed to Dubois. Nothing in there says that he is Marty. I want something conclusive. Everything is pointing that way: the fact he is Belgian, where Dubois is supposed to be French; the route he described to work; he told me that he had worked as a stockbroker. There is also the fact that there are no other outsiders in Vaour. His illness has left him looking older and thinner than he had been described, but even then he nearly fits the bill. If I can find one thing that says Marty, I'll go home and claim my fee.

Upstairs there's one long hallway with a few rooms coming off it. At the end of the hallway there's a window which overlooks the darkness between here and the village. The floorboards do their best to give me away. I walk along to my room which is next door to my host's. Oh, the devil take it!

I walk past my room to Marty's. I place my ear against his door and listen to him snoring. I can feel an electrical surge coursing up and down my body – a fearful excitement. I'm beginning to enjoy the sensation.

I would not have opened the door so carefully and slowly if I'd genuinely thought it to be my room. I doubt that Marty, in his drowsiness, will notice such a detail. The room is pitch black, except for the small amount of light following me from the hallway. Marty's breathing is low and guttural. My first step is onto a squeaking floorboard. I freeze. Marty is still breathing nice and slow. The wine must have sent him into a deep sleep. I leave the door open slightly so I can leave with as little noise as possible. Crouching down in the corner I wait for my eyes to adjust to the darkness.

I'm beginning to make out shapes in the room: a dressing table; a wardrobe; the bed. Upon the bed I can see the shape of Marty's curled-up body. The wardrobe is within arm's reach of me. I'm sitting between the bed and the dressing table. Let's get this over with. Stretching out my body and moving along on my elbows, I reach the dressing table. I open the drawers and feel around inside with my hands. Unable to see well enough I rely on my sense of touch.

The next few minutes are spent groping socks, under garments, braces and handkerchiefs. Ready to give up I push my hand in as far as I can force it and hit upon a small bundle. They feel like postcards. Why would he be hiding postcards in the sock drawer? They must be personal and if they are personal they must be addressed to Marty. I take them out for a look - there are about ten. I can't see well enough in this light. I lie down again and stretch myself out towards the door. I push it open a fraction and, with the scant extra light it provides, I take a look at the card on top. Strange – it's blank. I turn it over to reveal a naked woman kneeling upon a piano stool. The next one shows a naked woman standing in front of a painted jungle scene. I go through them one by one and each reveals a naked woman in a compromising pose. I return them to the drawer and wait a moment for my eyes to readjust to the darkness.

A cloud must have passed away from the moon allowing some light to get in through a crack in the shutters. Taking advantage of this light I stand up to get a good look around the room. On the far side of the bed I spot a cabinet with a drawer in it. I lie and crawl like a Boer commando. If it all goes horribly wrong I can run downstairs and get on my bike. Even if Marty has a gun he will be full of sleep. Christ, I hope he doesn't sleep with a gun though - a man silhouetted in the doorway makes for an easy target.

CHAPTER TWENTY-SIX

Crawling around the floor is an exceptionally uncomfortable way to travel. The unnatural position has caused my right leg to start aching. I'm on the verge of getting cramp, my leg muscles preparing to spasm. On the point of giving up I come face-to-face with his chamber pot. This is disgusting work. I should become an art dealer or an art thief – I could begin with that painting downstairs.

There is no way to crawl past the pot without tipping it over so I get up and step past it. Then I tip-toe the rest of the way to the cupboard. Once there I crouch down and wait - no need to rush. The bed starts grumbling. I can see Marty, under a cover, about two feet away. Unnervingly, he is facing right at me. His eyes are closed and his mouth is open. In this slight light he resembles a waxwork model. I wish he would roll over and face the other way.

I pull open the drawer. Medicine bottles and tins of pills ring out against each other. Nothing in there of use to me. I spend longer closing the drawer than I do shaving in the morning. The cupboard beneath the drawer opens with a click. A shelf divides it in half. On the top are cravats and silk ties – I dislike the sensation of the silk against my dry hands. The lower section holds a pair of shoes. I take them out to look inside; nothing but old newspaper. I place them back and, for want of any better ideas, I pull out the ties.

One of the ties has a different texture to the others. I place it on the floor and return the rest. All the other ties had been made of pure silk - this one isn't. I hold it up so it catches the scant light reaching the room. This tie is frayed. Marty strikes me as a man who would throw out a frayed tie. I move closer to the shutters and take a better look. Hey presto! It's his old school tie and his mother has been kind enough to sew his name onto it: Gustave Marty. That'll do for me. I return the tie to the cupboard and begin to crawl out of the room. Sod it. I get up and walk out, leaving Marty snoring on the bed.

*

Marty is in a jovial mood at breakfast. Having a house guest seems to have brought out the best in him. When I first met him on the deckchair he'd struck me as a grumpy sot. Nathalie is here too, and she's fussing over him. She behaves like a caring elder sister, wiping away a line of drool from his chin while handing him a coffee. She greets me with a warm smile; perhaps she realises I have put Marty in a good mood. Maybe, later, she'll ask him for a rise.

'Good morning, Mister,' she says in English.

I reply in broken French. Having gotten this simple protocol out of the way she goes into the garden and leaves us to our coffee.

'She really is a splendid woman, you know,' Marty says.

'I'm sure she is, Mr Dubois.'

'Please, call me Raymond.'

'Raymond.'

'I have been thinking about our conversation yesterday; maybe I ought to marry her. It wasn't so long ago I only thought of women as things for me to screw. Screw and, of course, perform the household chores. Now the illness, it has stolen much of my vibrancy.'

Even through his waxen face an odd, impish smile punctuates his sentences. In his prime he would have been a real charmer. Despite the things he says I find myself endeared to him. In his presence I forget that he is a man who tried to have me killed and that two other detectives were not so lucky. Only if I close my eyes tight can I recall his thievery and brutality.

I help myself to bread and jam which has been left on the table. Marty witters on about changes and new beginnings. Soon after he finishes I tell him I have to get going. He asks if I'd like to stay on for a couple more days. I tell him I have engagements elsewhere. Another few hours in his company and I might grow to like him.

I'm waved off by the pair of them and ten minutes later I'm cycling into Vaour. The sleepy main road seems to call out from centuries past. Even the petrol pump and its narcoleptic attendant could have witnessed the Knights Templar as they rode into town. The place creates an illusion of perpetual stability.

These pleasant daydreams burn away as I hit the hills to Saint-Antonin. Sweat and spit fall away from me as I reach the final summit. Downhill now, all the way to town. I will catch a train to Paris. I don't want to delay celebrating the end of the case by trying to cycle back.

Catching a train means cycling for an hour to the nearest station. A guard stows the bicycle in the luggage van while I take my compartment. For a flicker of a moment I think about buying a second class ticket. But the first class carriage has enough space for me to stretch out my legs. Once duly stretched I fall asleep. The rocking of the train is as good as any cradle. I'm woken three or four times – as we pull into stations or the conductor checks my ticket. Four hours of sleep later I stretch my legs by walking to the restaurant car. I find a table to myself and order a coffee and some fruit.

Having found Marty I'm left with one unresolved question: why? Why did Marie make me traipse around the country looking for this man? The more I think about it the less obvious it becomes. I had thought of her as being conned by Marty. I'm not so sure anymore. Maybe they were partners and he ran off with her share of the cash. She has money, not a lot, but she does not appear to work.

I know how she'll react when I tell her I've found him. She won't smile. She might say thank you. Then she'll bid me a good day and that'll be the end of it. I want more than that sort of pay-off. I want to know why. I would take that knowledge as payment in full; she could keep the cash. Clients are secretive; detectives are inquisitive.

If I can't finish a case without buying the lowdown I might as well shut up shop. I have to take the money as a point of principle. This should not stop me trying to find out why I was hired. I play over a few scenarios but fail to contrive a situation where Marie reveals her secret. Potential conversations are enacted in my mind. They never reach the point of her saying, 'Well, I suppose I should explain...'

The train meanders through the outskirts of Paris as the late afternoon sun lights up the tracks. For the whole journey, in-between sleeping and eating, I've been smirking and thinking of myself as something special. I haven't told Megan I'm coming home yet. I want to see her face when I tell her I found Marty.

My smugness is punctuated by the reality that it wasn't a great achievement. I only had to find someone. I didn't have to demonstrate how a seemingly impossible event actually occurred. I just followed a trail from one end of the country to the other. The achievement feels greater because it is the first thing I have completed since my demob. My other cases, and there have been two of them, left me with no sense of anything. For the first one I had to stand outside a hotel until a certain man entered and then I had to telephone his wife. The second one involved escorting an elderly gent to Reims. They didn't tell me why but I assume he was carrying a load of cash.

The train comes to its final halt and I pass among the crowds on the platform. An idea strikes me - the creepy kid, Stefan. There's always a chance that his persistence may have allowed him to discover something. Or for Marie to confide in him in the way old spinsters confide in their cats. Given that our last meeting involved a lot of violence on my part I do not expect the kid to be forthcoming. I do expect him to behave like a lovesick pup and I can play that. I'll wager he spends his time writing her name on bits of paper and letting out feeble sighs; that is when he isn't spying on her or masturbating.

I wheel my bicycle from the train to the street. People are giving me funny looks. I realise I'm muttering away to myself. I can't decide whether to ride home and drop off my bags or head straight to Montmartre and Stefan. I decide on Montmartre.

The kid is not in or not answering the door. I can't be fagged to track him down, or do much else for that matter. I flop down in a café and order a coffee. It's cold today, and grey too, even for Paris. I feel it more as it was so warm down south. A few people pass by wearing thick coats; it'll be June soon. Are we not getting a summer this year? There aren't actually that many people about. Four o'clock - too late for the Montmartre tourists and too early for the party-goers. This is an in-between time where the district gets to take a breath before it all starts up again.

The place is never actually empty, though. The area has its own stragglers - drunks, junkies and the insane. People wade about in their own vice and squalor. They stand on street corners talking to pet rats concealed in their coat pockets. They stare at you blankly; having lost all powers of recognition, every stranger could be an old friend come to help. The echo of the Communards' cannons has died, replaced by the shouts and laments of the street walkers. The struggling artists have crawled across to Montparnasse. Buildings lie empty which once held Zola, Maupassant, and Gambetta. The nightclubs dream their day-time dreams. An old man stoops to pick up a cigarette butt. The wind catches it making him stoop again further up the hill.

I wait for hours, or minutes, I don't know which. The waiter has taken my early saucers and the sun doesn't shine. My stomach rumbles. Across the street I perceive the greasy ghoulish form of the kid as he slithers among the dustbins and iron rails at the side of the street. He takes up no space and moves with occasional jerks as if dodging flies. I leave some cash on the table and slip out of the café. I want to catch him as he reaches his front door.

I move swiftly, timing my interception well. Stefan is fumbling in his pockets for his keys. He notices me standing next to him and does his best to pretend he hasn't. I follow him into the apartment as he puts the key in the lock. Without any conviction he attempts to shut the door on me.

The apartment is filthy. The grime on the cracked windows shuts out the scant light on offer today. Two chairs appear to have been discarded near a wooden table. The walls are bare and haven't been painted this century. Mould grows in the corners and the place feels damp. Empty tins of food sit around with forks still in them. The linoleum floor is strewn with old newspapers and old clothes. The mess is covering the holes in the floorboards. Altogether it's not too much better than my old place in Saint-Denis.

'A bit of a shit hole you have here, Stefan.'

'If you don't like it, the door is there. I never invited you in anyway.'

He turns to look at the door or simply away from me. I light a cigarette. I offer him one which he takes. He doesn't light it. His hair looks greasier than I remember. It hangs lank and lifeless over his face. Dandruff rests on the shoulders of his stained and tatty jacket. Marks down the front could be yoghurt, bird-shit, or semen. The trousers look shiny, cheap, and worn out. He looks a lot worse than when I last saw him.

'Have you washed since we last met?'

'I washed my cuts and bruises.'

'You know, Stefan, I want to apologise.' As I speak I feel a sudden remorse hit me in the stomach. 'Yes, in fact I really do. I'm sorry. I treated you badly and without good cause.'

'Thanks. Now can you go?'

'You're still in love with her, aren't you?'

'Fuck off, monsieur Salazar.'

'All right, I shall. Before I go I want to ask you a question. Do you imagine a woman like Marie would want you? The only woman who'd look twice at you is a hooker while deciding if you are worth the money. You stink; you are a foul and dirty creature. To be honest, you turn my stomach.'

'I thank you once more for your apology.'

'Let me do something. Let me get someone to clean up this dung heap of an apartment. We'll go out and get you cleaned up. If Marie is going to turn you down let her at least know what she is missing.'

'I don't really want to be pally with you, monsieur Salazar.'

'I don't blame you. But ask yourself: if I were Marie, would I rather be with a repugnant Stefan or a clean and presentable Stefan. Does she really want to walk down the street hand-in-hand with Quasimodo's little brother?'

'I judge people by what they are, not what they look like. Appearance is vanity, a superficial disguising of the soul.'

'All right, you win. I'm going to the café opposite for about an hour. If you want my help, come over. If not, then please accept my apologies once more.'

I don't have a backup plan. If Stefan doesn't come then I'll never find out why Marie wanted to find Marty. That will annoy me on occasion but it's an annoyance I can live with. Actually, I think I do want him to come so I can make it up to him. He'll never get anywhere with Marie but, if he smartens up, maybe he'll catch the eye of some other girl. I ought not to feel too guilty about him. I gave him that beating before my change of heart about violence. I can't go back in time and guilt is such a destructive emotion. So long as I never do it again, that is all that can be gained from it. Besides, I never have a backup plan.

Now that I think of it most of my planning never crawls above the level of instinct. Although this case is as good as over it would be wrong of me to carry on working this way. Unfair on me, and on my clients. If I decide to carry on with detective work I shall garner Megan's help and start planning my actions out in advance. I might not solve the cases any quicker but it might keep me out of trouble.

The bell above the café door tinkles. Stefan sits down opposite me in a state of high agitation while affecting a sulk.

'If you can help me with Marie then I'll forgive you.'

I speak to the café owner and within twenty minutes two old Breton women are sent to clean Stefan's apartment. I pay twice what they asked as I know what's in store for them.

I walk my greasy shadow down to the public baths. After a good scrubbing I tell him to apply a serious dose of Eau de Cologne. Most of the strange odours which hang about him are now gone. Once his hair is cleaned we oil it to keep it off his face. I have to explain the difference between the fragrant oil I was using and the oil that comes from not washing. He doesn't sound convinced. I'm not too sure I am either.

The scrubbing can't disguise the hideous clothes he is wearing. They will always be bad - in fact I'm not certain they would survive a launder. We journey to the centre of Paris and a gentleman's outfitters I use.

The shop window is crowded with mannequins wearing smart suits and dapper top hats. Silver-topped walking canes and elegant umbrellas complete their equipage. Inside there is a long table draped with cloth. There is a whole range of colour on display – from black to charcoal grey. I normally go for their less common colours, like pale blue, myself.

The assistant grins broadly and opens his arms in a gesture of welcome. The smile and arms drop when he catches sight of the kid lurking behind me. The assistant is reluctant to measure Stefan, afraid to touch his filthy clothes. I explain what we are after as the assistant stands, hesitant, with a tape measure dangling from his fingers. Somewhere in the void of his mind he places a set of scales; on the one side he puts the money from the sale and on the other he places Stefan's soiled garments.

'What exactly will sir be requiring?' he asks.

'This man is going to need the lot; vests; shirts; collars; a formal suit; a day suit; two pairs of shoes; and some tennis shoes. Have you got anything you can have ready for him in the next two hours?'

'It would not be our best, sir. We could not actually make a suit in that time.'

'Take a good look at him - he doesn't need your best. Your worst would be better than that lot. I want him out of those clothes and in something vaguely presentable by the close of play today.'

'Very good, sir.'

'Now go and fetch him something he can wear now. Fetch them from anywhere. I don't want him in these rags any longer. In fact, Stefan, you go in there and undress. Take anything you want to keep from your pockets and then throw your clothes out over here. You,' I say turning to the assistant, 'gather up the clothes and burn them. I don't want to hear anything else from either of you until this man is outfitted well enough for me to be seen with.'

We leave the outfitters with Stefan looking quite smart and devoid of his disagreeable odours. At some point it goes beyond getting him a few things to say sorry and turns into a project in its own right. Already I've spent significantly more than I'll get from Marie.

CHAPTER TWENTY-SEVEN

There are a few restaurants in Paris that don't dish up flesh. Then there are the anarchist syndicates which serve food for strict vegetarians – nice and cheap, but you do your own washing up. Stefan makes a fuss about not having meat. I ignore him and order for us both. The food arrives and he wolfs it down before complaining again.

We head over to a café for a moment of reflection. He looks presentable in his new clothes. Even his finger nails have lost their grime. To top it all he is smiling. He's not as ugly as I first thought him and he wouldn't look out of place on Marie's arm. However, I doubt he'll ever breach the absolute distance she maintains from other people. Two young ladies are casting Stefan favourable glances. I feel like Professor Higgins.

'I found Marty you know,' I say.

'Who is Marty?'

No one gives a detective a straight answer – conversations are games of give and take. I follow the protocol, like the dance of a scorpion before the sting.

'Marty is the man Marie hired me to find.'

'Tell her he's dead.'

'Interesting idea,' I say. 'Do you think she will be satisfied by that or will she want to visit his grave?'

'Tell her you can't find him. I'll get a job and pay you the money you lose on the case. Or you can keep the new clothes and make it up to me that way instead.'

'First, you might explain why I should tell my client all these lies.'

'From what I can fathom the man is a... better not use that word here. She doesn't talk about him, but I have found out a few things. I think they were lovers, when they lived in Belgium. One day he deserted her. I think he used to knock her about a bit too. Whatever it is she wants from him it will bring no good. Please listen to me; don't tell her where he is.'

Stefan holds my arm and fixes my eye like the ancient mariner. He and the mariner share a similar obsessive madness.

'I'll tell you what, Stefan; I'm going to see her now and you can tag along. If she needs someone, you'll be there. And look at you now; your shoulder is all nice and clean so she can cry on it without contracting Weil's disease.'

Stefan shows me a few shortcuts on the way over to Marie's. He also makes a few more attempts to change my mind. Eventually I warn him that I'll leave him behind if he doesn't stop whining. He sulks instead – I can take that, it's silent. On reaching the apartment I send Stefan over to the café Gondoles. Then I press her bell.

'Monsieur Salazar, come in.'

She holds the door open and waves her arm to guide me in. On my last visit she'd ushered me straight across to the café – this time I get to see her apartment. The cooking area and living are all one room. She has a long purple couch which sits under the window. The good quality of the item has told out; the thing has worn well. A wooden coffee table makes up most of the rest of the furniture. On the wall two paintings catch my eye. The first is a Dada montage. Not a bad one either – I wonder if she did it herself. The other looks like a painting by Otto Dix. I don't want to delay things by inspecting the signature. I wouldn't be able to tell if it were faked anyway.

'Sit anywhere, monsieur Salazar.' She makes a sweep of the room with her arm.

'You don't need the monsieur, remember.'

'You can still sit anywhere.'

She has taken the sofa so I sit opposite her on the coffee table. I can't see any other chairs.

'I have found your man. He lives near a village called Vaour. It's the middle of nowhere.'

'Nowhere?'

'He has a farmhouse a few kilometres from the village. The village is small and there are no nearby towns. The middle of nowhere. Marty himself is ill – Parkinson's.'

'Good. How much?'

'How much what?'

'Do I owe you?'

'I'm not sure off the top of my head. There was the trip to Vaour and a few minor expenses. I'll send you a bill.'

'I have seven hundred francs in the bedroom.'

'That will do then.'

She walks to her bedroom, returning with a roll of notes. 'You should send me the full bill – and deduct this from the total. Could you write down his address please?'

She walks over to a bureau and fetches some paper which she hands to me. I write the address and draw a map as she stands over me. She is trembling and has now lit a cigarette. I'm beginning to think that Stefan was right. None of my business I guess. 'And now I'll bid you good day, Salazar.'

'May I ask what you intend to do?'

'No. I am grateful to you. I really am grateful. I'll try to pay your bill promptly. Gustave Marty is a part of my private life and I don't discuss my private life.'

She has that look, the defiance she had when we first met. I'm not interested in the sordid details of their relationship. I reckon the kid summed it up pretty well; he's quite an insightful devil.

I take a long look at her before saying goodbye. This will be the last time I see her. I'm starting to get that satisfied feeling again. I can't wait to get home and tell Megan all about it.

On leaving the apartment I wave over at Stefan who

leaves the cafe and scampers across the road. I don't wait for him; I walk off up the rue Cavendish to the Métro. Everything feels as if it is in the right place. I find that disturbing. In chess we call it Zugzwang - if everything is in the right place, and you must move, things won't be in the right place any longer. If things don't move they grow stale and rot, the right place will cease to be right. Ah, the train, come to save me from these pervasive doubts.

I take the Métro to Stefan's apartment and pick up my bicycle, then I cycle home. Looks like Megan has been living here; her things are in the kitchen and the bedroom. Would be nice if she were here herself. Feeling done in I lie on the bed and fall asleep.

I wake in the early evening. Almost as soon as I put the coffee on Megan arrives. We embrace - she squeezes me so hard my ribs hurt.

'Did you see my note?' she asks.

'No. I found Marty. I've been over to tell Marie, my client. It's all over, and I did it.'

'I always knew you could.'

'What note were you talking about?'

'You won't need it now. Someone named mademoiselle Sordine called. She said you left her your card.'

'That's right. She was Marty's secretary at Lacman Brothers. I'll give her a ring and let her know I found him.'

'She doesn't have a telephone. She was using a public one. You could send her a telegram.'

'I wanted this to be over.' I take a sip from my coffee. 'I'll tell you what. I'll go and see her. Then I'll pick up some champagne on the way back. Have you seen Filatre?'

'Erm, he's gone to England.' She looks over at the floor as she speaks.

'England? What on Earth for?'

'Personal reasons.'

'Personal reasons? What are you going on about?'

'He's a really nice chap, Reggie.'

'Yes he is. Why has he gone to England?'

'Well, I'm not a detective but I imagine he has gone to seduce your Aunt Bess.'

'The little...well good luck to him.'

'So get a move on, Reggie. I want that champagne.'

Cycling over to mademoiselle Sordine's part of town doesn't feel as bad as it did when I went on the Métro. When you walk or cycle the city changes slowly as you pass from district to district. The Métro is a monotonous tunnel which spews you, without ceremony, onto the streets above.

This area of Paris, apart from being disgustingly bourgeoisie, is a place I would never ordinarily visit. Why travel this far from Paris without then leaving it all together? If I was coming from the other direction, why get this close to Paris without going all the way in? What's the point of these places that are nearly in the city but not?

I arrive at Sordine's apartment block and leave my bicycle in the lobby. I notice the concierge in her little observation booth, observing me. I say, 'Sordine' and wink at her as I head up the stairs. Before I reach the top Sordine appears on the stairwell.

'Monsieur Salazar?'

'Yes, mademoiselle Sordine?'

'Yes, do come up.'

Sordine is a slight woman in her mid-forties. Her eyebrows have been erased and then drawn in again as if she'd had second thoughts about removing them. Her hair is pale brown and wavy. Something is holding it off her face. Perhaps it is willpower or hidden wires. She has a sleek dress – a few years old but holding its own. The cardigan is there for comfort and warmth. It certainly isn't there for style. She has naked legs ending in comfortable slippers.

I meet her at the top of the stairs. We shake hands and she ushers me into the apartment. The building, although centuries old, has been refurbished in the last few years. Her rooms have been decorated like a Victorian parlour. Dark, heavy drapes cover the windows. Satin cloth covers small tables which overflow with delicate, ugly, paraphernalia. The dark wallpaper in the hall and living room lends the place a timeless quality. The sun has been permanently excluded – one way to avoid disappointment on a day like today.

'Monsieur Salazar, may I ask, you seem to be English?'

She holds her hand out towards an armchair which I sink into.

'Yes, I am English.'

'My dear departed grandparents were English. They moved to Paris not long after the Prussians left. I myself attended a school in England. Have you ever been to Cheltenham?'

Sordine has switched to speaking English. There is no trace of a French accent – only the over-emphasised tones of a Cheltenham school girl. Despite her reserve she exudes a certain warmth. At first glance I thought she was much older than she evidently is. Now I can see her face and hands I would place her closer to thirty than forty. There are no obvious wrinkles and her eyes almost sparkle. She has a sympathetic face which is pretty in its way. In a different era she would be happily married; in this one she will die a spinster.

Before I get the chance to speak she shuffles off to make lemon tea. I sit and listen to her pottering about. After five minutes she returns with a China tea set on a silver tray.

'Miss Sordine, I asked to see you about your old boss, Mr Marty...'

'I know, you said so in your note. I have been thinking it over. At first I didn't want to talk about him, didn't want to stir it all up again. Then I decided, no! I have been hiding from what happened for too long. Trying to pretend it isn't true. And seeing you, Mr Salazar, and as you are an Englishman like my dear Grandpa, I think I can tell you.'

Oh, God. What have I let myself in for?

'Do, please, go on,' I say.

'I will say it straight out loud.'

She has stopped talking, summoning the strength to continue. I feel uneasy - after all I don't need this information. There is something she wants to get off her chest and I'm in the firing line. She looks over at the fireplace. She's losing her impetus.

'Please continue, Miss Sordine. You don't really know me, so say what you want. Everything will be taken in the strictest confidence.'

I lean over, take her hand, and hold it gently.

'I find it hard to say it without remembering it. The truth is, he forced his attentions on me.'

'Forced his attentions?'

'He raped me, Mr Salazar.'

Her hand is shaking in mine. I crouch down next to her feeling weak and useless. She is still talking, going over the details. What else can I do but assume the role of her grandfather? I pat her head and say, 'My dear child.' She turns and cries into my jacket. She lets herself go for a few minutes. Now I can hear her trying to regain her composure.

'What must you think of me?'

'I think you are a very brave woman. Gustave Marty deserves a good hiding.'

I hold her for a moment longer. 'Oh, shit!'

'What is it?'

'Oh, double shit.'

'Please, Mr Salazar.'

'Excuse me, Miss Sordine, I must leave. Do you know where I can find a telephone?'

'There is one in the café on the corner. I use that one.'

'Ah yes, I know that café – I wrote your note there. Look, I know I'm being a total cad, but my client, the one who hired me to find Marty, is a woman. I think he might have raped her too. I'm afraid she's going to do something stupid. I have to stop her. I'm going to make a quick call then I'll be right back. Please wait for me, I'll be five minutes.'

I fly down the stairs and out of the apartment block. Luckily, the café telephone is working. I call Megan and tell her to borrow Filatre's automobile and get over here. Then I run back to mademoiselle Sordine's.

Sordine has washed her face and removed the smudged make-up.

'What do you think your client will do, Mr Salazar?'

'Whatever it is, I hope I can get there in time to stop her.'

CHAPTER TWENTY-EIGHT

Megan arrives and agrees to stay with Sordine. I take the keys and run downstairs to Filatre's automobile. A few gear crunches later I hit the road heading south. The first hour is spent getting properly out of Paris and into the country. After that I start to calm down – no point trying to maintain a sense of urgency on a seven-hour drive.

Every half hour I stop to give my leg a five-minute stretch. I limp around the auto a few times to get the muscles moving again. Each time I get back in the automobile the physical protest is greater. I have about two ampoules of morphine with me. They will ease the pain, but they'll also leave me drowsy. If I fall asleep I'll be reading about Marie in the morning papers.

Stupid girl. Poor girl. She said she last met him in 1919. That would make her about fifteen years old. Sordine was attacked around 1928. There must have been others victims in those nine years. Kuo had said something about the way he was with women and Céline described him as a creep. I had my eyes too firmly on the money – the sick bastard.

Night falls. The moon traces the horizon. I smoke a cigarette then toss the butt out the window. It blows back in and onto the rear seats. I skid to a halt and frantically search out the butt. I find it on the floor - the hole is almost undetectable.

These country roads are incredibly dark. Fatigue or the hypnotic nature of driving causes me to see things. Shadowy figures stand at the side of the road - they are scaring the hell out of me. There's someone in the back, hiding down below the seats, out of sight from the mirror. Perhaps they got in when I stopped to limp around. I stop to check. Nothing there. It's cold but I'm sweating.

Vaour once more. In the darkness the village might not even be here. It's lost its reality. I look at my watch – a few minutes past two o'clock. After passing through the village I head up the lonely track to Marty's place. Before reaching the farm I switch off the lights and let the moon guide me. The silence is eerie. What's happened to the crickets and frogs which sang all through the night on my last visit? Was that only two nights ago?

An automobile is parked near the house: Parisian plates. I pull up behind it and get out. The bonnet is still warm; can't have gotten here more than an hour ago. This auto was parked outside Marie's apartment earlier today.

There's no light coming from the house. I look in through the kitchen windows. Too dark to make anything out. I knock on the kitchen door which swings gently open under my touch.

'Hello,' I call. The sound of my voice only amplifies the silence.

Full of trepidation I enter the kitchen and light one of the gas lamps on the wall. Everything looks as I remember it. I can hear someone walking towards me from the hallway. If I had my revolver it would now be drawn. I'm ready to run. This could all be a coincidence. Marie may not be here. The automobile may belong to some lunatic from Paris.

'You!'

Stefan walks in with blood on his hands and clothes. He has no obvious wounds.

'What have you done?' I ask. I look him over as he approaches – no visible weapon.

'Nothing. I mean, I killed him.' He stands with his head down and his shoulders drooping. This doesn't feel right.

'Where is she, Stefan?'

'In the bedroom, but -'

I'm already on my way up. Light is coming from Marty's bedroom. I push the door open. There's blood splattered all over the walls. The bed is drenched in it. On the floor, between the bed and wardrobe, lies Marty's naked body. Belly down; his head is twisted so that his open eyes are staring straight up at me. Even from the doorway I can see the dark holes where a knife has entered him. I once found a soldier in this state. A bomb had blown all his clothes off leaving him naked and dead. His body was covered in dark shrapnel holes. I had shrugged it off. Today I feel like vomiting.

Stefan materialises at my side like a debt collector.

'I did it,' he says.

I look at him for a moment then enter the room. By the window, near the little cupboard where I'd found Marty's school tie, sits Marie. She is clutching a large kitchen knife. I step past Marty's body and stand next to her.

'Come with me,' I say.

She takes the hand I hold out for her and stands. She is breathing rapidly and staring directly ahead.

'I'm going to take you downstairs, Marie. Can you give me this first?'

I reach out and take the knife, then I lead her downstairs. Once there I take her outside and sit her in my automobile. I go back for Stefan. He's still upstairs standing in the bedroom doorway.

'Look, monsieur Salazar, I'll take the blame. You can say she wasn't here.'

'No, you look, Stefan. I want you to do what I tell you. Can you drive?'

'Yes.'

'Go down and sit with her in my automobile. It's out on the road.'

The smell of blood is repulsive; the butcher shop smell. I light a Gitane. If those two decide to drive off I'll be screwed. What do I do with this? My finger prints are on that

213

knife and all around the house. So are Marie's, including a few bloody hand prints on the wall. We could drive off and they would probably never find us - if it weren't for my previous visit. When the police drill the maid she is going to tell them all about the English visitor. People in the village will remember me and so will the guy from the Mayor's office. Next thing – my pictures in the papers and I have to start apartment hunting in Buenos Aires.

Marty's body is heavy - all bodies are. I gather blankets from Marty's death bed and wrap them around him. His eyes are still looking at me. Is he registering anything? I know he's dead, but is he all dead? Are there messages going around in his brain? Can he see me? Does he recognise me? I close his eyes.

A few days ago Marty and I were enjoying a drink and a laugh. If he were alive now I'd shun him. How do you shun a carcase and what difference does it make? A dead rapist is a dead person. His likes and dislikes, his traits and actions, are all irrelevant now. Everything he was is gone. He's a corpse, one of so many, only I have to lug this one down the stairs.

Using the blankets I drag his body to the top of the stairs. I could ask Stefan to help but I'd rather he kept an eye on Marie. Without ceremony I roll Marty down the stairs. He doesn't fall neatly – forcing me to give him a few kicks along the way. After replacing him on the blankets I start dragging him again. My back is aching and I'm breathing heavily. When this night's work is over I'm going to need a serious break. Stopping for a breather at the kitchen door I notice that I'm covered in blood. There's a line of red smeared along the floor. I remember something Marie said: 'A slug like Marty is bound to leave a trail.'

Logistics: if I stick the cadaver in their automobile, and take Marie in mine, that should control what Stefan does. If he decides to drive to the police and confess, they will spend five minutes beating the truth out of him - and then it's Devil's Island for me. Before we leave I'll make it clear to him - if he goes near the flics, I'll dump Marie in it.

After dragging the body to the kitchen door I go and fetch Stefan. They are both sitting in the front of my automobile. She's in the passenger seat, a blank expression on her face. Stefan is smoking and talking. I walk around to his side and open the door.

'Come with me, kid – I'm going to need a hand.'

I drive Marie's auto over to the farm door. We heave Marty up and into the boot. I tell Stefan he's driving the corpse to Paris. The worst part is we'll be arriving an hour or so after daybreak.

'We could stay in a hotel somewhere tonight, couldn't we?' Stefan asks.

'No. We'll have to risk it. When we get back, you park up normally outside Marie's place. I'll park right behind you. Make sure you stop every hour on the way back, or if I flash you, unless there are people about or we're in a town. I need to stretch my leg and we need to make sure everything is okay.'

'All right. Shall I start off now?'

'Not yet.'

He's getting jumpy. I hope he doesn't crack on the long drive home.

'Drive out to the road and park up. Keep the headlights off and wait for me.'

I wait until I hear him turn the engine off before I re-enter the house. Hopefully the corpse in his boot will stop him getting Marie and driving off. I make one more trip to the bedroom for a change of clothes. I'd rather people pointed out that my trousers are too short than the fact I'm covered in blood.

Going back inside is not at all pleasant. Along with the trail of blood there are red foot prints all over the place. They match my shoes. In the bedroom I try to look only at the wardrobe. Images of the horrible scenes which have taken place here flick through my mind. She must have gone at him in a frenzy. How did they get up to the bedroom?

Maybe Marty left the back door open. I grab a shirt and a pair of trousers. I left my coat in the automobile, so at least that's clean.

On Marty's dressing table I spot a large dictionary. I pick it up and pay another visit to the room I'd slept in. I get changed then take my bloodied clothes and throw them into the death room. Using the dictionary I start knocking the lamps out of the wall. The gas hisses at me. After doing three I realise what I'm doing – any one of those blows could have caused a spark. Three will do. In the kitchen I turn out the gas lamp and pile the wood from the stove onto the kitchen table. I shove the table into the doorway. There is some white spirit and rags under the basin which I use to set the table alight. If I can catch that doorframe and the door alight then the rest of the house will go up too. By the time the door starts turning black, the heat is too great to remain in the kitchen. I get out before the gas from upstairs catches.

Stefan has resisted the temptation to go and sit next to Marie. I flash my lights as a signal for him to get ready. A few minutes later I'm following him up the road towards Vaour. A few miles from the village I flash my lights again and he stops. I get out and look back. There's an orange glow coming from the area of Marty's house and smoke is rising into the sky. We hit the road again.

After two hours of driving Marie starts speaking: 'Do you think that I'm a bad person?'

'I don't know you well enough to judge.'

I look at her. She's looking back at me. There is a slight puzzlement in her eyes - she's coming back to reality. I turn to look at the road again.

'I was stabbing him and he kept shouting "No, don't do it!" He said it over and over. As he was saying it I was remembering saying the same thing to him but he wouldn't stop. Does that make me as bad as him?'

'I don't think so. What he did, he did to a child.'

'You can say yes if you think it.'

'I don't know if I do think it. Somewhere the morality and

the practice of life merge and dirty each other. I believe it's wrong to kill but I'm not prepared to condemn you for this killing.'

'I hired you to track him down. I'm not sure I planned on killing him. I'm not sure I planned anything beyond finding him. Will I go to jail?'

'That would be a crime in itself. I have no intention of telling the police about tonight. You need to keep quiet about it too. I've a feeling you can manage that.'

'What will we do?'

'You will do nothing. The kid and I will clean this up.'

'The kid, Stefan?'

'Yes.'

'He's changed recently,' she says. 'I think he did it to impress me – I've tried to tell him it's of no use.'

'Can you tolerate him?'

'He's not that bad. Now he cleans himself I almost like having him around.'

'At the moment he's infatuated with you. That will die down over time. Meanwhile, try to put up with him.'

'I keep seeing Marty on that bed, covered in blood, slipping to the floor,' she says.

'When we get to Paris, put my coat on and try to get up to the apartment without anyone seeing you. You've got a lot of blood on your clothes.'

She looks down at herself: 'God it's disgusting. I'm disgusting.'

'Try to keep calm until we're in your apartment. If the police stop us now it will be the guillotine for the kid and me. You're a woman, so they'll commute your sentence to life.'

A few miles of silence follow. Then: 'Do you want to know what happened?'

'No. I got a pretty good picture of what happened when I dragged him out the room.'

'I mean to me.'

I can't say no, although I don't want to hear a second

story like this.

'Maybe, if you are okay with it,' I say. 'It might help you get over what just happened.'

'You know, in the war, we were occupied.'

'Yes, that was a big recruiter for the army: think of Belgium.'

'Well, some people worked with the Germans and some people didn't. In my family we kept ourselves to ourselves. The Martys were different. I think Marty senior played both sides. During the day he co-operated, at night he went to freedom meetings. Anyway, after it was over there was a lot of retribution. People got beaten. Women had their heads shaved if someone claimed they'd slept with a German. All sorts of nastiness came out.

'One night Marty and a couple of his friends came to my street. They were drunk and causing trouble. My father went out to admonish them. One of them, I don't know who, hit him on the head with a walking-stick. Then they started kicking him. I saw it from my window. I ran out to stop them. Someone pushed me away. Then Marty saw me. He grabbed me, lifted me up, and took me into the house. He carried me up to my parent's room and raped me. I was crying and begging him to stop. Then I passed out. They wrote stuff on our house saying we had collaborated. We hadn't. My parents never spoke about it but they knew what had happened. My father lost an eye in that attack. The police behaved as if we'd deserved it. They knew we weren't collaborators - they pretended we were so they wouldn't have to go up against the Martys.'

'Must have been tough.'

'I suppose I have been thinking about tonight ever since. I guess I always did plan on killing him.'

We arrive in Paris with the sun riding high in a clear sky. Looks like being a beautiful day.

CHAPTER TWENTY-NINE

I'm so tired I don't know if I'm awake or asleep. There aren't too many people about. Everyone in this neighbourhood is already at work or sleeping after doing a night shift. Stefan parks and I pull up so close behind him that we're almost touching. This should stop anyone trying to steal from his boot. If someone steals the auto I'll claim they must have put the body in there.

Marie and I walk through the lobby of her apartment block. As I'm ushering her past the concierge Stefan lets go a loud fart. I don't know whether he did it on purpose but it provides an excellent distraction.

Once inside the apartment Marie begins pacing the floor looking like an anxious ghost. With some persuasion she washes the blood off and changes into her night clothes. Stefan's clothes are in a bad way too – and I only bought them for him yesterday. I sift through Marie's wardrobe and bring him a blouse and trousers which don't look too feminine. I light the stove and burn their bloodied attire.

For what I have in mind we're going to need the cover of darkness. Marie takes to her bed. I take the sofa. Stefan curls up on a rug.

There is something about this apartment which reminds me of the few years I spent in London. Between the opium and the all-night drinking I used to meet up with a few of my old university and army pals. We were young men who'd seen a lot of the bad side of life. People called us wastrels, bohemians, lost causes. I had a few happy moments then, as we each headed toward our own personal breakdowns.

Stefan sleeps, snoring quite gently. I light a cigarette and stare at the Dada montage on the wall. What will become of Marie now, and Stefan? I guess he'll meet someone else and gradually lose his connection with Marie. Years from now, in 1943 perhaps, he'll be in a shop, two children in tow, and Marie will be there buying some coffee. They'll smile at one another but not speak. 'If not for her distances...' he'll think and then feel a moment of yearning. A yearning for her and the passions of his youth. And what of me? What will I be doing in '43? Will I have two children of my own? Will I be stalking the streets of Paris, a detective of the old school?

I wake with a start. Marie enters the room and walks through to the kitchen area. I'm so tired I can't move. My hand reaches down and gropes for my cigarettes. The aroma of coffee, the burn of a cigarette, this is what mornings are about. Only this isn't morning and we have business. A pity really; if it weren't for the corpse outside this could make for the beginnings of a splendid evening.

'Make one for me please,' I call out.

The sound of clinking comes from the kitchen. Summoning up some inner strength I swing my legs around and sit up. Stefan and I have made the living room smell of men. Marie hands me a coffee. She looks sleepy and wistful - I want to hold her. She wakes Stefan, who stretches out on the floor. He looks like a waif with his tousled hair and woman's clothing. We drink the coffee in silence.

'What will happen now?' Marie asks.

'Stefan and I will go for a drive. Then it will all be over. Might be worth you and him going up to Brittany for a few days. Pull over somewhere secluded on the way and clean the blood out of the automobile.'

'Can it really be that easy?'

'Yes and no. You can forget these things for a while but they'll come back to you now and then. I don't reckon the flics in Vaour will come up with anything. When they start investigating monsieur Dubois and find out that he's really monsieur Marty they'll be occupied for a year or two interviewing all the people who had it in for him.'

'Will they interview you?'

'Quite probably, but I never found him and my client left the country. They may gather some circumstantial evidence but they'll need me to confess. It's dark enough out there now. Stefan, you go and check the coast is clear and wait for me downstairs.'

Stefan slopes off.

'Marie, the best thing you can do is return to Belgium. First you need to encourage Stefan to leave you.'

'How? I've tried to get rid of him before. He's very persistent.'

'Make sure he keeps himself clean and looking smart. Encourage him to go out with other girls. Do it subtlety; take him to cafés where he stands a chance of meeting them. Eventually he'll realise he's getting nowhere with you and attach himself to someone else.'

'But they'll see him with me.'

'And he'll be all the more alluring for it. I won't come back in when I return for my automobile. If you need me, you have my card. Take care of yourself, Marie.'

'You too, Salazar.'

Marie's vehicle handles a bit better than Filatre's. Maybe the corpse is acting as ballast. The drive through the city is a thrill, catching fleeting glimpses of lovers under street lights. We drive until the people grow fewer and the streets grow darker. The thrill recedes as we reach the edges of Saint-Denis. We pass through the very streets where I used to tramp. The sickness comes as old feelings stir within me. You should never go back.

I drive past an alley, then stop and reverse up it. A few metres from the river I park up. It's quiet here. Not surprising - this place is frightening enough in the daylight. A desolate spot where the locals come to rape and murder each other. With no decorum, we pull the body from the trunk. He falls on to the gravel pathway with a dull thud. We take a leg each and drag him over to the river's edge.

We scrape around on the river bank for some rocks. Marty doesn't have any pockets, so I pull his pyjama bottoms down a little and tie the ends of the legs. As I put the rocks in through his waistband I try not to look at the bloody mess that was once his stomach.

I can feel Marty's dead eyes watching me, even though I have closed his lids. Stefan is getting impatient, panicky. He doesn't say anything but I hear him behind me taking short paces to and fro. This is where it ends, on the river's edge in a northern slum.

After tonight I'll go back and share a drink with Megan. She'll be on edge after spending time with mademoiselle Sordine. Whatever it was she thought she was getting into with me I doubt it was anything like this. This will mark the end of our old life and the true beginning of our new one. Perhaps we can make a life for ourselves which is actually worth living.

I call Stefan over. He takes Marty's arms; I take the legs. A few swings and we toss him into the river. The current takes the body before it begins to sink. He's already invisible in the darkness. If the Seine ever dries up it's going to reveal a lot of truths about this city.

THE END

Acknowledgements

I'd like to thank Isla for proof-reading the chapters of this book (over and over, through many drafts) and providing valuable feedback. Dan and Dave for their encouragement. Chris Ewan, Heath Lowrance and Gary Corby, three excellent writers who gave up valuable time to read and blurb this book. Chris McVeigh for adding this book to the Fahrenheit list. Also the online writing communities and writer-bloggers who freely provide advice and feedback and time to the would-be writer. And luck, without which we'd never make it.

About the author

Born and brought up in the West of England, Seth has also lived in Carcassonne, Zurich and the Isle of Man. With two daughters, his writing time is the period spent in cafés as the girls do gym, dance, drama lessons. Previous novels include Salazar and A Dead American in Paris.

More books from Fahrenheit Press

If you enjoyed this book by Seth Lynch you might also like these other Fahrenheit titles from his 3rd Republic series

A Dead American In Paris (Vol 2)

The Paris Ripper (Vol 3)

Veronique (Vol 4)

Printed in Great
Britain
by Amazon